The Rule of Last Clear Chance

THE RULE
of Last Clear Chance

Judith McCormack

The Porcupine's Quill

NATIONAL LIBRARY OF CANADA CATALOGUING IN PUBLICATION DATA

McCormack, Judith, 1954–
The rule of last clear chance / Judith McCormack.

Short stories.
ISBN 0-88984-264-7

I. Title.

PS8575.C668R85 2003   C813'.6   C2003-901399-5
PR9199.4.M423R85 2003

1 2 3 4 • 05 04 03

Published by The Porcupine's Quill,
68 Main Street, Erin, Ontario NOB 1TO.
www.sentex.net/~pql

Readied for the press by John Metcalf; copy edited by Doris Cowan.
Typeset in Bauer Bodoni, printed on Zephyr Antique laid
and bound at the Porcupine's Quill.

We acknowledge the support of the Ontario Arts Council,
and the Canada Council for the Arts for our publishing program.
The financial support of the Government of Canada
through the Book Publishing Industry Development Program
is also gratefully acknowledged. Thanks, also, to the Government of
Ontario through the Ontario Media Development Corporation's
Ontario Book Initiative.

 Conseil des Arts   Canada Council
du Canada   for the Arts

Canadä

ONTARIO ARTS COUNCIL
CONSEIL DES ARTS DE L'ONTARIO

To Peter, Julia and Daniel

Table of Contents

The Rule of Last Clear Chance

Andrea is surprised by how much the pages of the Highway Traffic Act smell like burnt sugar, but she doesn't mention this to Liam because he already suspects that she is not a serious person, and she does not want to add to his suspicions. It goes without saying that he is mistaken, but she knows this is an easy mistake to make because she is not a ponderous person, or even a studied person, although, of course, these are not the same things as being serious.

She is thinking about the smell of the Highway Traffic Act because she is reading the Highway Traffic Act, or at least she has it open in front of her, although for all the good this is doing, she might as well be reading the television guide. She wonders whether the smell could be caused by some chemical process, like oxidization, except she is vague about what this means. For all she knows, the source of the smell is bacteria, or even microscopic mites.

In fact, she is now leaning towards the bacteria theory, because the thought has occurred to her that the bacteria might actually be producing the law itself, rather than merely the smell. She pictures penicillin-like colonies of legal cells busily multiplying into statutes and regulations, and then has to muffle a little spurt of laughter, which makes her realize exactly how easily Liam might make his mistake.

All the same, she lifts up the volume of statutes and holds one of the pages up to the fluorescent light in the boardroom. The edge of the page is caramel-coloured with age, although it is so thin that she can see the black ant print on both sides of the paper, which makes it unreadable.

There is a rustle at the other end of the boardroom table, and she glances up to see Liam looking at her in a pointed way.

'I'm thinking,' she says hastily, putting the book down and turning another page.

'Right,' he says. 'So am I. Thinking. Of course, I'm thinking about the case, instead of book-binding, or whatever it is that you're thinking about, but still – thinking.'

This is what Liam looks like: his body is sudden, no outline in the air around it, just the instant edge of his skin, pale and flecked, almost unripe looking. His skin is translucent, and there are thick blue veins visible underneath it. (If you look hard enough, he says, you can probably see my pancreas.) He has brown-blond hair, a colour that officials in passport offices look at, pen in hand, and say doubtfully: what colour *is* that, anyway? The pupils of his eyes are made up of dark grey dots crowded together in a bluish-grey background. He has stringy muscles, and he lopes when he walks. Andrea knows that his loping is purely a physical matter, a question of leg length and gait and rhythm. He is not in the least predatory, but there is no other word to describe how he walks. He is a born loper.

'Think we should take a break?' says Andrea, yawning. 'Wrap it up for the night?' She thinks they should take a break and wrap it up for the night, but she wants to know what he thinks. The reason why she wants to take a break is that it is eleven-thirty, and half of her brain synapses are curled into little balls and sucking their fingers, while the other half would like to go drinking. This may also explain why she is not making much headway with the Highway Traffic Act.

Not that she is a good drinker. In fact, she is a bad drinker, almost an inept drinker. She moves through certain stages of inebriation very quickly, often in the course of two drinks: an initial warming-up stage; a stage of astonishment and high glee about almost everything; a stage of genuine elation; a stage where she feels log-tongued, but compelled to explain things to people gently and carefully; and finally and most unpleasantly, a room-spinning stage. She also dislikes the taste of alcohol – the mealy taste of beer, the surgical taste of martinis, the astringent taste of wine.

However, all of this sounds better than sitting at an oval table in a law firm boardroom, surrounded by chairs with nubby purple fabric, breathing dry air and listening to the fluorescent lights buzz, while she and Liam try to fit together the various pieces of Harry Singh's existence.

'Give it another half hour?' says Liam.

'Sure,' says Andrea.

She thinks that another half hour will be a waste of time because her concentration is at such a low ebb, but she doesn't say so, both because of the seriousness problem, and because she feels that anyone she is sleeping with is entitled to some latitude for that reason alone.

So instead, she goes back to thinking about Harry Singh.

Harry Singh is their client, or at least he is the client of a more senior lawyer in their law firm, and the various pieces of his life have been sorted into files, which are spread out over the table and labeled Medical Reports or Family or Employment History or Special Damages. Working from these files is a strange process, like trying to fit body parts together without any idea of the shape of the original body. They are engaged in this process because they are trying to build a case for him, but Andrea, who has been a lawyer for ten months and six days, cannot help wondering how closely the legal version of Harry Singh they are pasting together resembles the real Harry Singh.

This is what their current model, their working model, looks like:

Harry Singh's employment: he is a forty-eight year old school janitor at East Scarborough Technical School; he smokes occasionally in the janitors' room, which is prohibited; he insists on waxing the school floors too often without stripping them first; he is the United Way canvasser for the school because no one else wants to do it; and he unlocks classroom doors after school for anxious students who have forgotten their glasses or their ecology assignments or their trip permission slips, although he is bad-tempered about it. (Do we want to admit the bad-tempered part? says Liam. It has to be credible, he can't be a saint, says Andrea. Besides, it's better if it comes from us first, instead of from the other side.)

Harry Singh's personal life: his face is lumpy with an acne pit on one cheek (this part is not difficult – they have pictures of him); he has a heavy nose and a faintly sheepish smile, both of which make him look kinder than he is; he is the father of two girls, both of whom he has taught to play a sleepy game of chess (one hates it, one likes it, but doesn't want anyone to know); he grows English cucumbers in his backyard, and keeps records of particularly productive years in an old pink Hilroy; he gets chapped lips in the winter; he likes soft cheeses – cottage cheese, cream cheese – although his wife worries about his cholesterol; and he does the double acrostic in the newspaper.

Most of these characteristics should be in the past tense, though. He *grew* cucumbers. He *did* the double acrostic.

This is because Harry Singh left his home on a rainy evening to pick up a video, some microwave popcorn and his youngest daughter at her ballet class, and instead drove through a four-way stop intersection, hitting a radiologist on her way home from work in her 1999 Subaru. He ended up with severe head and pelvic injuries, and one of his legs was torn off in the impact.

The neurological assessments indicate that Mr Singh may never recover his powers of speech, and he does not appear to comprehend simple events (says one of the file memos). *His wife is on antidepressants, and his younger daughter, his 'darling' according to his wife, and the reason he was out that night, has been using a razor to make small cuts in her forearms, leaving threads of blood on the bathroom sink. Mr Singh is incontinent as a result of his pelvic injuries and he spends most of his time watching television, although it is not apparent that he understands what he is seeing.*

And on top of that, he has been sued.

Andrea winces, although she has read this memo before.

'Why weren't there any witnesses?' she says to Liam, as if he were responsible for this oversight. The two of them are the most junior associates in the law firm, which specializes in civil litigation, and which has twenty-eight lawyers, sixteen secretaries, an office manager, a receptionist and a paralegal.

'It was a residential intersection,' he says. 'I guess it was too early in the evening for dog walkers.'

'Well, why were they both going so fast, anyway? And why didn't he see her?' Such a little intersection. So much damage.

'You mean why couldn't she avoid him?' says Liam. 'He's the one we represent.'

'How about this, then – why didn't either of them stop at their stop signs?'

'Very good questions, possibly excellent questions,' says Liam, 'but they would be more helpful if we hadn't asked them several hundred times already.'

Of course, this almost complete lack of knowledge about what happened has not prevented anyone from taking legal action, thinks Andrea. Not at all. What a thought. On the contrary. In addition to the lawsuit against Harry Singh, his family is counterclaiming against the radiologist.

A claim and a counterclaim. Andrea is interested in the tinny, tocky sound of this. A claim and a counterclaim. If anyone asks her why she went to law school, she thinks, leaning back in her chair and twisting her hair up onto the top of her head, she'll say it was the language, the stale elegance of the words. This is a good phrase as well, and she starts picturing the interview, the interviewer leaning forward intently, herself relaxed and witty – *Thank you, Bob, it's a pleasure to be here, too. Here, let me tell you about some of the other words.*

Listen to this:
inter alia
writs of fieri fascias
the party of the first part

locus delecti
the rules of affinity and consanguinity
lucri causa

Was it possible that she went to law school out of a kind of linguistic incredulity?

This would make a good line for the interview.

Liam is looking at her again.

'All right, all right,' she says, dropping her arms from where they are holding up her hair. She picks up one of the files in front of her.

As bad as things are for Harry Singh, he is better off than the radiologist. He must be. The radiologist is dead.

She was thirty-four, and in good health, except for minor problems — tennis elbow, occasional lower back pain which might have turned into a disc problem over time — and she was taking a short cut home to avoid the traffic, and to let the nanny go home on time. Her skull was fractured, and some of her dark, curly hair was torn out. Because of the angle of the impact, her spine was crushed as well, so there will be no disc problem in the future, and, in fact, no future.

She died in the ambulance from internal bleeding, although she wasn't officially labelled dead until they reached the hospital. Her husband, a benefits administrator, has sued on behalf of himself and their three-year-old son.

This is bad, Bob, this is very bad.

Andrea gets up stiffly, shaking a numb foot.

'I'm going to look up some things on negligence,' she says to Liam. 'I'm not getting anywhere here.'

She walks down the hall to the firm's library, still shaking her foot every two or three steps. There is no one else there at this hour, and the library smells like the turquoise nylon broadloom on the floor, like the blond wood furniture. The shelves are full of law reports, so that whole sections are stocked with identical-looking volumes that are dark green or red or cigarbrown. They look impressive, but Andrea knows that many of them amount to a form of wallpaper. Most of her research is done on a computer.

But not all. Negligence is a tort, so she pulls a book on torts off the shelf (*torts, Bob, torts!*), and starts flipping through it in a desultory way, looking for legal propositions which might be helpful. This is what she finds:

The rule of inevitable accident: an accident which cannot be prevented by human skill and foresight.

The rule of inescapable peril: peril which one party is helpless to avoid by his own efforts, and which requires action on the part of the other party.

The rule of last clear chance: the party who has the last clear chance to avoid injury or damage is responsible for the accident.

Amazing, she thinks. Out of this accident, out of this violent conjunction of speed and metal and glass and flesh, out of this mess of splintered bones, torn arteries, cracked and twisted lives, out of this eruption of rogue physics and metaphysics, there is only one thing which really matters. Legally.

Whose fault was it?

Of course, Andrea is still startled to find that she is sleeping with Liam. Of course she is. Startled, that is.

She feels as if this must have happened one night when she wasn't really paying sufficient attention. Not only that, she knows it is a bad idea, possibly a very bad idea, not simply because they work together, although this is bad enough, but also because he is so different from her. Their relationship is a testament to the combination of proximity and physicality.

Well, maybe this is a little harsh, she thinks. A little cynical. However, it is difficult to imagine them being together otherwise, she and Liam and his career path, which is almost as substantial as a third person. Liam is eager, possibly the most eager human being she has ever met, every part of him straining towards success. Like a dog with its head out the window of a moving car, she thinks – bright eyes, tongue lolling, nose in high gear, ears ruffled by the slipstream.

So why *are* you sleeping with him then? Gaby said a few weeks ago. If it's such a bad idea.

Andrea doesn't have an answer for this, or at least a fact that she can serve up that would provide a satisfactory explanation. *Oh, I see. Now I get it.* She can't say to her sister, someone who has the ruthless clarity of an athlete: it's because of his blind white tube of a penis, because he can't sit still, because of his small ears, because of his smell. She knows that this is completely unconvincing.

In her own defence: it isn't simply his smell, it's his *smells*. Plural. The live hormonal smell of his hair; the smell of his jaw – equal parts shaving cream, and the baked smell of skin; the metallic smell that eddies out of the fillings in his teeth; the hard white bone smell from his rib cage; the milky glue of his semen; the sweat in the creases where his thighs join his torso. Smells that are so wild and irritable that she can almost see them if she closes her eyes.

But why is he sleeping with her? Now, this is a good question, a very good question. Nót that she thinks she is unattractive, or so she understands.

This is the way Andrea looks: tall, with dark hair which is unusually dense with pigment, short bangs, shoulders and hips and arms that slide around a lot when she walks, small breasts which make her look thinner than she is, large wrist and ankle bones, opaque skin. (You look like your molecules are closer together, like a person could slip right off you, says Liam.)

This is untrue. Bodies are such liars.

In fact, she usually feels exactly the opposite of the way she looks; as if her skin were particularly spongy, with the effect that the various scenes and events of each day leave large sense prints on her. A heat picture of her in the evening would show her covered with coloured aromatic shapes.

But attractiveness is not the question, anyway. Sleeping with another junior lawyer is simply not a good career move for Liam.

Although in his defence: everyone needs to tread some water from time to time, and she and Liam are friends. If you can't sleep with a friend, who can you sleep with? Enemies?

She suspects that he is sleeping with her in part because she is handy and quick, a snack of a relationship, something to nibble on between gulps of law and ambition. She also suspects that this relationship – or whatever it is – at least the sexual part of it, will last about as long as it takes to walk across a room.

Bicycling in the rain is not something Andrea recommends, even in a warm October. When she woke this morning, it had rained overnight, but the sky was a calm grey, so she thought she would be safe taking her bicycle. Tiny pindrops started coming down a minute or two after she left the house, like a series of dotted lines. She was hoping that this might be the end of it, but bigger drops followed, and now they are splattering on the street around her, getting in her eyes, and soaking her clothes.

Between the overnight rain and this rain, the trees along the street are sodden, intensifying their colours. A small tree with wet black branches and apricot leaves goes by, followed by a scraggly shrub in translucent red. The sidewalk is plastered with yellow and green leaves, and a clump of deadhead coneflowers rushes up and then disappears past her. The damp fabric of her pant legs is sticking to her thighs, and her handlebars are slippery with rain. She wipes her face with her sleeve, but it is wet again in a second.

Now it is raining hard enough that her wheels are splashing through puddles, sending up sprays of water. Good start, she thinks. This will help the well-groomed look.

A ginger-coloured oak tree goes by, and then another red shrub, but this one is darker, like red leather. A birch with hectic yellow leaves and some brown stalks in front of it passes by. Reddish-orange is creeping across a wall of ivy on her left, as if the ivy were heating up, and a bush with deep amber leaves slides past. Wet and uncomfortable as she is, she can't help exulting in this jumble of colour.

While she is exulting, she almost runs into a traffic island.

At work, she uses the paper towels in the women's washroom to dry herself off, and then blow-dries her hair under the hand-dryer.

'You look a little damp,' says Liam, when she walks into the boardroom. He has obviously been there for some time, since the table is littered with coffee cups and sugar tubes and stir sticks, and the remains of a muffin.

Carolyn puts her head in the doorway.

'I need someone to come with me on a motion today,' she says. She is a senior partner, a woman with dark brown hair and unusually good manners, who talks with the overconfident resonance of someone who has spent her life persuading people of things. She seems unflappable, almost languid, as if the water in her body had been replaced by something smoother and thicker, except that her nails are bitten down.

'What's the motion about?' says Andrea, trying not to look damp.

'It's a stock fraud. It should be interesting. In a way. I need someone to take notes.'

'I'll go,' says Liam. 'I mean, if –'

Carolyn looks inquiringly at Andrea. She is a woman who tries to be fair to women.

'Sure, go ahead,' Andrea says. She isn't interested in stock fraud, and she knows that Liam wants to work with Carolyn.

After Liam has gone, Andrea turns back to the papers in front of her, and picks up an affidavit.

1. *I, Carl Morthau, of the City of Toronto, make oath and say as follows: I am the spouse of the late Dr Rita Morthau, and as*

such have knowledge of the matters hereinafter deposed to.

2. Our son Gerard is three years old and was very close to his mother. Every night she would cut up a banana in milk for him, give him his bath, and read him Goodnight Moon before putting him to bed. Sometimes in the morning she would get up early and make date bread and then bring it upstairs to his bed. She would hang a sheet over his bed to make a tent, and then come and get me and we would eat breakfast in this way.

3. Since the accident, Gerard has become withdrawn and anxious, refusing to play with other children. I have retained the services of a child psychologist who meets with him every week, but she advises me, and I verily believe, that his progress is stalled, and that he has been traumatized by his mother's death.

4. Since my wife died, I have had endless migraines. I had no history of migraines previously. I have undergone numerous diagnostic and treatment procedures and there is nothing, which relieves the pain and still allows me to function normally. Medication that is strong enough to prevent the pain also puts me to sleep.

5. As a result of these migraines, I have been unable to work at my job as a pension benefits administrator.

Andrea skims through the rest of the affidavit until the last paragraph catches her eye.

I estimate the general and special damages suffered by myself and my son at $14.3 million dollars.

What are they going to do with the money? she thinks. Buy a new mother? A new wife? A bakery? But then she is ashamed of this thought. *These are tragedies, Bob. Real tragedies.*

She twists her hair up again. Why was Harry Singh going so fast? Was he worried about being late to pick up his daughter, a nine-year-old girl standing on the Danforth outside a closed ballet studio on a rainy night? Was he thinking about which video to get – *Air Bud* instead of *Lethal Weapon 2* (oh, Daddy, not *again*)?

And the radiologist? Was she hurrying home to see her son, finding it unbearable to spend another minute without him? Or thinking about a staff meeting that morning, those ridiculous new forms?

Who knows? Not Andrea.

She works steadily on the case for most of the morning, even though her mind feels slow, as if she were manually moving her thoughts from one location to another inside her head. Finally, she stretches and looks out the window. There are vertical strips of sky between the office buildings outside, and a gaseous October sun is partly visible. Below on the street, the leaves of a row of stunted trees in cement containers are turning rust-coloured at the edges, and people are sprinkled on the side-walk, like moving confetti.

The building next door is an insurance company building, shorter than Andrea's building, which means that she can look down on its roof. A security guard comes up and checks the roof at intervals, circling the enormous ventilation units. The guard this morning is a slight man with a sandy brush cut and a flat face, who looks young, even to Andrea. His hair is almost the same colour as his face and his khaki uniform, which makes him seem tidy, but undefined. After he does his circle, he sits down on a cinder block and smokes a cigarette, with his face turned up to the diluted sun.

'Not very professional,' Andrea says to him sternly, although of course he can't hear her. 'What about an aerial assault?' She pictures a group of men in camouflage outfits pouring out of a helicopter on the roof, even though an insurance company seems an unlikely candidate for a raid. Hand over all your casualty policies, or we shoot the receptionist.

The guard pulls up a trouser leg, and scratches his ankle, turning it to one side to look at it in the sun.

Andrea catches a trace of the smell of the soap she used this morning, a smell like irises. Her sense of smell is anomalous, a doctor said once to her mother when she was younger. *She's an anomaly.* An anomaly. She still likes the lolloping sound of this.

Isn't the nose too big? says her mother. They are in a small kitchen with cracked grey-green linoleum, and fiery-red geraniums on the counter. The geranium pots have old saucers underneath which are stained with calcium rings. Her mother is studying a sheet of poster paper that has a blue stick figure on it. The blue stick figure has big hands with many fingers, and a trumpet-like appendage growing out of its face.

No, says four-year-old Andrea. She is painting her toes blue with what is left on her paintbrush.

How about making another one? says her mother.

No, says Andrea.

Up it goes, then, says her mother. She rummages around in a drawer for Scotch tape, and tears off four pieces, sticking one on each finger. Then she holds the picture up to the wall with the heel of her hand, while she takes the tape off each finger and transfers it to the corners of the picture.

She steps back to look at it, and starts to laugh.

Andrea is stiff with indignation.

That's a real schnozz, her mother says. That is one big schnozzola.

'I have something for the ridiculous law contest,' Liam says. This is Andrea's project, the ridiculous law project, but he has now become an enthusiastic participant, and has turned it into a contest. 'There's a legal rule against absurdity.'

'You're making that up,' says Andrea.

'No, really,' he says. 'It's a rule of statutory interpretation.'

Andrea is speechless. She can't think of anything more absurd, more side-splitting, roll-on-the-ground-in-stitches and pound-your-feet-with-tears-in-your-eyes absurd, than a rule against absurdity.

'Does this mean I'm in the lead?' he says.

'You're in the lead,' she says.

At the end of the day, Andrea takes the elevator down to the parking garage, where she releases her bicycle from its kryptonite headlock and wobbles up the ramp to the street. Outside the sky is dark grey, with a lemon-coloured rim on one side. She tries to remember whether she has something to eat in her flat, and decides to stop at the supermarket.

The supermarket is brightly-lit, which looks oddly cheerful against the dark sky. She locks up her bicycle again, and takes a shopping cart on the way inside.

As she rounds the first corner, she is surrounded by a soft, smoky smell from a pile of eggplants on a display table. *Eggplants, Bob. Admit it, a ridiculous vegetable, a cartoon vegetable. The shape. The shiny purple skin. Even the name.* Of course, this is irresistible, so she puts one in the cart, even though she is almost certain it will end up rotting in her refrigerator.

The waxy smell of milk follows her into the next aisle, where there is a scratchy blast of Parmesan cheese, a smell so strong that it is almost aggressive. She walks more quickly, relieved when she reaches the canned goods, where only a light aluminum smell is humming around the shelves.

By the time she gets to her flat, she is late. Gaby is coming for dinner, and she plays basketball at eight. Their parents are in Victoria for a week in a time-share condo.

Like I can't feed myself, says Gaby when Andrea calls her at the prompting of her mother.

Who cares, come anyway, says Andrea. I'd rather feed you than listen to her.

She throws her backpack with files spilling out of it onto the couch, and starts pulling out groceries on the kitchen counter. The flat has a still feeling, an almost breathless feeling, so she turns on all the lights, and puts on a CD to stir up the air.

She cuts up some black olives and basil leaves, tips them into tomato sauce from a container, and boils water for linguini. Then Gaby is there, hauling a sports bag up the stairs.

She is taller than Andrea, even at seventeen, with straight legs, her hair short but bleached platinum. She has a faint air of exhilaration about her, but she is always like this, as if she had just plunged into a cold lake. When she talks, the *ch*'s in her words stand out, a slight *sh* sound underlying them.

Her room is full of sports trophies that she treats with contempt, at least for the benefit of other people, using them as hooks for old sweatshirts or tank tops. Sometimes Andrea wonders whether she clears off the trophies at night, and holds their cool surfaces up to her face. That's what Andrea would do. The idea of trophies is seductive – so tangible, so unambiguous. You won! Too bad they don't give them out to lawyers – a tasteful silver cup for a big case. Or maybe something more modern, more stylish, in Lucite.

'Hey,' says Gaby, 'what are all the files?'

'Just a case,' says Andrea. 'A car crash. Pretty ugly. One dead, one in bad shape.'

Gaby screws up her face.

The idea that a few seconds of inattention can fracture the worlds people take years constructing – the bananas and milk, the chess games, the cucumbers – is bothering Andrea.

'You look the wrong way, and it's *Goodnight Moon* forever,' she says.

Gaby drapes herself over a chair and starts leafing through an outdoor equipment catalogue.

'That's why you have to stay awake,' she says, surprisingly. 'Keep your eyes open.'

Andrea hands her two plates to put on the table.

'Regional finals on Saturday,' says Gaby.

'What does it feel like, anyway, when you win?' Andrea says suddenly.

'Good,' says Gaby, puzzled. 'It's good.'

'Really, really good? Incredible? Or just good?'

'It depends, I guess. If it's a big game, there's that glittery feeling. That's pretty good.'

Andrea tries to remember feeling this way. It sounds familiar, but maybe this is because she has seen Gaby after a game. Although usually her parents are the ones who go, both of them – her red-faced, round father, thinning hair, a runny kindness seeping through him which should be more appealing than it is, and his fiercely cheerful wife, a collector of pink Depression glass and a member of the Humber Tango and Rhumba Association, someone who lost eighty-seven pounds and has kept it off for nine years. *I used to be a big girl*, she likes to say, speaking of her transformation with a combination of confession, smugness and wonder. She is still short and stocky, but now she wears high heels everywhere, to Gaby's games, the drug store, all kinds – wedgies, pumps, stilettos, platforms – as if they were the defining symbol for her new, sleeker self.

Or just to look taller.

Is there such a thing as parents who are *too* supportive? Gaby said once. Andrea knows what she means – something about their devotion makes her feel uneasy as well, a certain heavy sensation at the bottom of her chest. Is it sadness? The knowledge that this extravagant dedication can never really be reciprocated? Or is it a sense of looming debt, that sooner or later a bill of some kind will be presented to her, that she will have to pay for all those years of nose-wiping and hand-holding and rides to the mall. A childhood with a deferred payment plan.

'How's the Bad Idea?' says Gaby.

'He's happy, he got to go to court with a senior partner today.'

'Still being careful?'

'Absolutely,' says Andrea, more confidently than she feels.

She is determined not to get caught with her feelings

hanging out this time. She is already wary of the various ways in which she has been infatuated before – the tiny, quartz crushes that settle into her chest, the binges of wrenching anxiety, the waves of high-octane euphoria, the sandy, teary explosions of affection. This is not happening to her again. Absolutely not. Is she stupid? No, she is not stupid.

Gaby eats two bowls of pistachio ice cream, and then she is gone, hauling her sports bag down the stairs again.

Liam calls later. Andrea is smoking the end of a joint she has discovered in a drawer while she was looking for a pen. The room has softened and lengthened, like an animal stretching, and Liam is buzzing in her ear. He is talking about working with Carolyn. You have to see her in court. She's so good, it's almost depressing. You wouldn't believe it. The strategy. The skill. The nerve.

'You realize you're fawning?' says Andrea.

'All right, all right,' says Liam. 'You talk, then, and I'll make snide remarks.'

'That's not snide,' she says. 'I'm just trying to keep you from a fate that includes Sycophants Anonymous.'

'No danger there for you,' he says. 'Although you might want to consider at least faking some interest. Carolyn was talking at lunch about fast-tracking you.'

'If I get fast-tracked any faster, I'll get motion sickness,' says Andrea, although she suspects that it was Liam who suggested the fast-tracking. He sometimes functions as an exasperated advocate for her – a few months ago he got raises for them both.

'And this is because you want to spend your life on car accident cases?'

'Not exactly,' says Andrea, although she immediately feels a streak of loyalty to Harry Singh. There is nothing wrong with car accident cases, at least a case like his. It has everything, all the issues – fault, liability, chance.

The word *fault* starts revolving around in her head. It must be a way of trying to impose order, she thinks, to make sense of something random like a car accident. A way of looking for cause and effect – no, *hoping* for cause and effect. For an explanation. If something bad happens, someone must have been bad. So who was it?

'Are you smoking dope?' says Liam. She can hear him sigh, hear him drumming the side of his thumb and his forefinger against something.

She ignores him. Her thoughts have started to disintegrate into tiny sparkling pieces. 'Do you ever feel like you're just pretending to be a lawyer?' she says. 'Like an imposter?'

'A lawyer *is* an imposter,' he says. 'I'm going to watch the news.'

Liam is baking, something he does when he is tense. This time he has made gingerbread men.

'This is stunningly domestic,' says Andrea with genuine admiration. He has brought them over to her flat, so that they can decorate them with icing.

'Great, maybe I can be a wife,' he says gloomily. 'Something to fall back on when I don't get into the partnership. Or a husband. Although then I'd have to get a Labrador retriever.'

'You'll be a partner,' says Andrea, in what she hopes is a heartily confident way. 'Any day now. Any minute now. Ahead of schedule.'

Despite his eagerness, despite his ambitions, Liam often becomes depressed, and she turns into the resident optimist for the duration. She is still a little rusty at this – she doesn't have the stock phrases or tones that a more experienced optimist would have, but she makes them up as she goes along. It seems odd to her that her personality is so mutable, as if its contours were shaped by echolocation, some kind of human waves bouncing off other people and then returning to define her self. She had assumed she was less relative, more absolute. Maybe that happens later, she thinks, the edges of her personality will harden as she gets older, by thirty she will have fixed, clean lines.

Or maybe she won't.

'Do you think we're regressing?' says Liam, as he drips icing onto a gingerbread man.

'Maybe this is a way of dealing with the testosterone fest at work,' says Andrea.

'Speak for yourself,' says Liam. 'Testosterone is a perfectly good hormone when used according to instructions.'

'What's that?' says Andrea, pointing to his gingerbread man, which has zigzag icing lines.

'He's a villain,' he says. 'I meant to tell you. These are bad gingerbread men. Very, very bad.'

'Is this where the "run, run, as fast as you can" thing comes in?'

'Exactly,' says Liam. 'Most of these gingerbread men are out on bail for unspeakable crimes. This one's a junk bonds artist. And this one's a priest who's been doing the altar boys.'

'I didn't know you could get bail for unspeakable crimes,' says Andrea.

'Hah,' says Liam. 'The more unspeakable the crime, the more likely you are to be released. Spectacular evil is full of ambiguity. It's your petty thief who's cooked.'

'In this case, baked,' says Andrea, handing him the blue icing tube.

Liam bites the leg off his gingerbread man.

'Then there's the personal injuries litigation,' she says.

Carolyn is also the senior lawyer on the Singh case, and she stops by Andrea's office to tell her that she is expecting another medical report about him. She is someone who can be suddenly charming, especially with clients – witty, but not too witty; self-deprecating, but not too self-deprecating; warm, but not effusive. This is so expertly done that Andrea sometimes has the impression that Carolyn puts this side of herself on in the morning, like a beautifully cut jacket.

She seems more normal today, and she sits down with her green tea in Andrea's office for a minute. She had been scheduled for court, but her case has adjourned, so she has a little pocket of unexpected time. How are things going? she says first (such good manners!), and listens carefully to the reply. They talk for a few minutes, and then she starts talking about her son, who has overnight become a bad-tempered adolescent. She is laughing about this – think I should get an exorcist? – but Andrea can see that she really is bewildered and hurt.

Andrea can't think of anything helpful to say, but then she realizes she doesn't have to say anything. Her role in this part of the conversation is to listen. This isn't hard. She is content to sit and smell the fibre smell of Carolyn's silk suit, her clear fingernail polish, her soapy hand cream.

'I should get going,' Carolyn says abruptly, as if she regrets having said so much. 'I should let you go. You probably come to the office to work.'

While she is standing up, Liam charges in and then stops. Instantly, the atmosphere in the office changes. Carolyn becomes glossier, and Liam becomes more physically present, as if his body had become outlined in black marker. They leave together, talking about the stock fraud case.

'Did you see that?' says Andrea to the security guard, a building away, who is doing his roof circle. He pulls his cinder block over a little, so that he can lean his back against the ventilation unit, and sits down, patting his shirt pocket for his cigarettes. Today, he has a cup of coffee with him as well, which he sets down carefully near his feet while he lights his cigarette. Then he picks up the coffee, takes off the lid and sips it. The sun is a little stronger today, and he unbuttons his jacket and stretches out his legs.

'Maybe you should come to the office to work,' says Andrea. She watches him smoke, and thinks about Liam. After a few minutes, he checks his wristwatch.

'So you think I'm making a mistake?' she says. He steps on his cigarette, picks up the butt and puts it in his coffee cup.

'Oh, come on,' she says. 'You'd be sleeping with him too, wouldn't you? If you were me?'

No?

What a liar.

Liam is back at the end of the day, moving restlessly around her office. I'm bored, he says. Let's hit the Royal, he says. If we leave now, we can make the seven o'clock.

The movie is about an African woman and the eccentric musician she works for in Italy. The movie is full of heat and colour − terra cotta, gold, straw − and light playing on walls blistered with age. The music is urgent, and Andrea feels saturated afterwards.

The night is dark and warm for October, and they walk down the street in silence to an outdoor patio. In the shadows, the young street trees look as if their branches are made of black felt. The patio has lights in the shape of fruit strung around it, and they sit at a table and drink beer in the grainy air, watching people streaming by on the wide sidewalk. Most of them carrying things, backpacks, satchels, shopping bags, handbags.

'Look at them, they look like they're evacuating,' Andrea says. 'Like an old sci-fi movie.'

'Except they're going in both directions,' says Liam. 'Better to go in one direction.'

'So what's happening with the stock fraud case?' says Andrea, although she really wants to know what's happening with Carolyn.

'I'm working on Carolyn,' he says, because he knows what she wants to know. 'If I can impress her, if she likes me, the sky's the limit.'

He has been tapping a stir stick on the table, and now he makes it travel up her arm.

'Ugh. How can you say "the sky's the limit" with a straight face?'

'I'm officially pro-ambition. Ambition is full of vitamins, it's low fat, good for the complexion. Gets you places.'

'Seriously,' she says. 'How do you know you'll like those places when you get there? *If* you get there,' she adds.

'I don't, I guess. I don't know any other way to do it. I mean, what's the alternative? Running in one spot?'

He has traded the stir stick for a coaster, which he is rolling back and forth on its side along the table. He can't help this constant movement. Even in his sleep, Andrea has seen one of his feet jiggling. How can you be asleep and moving at the same time? she says. People grind their teeth in their sleep, he says. Not to mention sleepwalking.

They drink until Liam is a little drunk, and Andrea is hovering near the explaining-things-gently-and-carefully stage. Then they join the migration, and their own shadows stretch out in front of them under the street lights, impossibly tall stick people. Liam rubs the back of her neck while they walk, something he does when he feels affectionate.

'I should really go home,' says Liam, when they get to her street.

'You should really go home,' says Andrea.

'I don't want to go home,' he says.

'Then don't,' she says.

Just one more time, she thinks. Soon, I will quit doing this. Very soon.

They lie in her bed afterwards and watch shadows flitting across the wall from passing headlights. His skin looks white and rubbery in this light, like the white of a hard-boiled egg.

This seems unflattering, so she tries to think of something friendly to say to make up for it.

'That torts book,' she says. This is the first thing that floats into her head.

'I don't know how you can give me a hard time about

ambition,' he says sleepily 'when you're thinking about torts in bed.'

Well, look at the name, Bob. Surely torts belong in bed?

'There were old chapters in there,' she says, ignoring this. 'Old chapters for when they had categories called idiots and lunatics.'

'You're kidding,' he says. 'That's stupid.'

'No, it's crazy,' she says, and they both laugh.

'What made you think of that?' he says.

'Nothing,' she says. 'Am I in the lead?'

'You're in the lead,' he says.

Then he falls asleep with one arm across her chest. Something about the protectiveness of this touches off a trickle of feeling in her, like the secretion of a gland. A minute later, she is drifting off to sleep as well, a subterranean sleep under his arm.

'Carolyn wants to be a judge,' says Liam. He is shaving the next morning, using her mirror and one of her pastel disposable razors.

'Me, too,' says Andrea, who is searching for a shirt she won't have to iron, although the thought of being a judge has never entered her mind until this second. It sounds good though. Why not be a judge? She likes the sinewy, gelatinous sound of the word – *judging*.

'You can't even pick the right person on *To Tell the Truth* reruns,' says Liam.

'I can get three out of five.'

'Well, judges need pomp and circumstance,' says Liam. 'Face it, you don't have the pomp.'

'Maybe not, but I have plenty of circumstance,' says Andrea.

'Look at this,' says Liam, taking out an envelope. They are eating a quick lunch at a falafel place a few weeks later, a tiny place with trays of tabbouleh and hummus, plates of pastry with honey and pistachios. The air is full of brown smells, cumin, turmeric, garlic, deep frying oil, grilled meat, cut with the smells of lemon rind and mint.

'Give me the short version,' says Andrea. She is holding a black olive in one hand and she can smell the report across the table, a bleached, pulpy smell.

'Singh had a stroke. A very minor one, he was probably only unconscious for a few seconds. Hardly any damage to his brain, they say. He might not have known about it if he had been in his bed, sleeping, at the time. He might have just woken up and carried on the next day.'

If he hadn't been driving. If he hadn't been at an intersection. If Rita Morthau hadn't been rushing home from work.

'I met them,' says Liam suddenly. He is tearing flatbread into strips. 'The Singhs. They came in one day, or at least the mother and the daughters came in, because she had to sign an affidavit. The older daughter is skinny, one of those bright faces, the other is a bit of smart-mouth, but in a good way. The mother is gorgeous, brown eyes, black hair, the whole thing. Somehow you think a person that gorgeous would end up with a better life than changing her husband's diapers.'

'Not much of a life for anybody.'

'You know what I mean. It seems like she ended up with the wrong life.'

How can you tell? thinks Andrea. Some kind of matching bar code?

'Things didn't work out so well for the daughters, either,' she says. 'Not to mention the radiologist's three-year-old. Who ended up with their lives?'

'Right, the whole thing,' he says. He is arranging his flatbread strips in a cross-hatch pattern. 'Anyway, Carolyn says it's going to settle now. It's all insurance money, anyway.'

Andrea feels relieved, but a little guilty, that she doesn't have to think about these people and their tragedies any more. Goodbye, Harry. Goodbye, gorgeous wife. Goodbye, Carl and Gerard. Hope it works out for you. Hope you find the right life.

Now Liam is tearing his flatbread strips into even smaller pieces, and dropping them into a small pile on his plate.

'What's the matter?' she says.

'I'm in love,' he says to his plate. The way he says this, though, it sounds final, as if he is climbing into a hard pink box and bringing the top down over himself.

In love? This is so banal that it makes him seem naked.

'You need a cliché doctor,' she says.

'No, really,' he says. 'With Carolyn.'

How long does it take to walk across a room?

She feels forlorn and awestruck by this. The nerve. The ambition. The strategy.

'Congratulations,' she says. 'I guess.'

He looks up, and for a second, she thinks she can almost see in the back of his eyes a tiny version of himself rolled into a ball, screaming, until he is swallowed up by his ambition. Then she realizes she is imagining things.

'No hard feelings?' says Liam.

No hard feelings, Bob? No hard feelings?

Are her feelings hard or soft? She feels like a corrosive gel is spreading into her lungs.

'All right,' he says, when she doesn't answer. 'Maybe that was the wrong question.'

'Don't talk to me,' she says, standing up.

'I hate you,' she says, putting on her coat.

'You're a bastard,' she says as she squeezes between the tables, and walks towards the door. Except that she's not sure she actually said any of these things.

Outside, the wind is swirling yellow leaves around on the sidewalk, pinning a piece of newspaper up against the pole of a parking meter.

She should have seen this coming.

Or maybe it was an inescapable peril.

She estimates her damages at $1.2 million.

* * *

33

Liam hovers around her for the next few days, coming into her office to talk about legal issues, borrowing things. Andrea doesn't want to see him, the sight of him sends a thin ache up the side of her body. She spends a lot of time looking out her window with her knees drawn up, looking down at the confetti people.

Maybe she does want to see him, though. He seems apologetic, but is he apologetic enough? What is enough, in this situation? Although even an unreliable friend, even an obsessively ambitious friend is distracting. What she would really like to do is complain to Liam about himself, to do a caustic inventory with him of all his faults, to make sardonic jokes together, to have him take her out for a drink and tell her that he wasn't worth it. You're lucky it didn't go further, she can hear him say. At least you found out quickly.

She is still looking out the window when the security guard comes out, does his circle in a deliberate way, and then sits down on his concrete block. He has a newspaper today, as well as his coffee, and one of the pages is fluttering in the breeze. A traffic helicopter buzzes by, and he turns to look at it.

'I'm sorry to be the one to tell you this,' she says to him, 'but your life is a lie. There is no such thing as security. It's a trick.'

A school janitor gets into his Ford Taurus to do the most ordinary things – get his daughter, pick up a video – things he has done safely a thousand times before, and then a few seconds of unconsciousness at an intersection, and his ordinary life implodes.

So casual. So vicious. Just a flip of some existential coin, spinning aimlessly in the air for a second, and then coming down with a light *plink*. Heads, a video with microwave popcorn tonight. Tails, brain damage and incontinence.

No warning, Bob. No margin of error. No appeal.

Although if this kind of thing can happen in such a random way, perhaps this leaves open the possibility of accidental good luck as well. Some astounding, jubilant fluke should be just as likely, at least in theory.

Unless, of course, the good luck is simply a matter of avoiding the bad luck.

Perhaps the point is to avoid making a lot of plans.

She looks at the time on her computer screen – 6:47. She has told Gaby that she will come to the regional finals because their parents are still away.

She takes the subway out to Etobicoke, where the game is being held in an old school gym, a school that has wooden scaffolding around the entrance to support the stained brick archway. The gym is cold, and has high ceilings and enormous light fixtures on heavy metal racks. The air is filled with acrid smells, like rubber and sweat and urethane, so many smells that the gym seems even more crowded than it is. Andrea slides onto a bench at the back, far above the court, next to a heavy woman in a dirty pink jacket. Down on the court, Gaby is ducking and feinting and dribbling and jumping as if she were electrically charged. Andrea doesn't watch basketball, other than Gaby's games, but she is surprised again by its fluidity, the way the taller players palm the ball into the basket, and the herky-jerky moves they make around each other. The game has a buzz/relax cycle, so that when the play starts, there is a frenzied knot of activity roaming back and forth across the court. This dissolves into the players sauntering around when the play stops, only to bunch up again a minute later.

The crowd is chanting, and now there is a discussion going on the court with the referee. Andrea looks around the arena, and up at the high ceiling. One of the wide light fixtures is sagging. They should do something about that, she thinks idly. She wonders how long it has been hanging there like that. Then she sees it shift another couple of centimetres, and feels a chill seeping down her back.

She must be imagining it. Too much thinking about Harry Singh, too much thinking about disaster. Or too much imagination. Clearly, there is a lesson here. What is the lesson? She should keep more distance between herself and her cases. Or she should smoke less dope. Or more. Or something like that.

The play has started again, but Andrea keeps her eyes glued to the light fixture, trying not to blink. Is it shifting again? She can't see it well enough from where she is. There must be building standards for a school.

There is a throaty tearing sound, and half of the fixture is no longer attached to the ceiling, hanging by one support, bits of plaster and dust spattering the court.

She tries to yell, but the sound of the crowd drowns her out. She leaps off the bench and is running down the cement steps of the bleachers, as fast as she can without falling herself, her feet clattering at top speed, like some kind of crazed dance step, her breath coming more quickly now, she is focused on trying not to trip herself. There is no sound except the crowd roaring. She can see people in her peripheral vision, a blur at the sides of the aisle, turning slowly to look at her, and she almost falls.

'Are you all right?' says the woman in the dirty pink jacket. Andrea looks up and finds that she is holding grimly on to her bench, still sitting at the top of the arena.

She closes and opens her eyes. Then she looks at the ceiling where the light fixture is still solidly anchored to the ceiling. This is ridiculous, she thinks, but blood is roaring in her ears, and her hands are sweating. She uncurls her hands stiffly from the bench, and opens them up.

I have a question, Bob. I realize that you're the one who is supposed to ask the questions, but this won't take long. I just want to know this one thing about bad luck, about the random selection of people for brain cancer or fires or flash floods or earthquakes, or even plain, ordinary car accidents. I just want to know this one thing:

How do you get to be one of the lucky ones?

Fish Responsible

Frank Merton believes that there is a point in the middle of every summer when the thick heat starts making people stupid. He sees them wandering into the Foodmaster store where he works, looking for cold things to eat or drink, ice cream bars, cantaloupes, ginger ale, their eyes crusty from lack of sleep because of the stifling nights. In the frozen food aisles, they have a slightly dazed look on their faces, as if they've spent the day banging their shins on open drawers or knocking over their drinks, the ice cubes spinning out across the floor.

This is the point in the summer, the stupid point, when he finds out that he has been promoted to Fish Responsible.

'Hey, what can I say?' says the store manager, who comes over to the produce section in the late afternoon to tell him that he has the position. 'You're a natural, know what I mean?' He sticks out his hand to shake Frank's – *put it there, buddy* – except that Frank's hands are filled with the yellow peppers that he's been unpacking, so the manager claps him on the back instead. Then they talk a little longer because the manager wants to stretch out this moment, make the most of his own generosity, and provide the maximum opportunity for Frank to appreciate it as well. Frank keeps on working while they talk because he's a little embarrassed by the attention.

'Not exactly a big surprise,' says the manager, picking up a grape from the floor, and looking around for a place to throw it.

'I guess not,' says Frank. In fact, he's been waiting for this news since the previous Fish Responsible took an early retirement buy-out in June, talking about his restless leg syndrome. *I've had it, Frank, I'm just beat during the day. My legs are going all night like one of those dogs chasing squirrels in its sleep.* Frank is not the kind of person who would raise the

subject of Gord's other small problem – the sour morning hang-
overs, and the miniature bourbon bottles in the garbage can in
the men's toilet. More like restless arm syndrome, says the bakery assistant to Frank at Gord's retirement party, and some of
the people around them snicker.

'Will you get a load of that?' says the manager. He takes the
empty yellow pepper carton from Frank, and puts the grape in
it, while he watches one of the stock boys manoeuvre a
hydraulic dolly stacked with cases of romaine and iceberg lettuce down an aisle. The stock boy, whose name is Marco and
who has heavy black eyebrows and pebbly skin, is pointedly
ignoring the manager and Frank. He was the other candidate
for the Fish Responsible position, the unsuccessful candidate.

'Nose out of joint,' says the manager. He raises his voice
slightly. 'Well, that's the way the old cookie crumbles. C'est la
goddamn vie.'

The manager turns toward Frank again and shrugs slightly.
'Let's face it, not many people been here as long as you, that's
gotta count for something.' He starts fixing the hair above one
of his ears by making quick motions with his half-cupped
hand, the thumb and forefinger of his other hand resting on his
hip.

Twenty-three years, Frank thinks. Twenty-three years in the
same store. This thought surprises him again, as if he keeps
bumping into these years, piled up like a stack of used tires. It's
true, they *should* get you something, he thinks – or at least
something besides a chance at a pension that wouldn't keep a
cockroach alive.

The opportunities for career advancement at the store are
limited, though, even for the most unambitious, a category
which probably includes Frank by default. He has already
done almost every other job in the store, except the Meat
Responsible, and this is only because the idea of spending his
days sinking cleavers into white fat, pork blood draining into a
table gutter, doesn't appeal to him. The fish job is a different

proposition – most of the stock arrives at the store already filleted, slick pieces of fish flesh.

He fits the last two peppers into place in the pile on the display table, feeling their cool skins.

'I shouldn't be telling you this,' says the manager, lowering his voice, 'but about the job? Confidentially? Between you and me? It wasn't even close.'

'Christ, those fish are ugly,' says the bakery assistant, whose name is Louise. She is standing by the fish counter with Frank, eight months later, stuffing the bunchy brown mass of her hair into a store issue hairnet with quick, bird-like motions.

'Tell me something I don't know,' he says.

'That wouldn't be tough,' she says.

'Hardy har har.' He leans over to rearrange some of the plastic greenery around the fish, which are spread out over piles of crushed ice. The fish counter is a new one, designed to look like a fish market stand, with black and white tiles around the base and nothing but a Plexiglas guard between the customers and the fish. So they can stare at each other, eyeball to glassy eyeball, he thinks. At least for the fish that still have their eyeballs.

Louise gives her hair a final push, and then yanks a sack over to the self-serve bins a few feet away from the fish counter so that she can fill them up with cheese buns and hard rolls. She has a long, curious nose and a tense forehead, and her fingers are twiggy but flattened at the ends, as if years of sliding loaves of bread into paper sleeves had moulded her hands into the most efficient design for handling them. Her body is large and lumpy under the white coat she is required to wear (like we're a bunch of frigging scientists, she says), although her legs are thinner, and she crosses them as if they were expensive.

She needs a warning label, a cashier said to Frank once. Like the cleaning stuff in aisle 5: *Caustic. Avoid contact with skin. Flush affected area with water.*

Frank finds her particularly difficult to take in the early mornings, when he is less alert – his brain seems to wake up in sections, one after another, rather than all at once. If he were being truthful, though, he would have to admit that she is too fast for him at almost any time of the day, since quick retorts are not one of his strong points. Or one of his any points. He is still willing to put up with her, though, because – because why? Because he is that kind of person, he supposes, someone who puts up with things, and because she is funny, and because she leaves a small trail of bleary warmth behind her.

She's right about the fish, anyway, he thinks. Ugly is the word. He looks over at the counter, at the dead-white squid, the octopus with purple suckers, the grubby clam shells, the shiny grey piles of raw tiger shrimp. They seem more naked than the other items in the store.

'You want to see ugly?' says Wilson Lee, one of the other stock boys who is bending over a few feet away from Frank and Louise, slitting open a case of butterscotch pudding cups. 'Check out those lobsters. Now that's *ugly*. Like giant bugs. Or aliens. Yeah, that's it,' he says, pleased with himself. 'Aliens. Probably smarter than us, and here we are, eating them.' He straightens up and waves his box knife over towards the live lobster tank beside the fish counter. He has an earring in one ear and a sparse goatee, which is wiggling a little because he is chewing sugarless gum.

'Not me, buster,' says Louise. 'I don't eat anything that looks like that.'

Frank glances over to where the lobsters are hanging in the water in the tank, their bodies dark green with purplish-brown blotches. They have eye beads on small stalks, and their antennae and claws are bobbing. One makes a half-hearted attempt to crawl over another one, and then gives up.

'They're crustaceans,' he says. 'They're supposed to look like that.' He has a Basic Fish I manual he inherited from the previous Fish Responsible, a dog-eared blue binder divided into sections. Lobsters have a section to themselves:

Q. How large is a lobster's brain?
A. Lobsters have relatively small brains. As a result, they do not feel pain, at least not in the way that human beings do. You may assure customers that they can lower the live lobster into a pot of boiling water without being cruel.

'If I looked like that, I would kill myself,' says Wilson.
'Well, that's something,' says Louise.

Eating fish is an acquired taste for many people, and Frank has never acquired it.

Fortunately, he has a number of good excuses. While he was married, for instance, his wife didn't like the taste. Like boiled rubber, Doreen said. She was talking about fish in general, though, because she left long before Frank was promoted, walking out the door of their brick bungalow in Mimico with her orange and turquoise flowered suitcase in one hand, her matching overnight case in the other, and the cat carrier balanced under one arm.

So this is one excuse. Another is that he has the sweetish, rank smell of the fish in his nose and on his fingers all day, now that he is the Fish Responsible. This means that fish are the very last thing he wants to see on his plate at night. At first he tries rubbing lemon wedges on his hands to get rid of the smell, but the lemon juice works into little dry cracks in his skin and stings, so he gives up.

'Who's going to smell it, anyway?' says Wilson tactlessly.

May, 1985, the Victoria Day weekend. One of those sleepy, sunny weekends when the drone of lawnmowers on crewcut grass makes it seem as if time is eddying around, instead of proceeding in the usual brisk line. People step outside in the morning to get their newspapers, and then stop and sniff the damp air, surprised at how many smells are mingled into it, car exhaust fumes and honey locust trees mixing with sulphur and a freshwater smell from the lake, and some familiar smell they can't place. A long weekend, which means they can count the extra day over and over. Saturday – and there's still two full days to go! Sunday – another whole day after this! Monday – here we are, not working! Not that we don't goddamn deserve it.

The last weekend in the world that a wife would leave her husband.

All three days are still clear in Frank's mind, a jumble of sharp details he spent months raking over after she left, looking for clues, hints, anything. Months reviewing his own movements – putting a new cord on the weedwhacker, eating a cheese and pickle sandwich, reading a hardware store catalogue cover to cover, planting some zinnias and marigolds for her along the driveway, drinking a slow beer or two with the sports showcase on television. Which one of these things was the trigger, the moment when some sour part of himself was revealed, some rotting defect that made him unfit to be a husband? Even after all these years, he is still bewildered. What he remembers most about the weekend is that he was relaxed – since when is that a crime? – sitting outside in a webbed lawn chair without thinking about whether he should be doing something else. Sitting there, content to have the warm sun on his face and arms, and to watch an airplane sawing across the sky, leaving a trail like a scrape of white chalk.

Hey, here's a thought. Gord called on the Monday. *Forget about fighting the traffic, skip the fireworks – just come on out to the house and Patty'll make her pork chops with that cream of mushroom soup sauce.*

Patty produces a macaroni-celery salad and a cherry cheesecake as well as the pork chops, and they eat hungrily, sitting out on the patio, watching the evening light get greyer and denser. The conversation drifts easily from one thing to another, and when it gets dark enough, Gord switches on the new torch lights he has installed. They can hear the banging and whistling of the fireworks in the distance, and Frank slowly peels the label off his beer bottle while he and Gord talk about baseball until Doreen and Patty get bored, and start a side conversation about one of the cashiers who has a mentally retarded daughter, and whether gelatin will make their fingernails stronger. The smoke from Doreen's Du Mauriers curls up into the night air, and when Frank finishes peeling his label, he begins twisting the foil liners from her cigarette package into the shape of tiny cups. Then he makes a little foil table, and puts the cups on it.

On the way home in the car, Doreen is suddenly irritable.

'We should have gone to the fireworks,' she says accusingly, as if Frank had been the one standing in her way. (Was that it? A few showers of coloured stars and things would have been all right?)

'Well, now,' he says. 'I guess we can always go to the ones in July.'

'Blah, blah, blah, all night about baseball.' She pushes in the car lighter.

'It wasn't all night.' (If they had talked about something else?)

'Him and his drinking,' she says. 'I don't know how Patty puts up with it.'

'I don't see that it's any of our business.' He feels his chest stiffening. (If he hadn't defended Gord?)

She takes her cigarettes out of her purse, without the foil.

'Well, whatever it is she sees in him,' she says, 'it's lost on me.'

The fact that Frank doesn't eat fish himself doesn't prevent him from telling other people how to cook it. This culinary advice is one of the store manager's marketing ideas, the same manager who announced Frank's promotion. Kenny Peruccio has thick hair, a high, stretchy voice and a shelf full of exercise videos. Abs of Steel. Biceps of Steel. Thighs of Steel. He is someone who has laboriously built himself from scratch, a container of muscles filled up with manufactured confidence. I'm a go-getter, he says, with utter sincerity.

He is still stocky, though, still slightly pigeon-shaped, but tighter looking, especially because he usually wears tight clothes as well. Around his neck he has a small cross, even though he is not particularly religious. He likes the look, though, the impression that he is connected, particularly to something important and powerful. 'The Pope and I, we're like that,' Frank half expects him to say one day, holding up two fingers twisted together.

Kenny is an eager participant in company training courses, which means that he likes to talk about ambiance, or selling to market niches, or brainstorming the shopping experience. *They're dynamite, these courses, they've got it all down cold.* He is a fervent brainstormer, a true believer. Except that most of his brainstormed ideas are ridiculous.

'It's only brainstorming if you have a brain,' says Louise.

Frank is often assigned the tricky job of talking him out of these ideas.

'You have to do it, Frank,' says Wilson. 'You're the only one older than him, and you're kind of easygoing, so he'll listen to you. Louise has too much of a mouth, and he's not going to take it from a stock boy or a cashier.'

Frank isn't particularly skilful at this job, this uncomfort-able responsibility. It requires a kind of a conversational agility that doesn't come naturally to him. His sentences normally come clumping out in quiet straight lines. But no one else can (or will) do it – the Meat Responsible is spineless, someone who would never risk offending Kenny unless there was something in it for him.

As Kenny's ideas go, however, the Recipe of the Day is one of the more innocuous ones.

You know the blackboard where you write up the specials, Frank? Put some recipes up there. They're gonna buy more fish if they know how to cook it.

So Frank begins writing out short recipes on the blackboard, and Wilson, who is taking courses in computer animation at night, uses coloured chalk to sketch a border or add a picture of a little fish leaping with a lemon slice in the corner. Louise lugs in some cookbooks – *be my guest, it's not like I'm using them* – and Frank picks out recipes based on the kind of fish they have in stock that day, particularly whatever they are trying to unload.

Unexpectedly, the Recipe of the Day blackboard prompts people to ask Frank how to cook other kinds of fish. *How about this one? Think it would be good grilled?* At first he is taken aback, but the more he reads, the more knowledgeable he sounds, as if he really knows his fish cuisine. In fact, he has no idea whether the recipes are any good or not, but no one complains about them. If they don't turn out well, he suspects that the customers assume this is their own fault, that they must have forgotten a step, or done something else wrong.

'You take a piece of that nice fresh salmon,' he says, 'and poach it for eight minutes in some chicken stock, aisle 4, with a little white wine, and some tarragon sprigs from produce, aisle 9.' This is one of his best recipes because it sounds stylish, but it's also easy to remember. 'Then arrange it on a bed of arugula, also in produce, put some lemon slices on top, dice some red pepper finely and sprinkle it over the fish, and then put some more tarragon sprigs here and there on the plate.'

Of course, that nice fresh salmon is probably on special because it's already been sitting around for a few days. And the truth is that he has never poached anything in his life – fifty-four years old, and not even a poached egg has emerged from his hands. When Doreen was still around, she did all the cooking, part of a nightly marital ritual in which she offered up dinner to him, and he accepted it gravely. He would taste the food, and then carefully and unfailingly praise each part of it, offering his appreciation, his quiet enjoyment of it to her in return. *Nice chicken. Like those potatoes that way.* When she left, the idea that he could start cooking, that he could take on her role in this exchange seemed almost perverted, with the result that he acquired only the culinary skills necessary to take food out of a microwave container and put it on a plate.

But now he can at least speak the language, a grammar of peppercorn-crusted tuna steaks, mussels in garlic-coriander broth, orange roughy with brandy, pan-fried sole with lemon-basil sauce, lobster and cucumber salad. He even includes tips from other customers – *add the oil slowly to the dill mayonnaise, too quick, and it just sits on top.* His list of recipes has become so long that he has started to feel that he is part of this cookbook world, this place where people cook blackened red snapper, or scallops with angel hair pasta, or lime-ginger shrimp. He realizes that he is not a resident of this world himself, but he sees himself as expert help, a consultant, in the same category as a landscaping contractor or a renovator – someone who provides indispensable advice to the real residents. He would never actually eat anything so elaborate anyway. Except for maybe the beer-battered cod and chips. They sound good. They sound edible.

'A regular frigging Martha Stewart,' Louise says, one morning when he has been talking to customers more than usual.

She and Frank are sitting with Wilson in the lunchroom, which consists of a green and black card table and folding chairs set up in one corner of the backroom storage area. The cement floor is dirty, and a piece of old lettuce is plastered to it. Most of the catches on the lockers are broken, so that the doors hang open, the paint coming off them in spots. (That head office, they don't like to go overboard with their employees, says Louise.)

'You mean *Mr* Stewart,' says Wilson. 'Martin Stewart. Marty Stewart. Could be a whole new line.'

'Unless you've gone and gotten one of them sex change operations and just forgot to tell us,' says Louise.

'Ha. Ha. Ha.' says Frank.

'Seriously, Frank,' Wilson says. 'Maybe you should write a
cookbook or something.'

'Sure,' says Louise. 'Like the Seniors' Guide to Crustaceans.'

'I'm glad you think this is so funny,' says Frank.

'Don't get your shorts in a knot,' Louise says, taking a gulp
of her coffee from the vending machine and making a face.
Frank looks at his own styrofoam cup. The vending machine
dispenses the same muddy, lukewarm liquid regardless of the
button pushed – coffee, tea, hot chocolate, even the chicken
soup. Usually they end up in the Donut Delight across the parking lot for their breaks, where Wilson smokes and Louise eats
an apple cruller, but Wilson has a nicotine patch now. *You're
supposed to stay away from places that remind you of smoking,*
he says. *It's a mental thing.*

'Christ, it's hot,' says Wilson. The air-conditioning system is
down for an hour, while a technician performs a series of main-
tenance functions, his tools laid out on a grimy cloth in the corner. Frank is trying to breathe deeply so that he doesn't sweat
too much, but this is the second week of a heat wave, and the
effect of all those hot days in a row seems to be cumulative, as if
his internal body temperature has been slowly rising. Although
the coffee is probably not helping.

The heat has been a strange, hard heat, so intense that he
lies in bed at night covered with a film of sweat, until he feels as
if he is suffocating. Then he gets up and goes into the bathroom
where he sits on the side of the bathtub and wipes his face and
arms and legs down with a wet washcloth. Sometimes he brings
the washcloth back to bed with him and puts it in reach on the
bottom sheet, where it leaves a wet mark. He has a fan on his
dresser, and he lies in the bed watching a ribbon attached to the
fan's wire hood flutter in the air flow. Usually he finds the hum

of the blades hypnotic, except that now the fan has developed a clicking noise. Outside, the heat is even worse – when he walks out of his house in the morning, the same heavy, polluted air is still squatting there, as if it hasn't moved all night.

'Or how about one of them self-help books,' says Louise. 'I bet you can make a good buck off them.'

'Yeah, well,' Frank says. 'If I knew anything about self-help, I would have helped myself a long time ago.'

Wilson is talking about his parents again. 'They don't get it about animation,' he says morosely. They want him to be a doctor or, in the worst case scenario, a lawyer, but at least a professional. They didn't bring the whole family over from Taiwan (like they swam all the way, says Wilson) so that he could learn how to make cartoons.

'And who the hell wants to be a doctor, anyway?' The energy that usually goes into smoking is making him twitchy, so that he is talking faster and more emphatically than usual, although talking about his parents always upsets him. 'You go to school for about a hundred years, and then you end up giving people rectal exams. You want to look up their noses? Lance their abscesses? Or you could be a surgeon, and just cut open people's guts.'

'All righty,' says Frank. 'I think we got your point there. In fact, maybe I won't be a doctor either.'

'Okay, then,' says Louise, with a sigh. 'I guess I'll skip medical school too. Just to be a real pal. After all, look at all the job satisfaction I got putting out the kaiser rolls. Can't beat that with a stick.'

'Not to mention all the new ambiance.' Frank looks around the storeroom. One wall has a health and safety poster and a tarnished face mirror on it, and there is a cracked tub sink with a sign over it, showing a pair of hands crawling with magnified germs. *Don't forget – Get them wet*, it says. A broken paper towel dispenser is sitting beside it with an empty cardboard roll.

'Yeah, that's it,' says Louise. 'That's what I like too, all the ambiance.'

She makes her voice higher and gives herself an English accent.

'Would you care for a little ambiance? Do you take milk or sugar with your ambiance? Why don't you stick it up your ambiance?'

Wilson laughs.

'You know those lobsters, Frank?' he says a few minutes later.

'Yeah,' says Frank.

'Do you really need those bands on their claws? I mean, what are the chances of them grabbing you?'

'You could get a pretty good pinch from them, I guess.' Frank swirls the dregs around in the bottom of his cup where all the sugar has collected, and then drains it. 'But the bands are mainly so they don't try to eat each other. They get cannibalistic because they're not used to being cooped up together like that.'

Q. Can you cook a lobster with the bands on?
A. Yes. You can assure customers that studies have shown this does not change the taste when they are immersed in boiling water. Also, it is not advisable to remove the bands, as injury may occur.

'Well, isn't that just charming,' says Louise.

'Fish are the last to discover water,' says Wilson, looking at the lobster tank later that day. He taps on the glass.

'What's that, some Chinese saying?' says Louise. She says this as if she is genuinely curious, though, instead of being sarcastic.

'Beats me,' says Wilson.

* * *

One of the advantages of being the Fish Responsible is that there isn't very much cutting and slicing required, especially in contrast to the meat department, where the butchers split chicken breasts and butterfly pork chops almost continuously. If there are special requests for fish, Frank uses the work station in the back which has a set of German fish knives, but this doesn't happen often, particularly since he ensures that his recipes involve cuts of fish that are already available. When a loin of tuna or salmon comes in, he cuts it into steaks, but this is about the extent of it, which suits him. The cutting itself involves wearing metal mesh gloves so that he doesn't slice off a finger by mistake, and trying to cut one-inch steaks off a slippery, cold piece of fish while he is wearing these gloves is not something he particularly enjoys, especially since he has bursitis in his left hand. The rest of the fish comes off the truck in fillets, or in net bags for the mussels and the little neck clams. He unpacks it, thaws the frozen stock, rinses it and sets it up on the display counter.

And it's not always ugly, thinks Frank. Sometimes the colours of the fish – the orange salmon, the pink and white cooked shrimps, the red snapper, the silver blue of the trout skin – are actually striking. This makes him wonder what they looked like in the ocean or the lake, before they were netted. Gliding around in their silent, watery universe, slipping behind seaweed, their fins waving slowly, a flash of brilliant scales as they turn their flat bodies one way and then the other, their staring eyes fixed on the sides of their heads. Although half of them probably come from fish-farming operations. He can't imagine lobsters doing any gliding either. They must scuttle around. Shrimps? Who knows? They don't seem likely to be gliders, though. And the squid – do they swim with all those tentacles waving around them? Or streaming behind them like hair blowing in the wind?

Kenny usually comes by the counter about eight-thirty in the morning.

'Looking good there, Frank.'

Positive feedback is something else Kenny picked up in another one of his corporate courses. Frank suspects that the trainer didn't realize his students would go back and tell their employees all the details of the course, the theories of rewarding performance and enforcing negative consequences. 'Why don't they just call it the carrot and the stick?' says Louise. 'Kenny's a moron.'

Hard to argue with that, Frank thinks. On the other hand, things could be worse than having a manager who runs on about his courses, or passes out oily compliments. Kenny might be a little vain, a little weak, a little too much of a go-getter or an up-and-comer, but he isn't a bully. 'Not like Vic,' he says to Louise. The previous store manager changed the cashiers' schedules almost daily, and then watched them frantically trying to salvage their babysitting arrangements.

'Not much of a comparison,' says Louise.

'Well, Kenny expanded the deli counter,' says Frank. Instead of mock chicken loaf and cole slaw, there are now antipastos, feta cheese in brine, dried tomatoes, marinated portobello mushrooms, and an olive table with a little roof over it.

Upscaling. *Upscale* reminds Frank of dressing a fish. Can I upscale that for you, ma'am? Downscale it?

Or a measuring term. Put the fillet on the scale, put your finger on, and there you are – upscaled.

Of course, they still have to deal with Kenny's brainstorming.

'Listen up, Frank, I got an idea,' says Kenny one day.

An idea. Frank tries to smooth out his face, so that he doesn't look irritated, and waits. 'How about we set up the lobster tank like a little aquarium? You know, put in some of that coloured gravel, some of those aquarium things, people come over to look at it, they see the fresh fish beside it, and then – bingo – they buy some fish.'

'Well,' says Frank. But this is such an awful idea that he can't think of anything to say quickly enough, he doesn't know where to start.

Kenny begins rubbing his hands together.

'Do I know marketing, or what?'

Several days later, the tank is equipped with coloured gravel, plastic weeds and a skeleton sitting beside a little treasure chest. There is also a large clam shell that opens and closes, up and down. The lobsters keep dislodging these things, and Frank is worried they might try to eat some of the plastic weeds. *There's nothing against it, no health regs or anything, says Kenny.* No kidding, Frank thinks. What health inspector could possibly have anticipated an idea like this?

People do wander over to look at it, although it doesn't seem to inspire anyone to buy more fish.

Louise is not as scathing as Frank thought she would be, but this is only because she can't stop laughing. She puts down her case of packaged apple strudels to inspect the tank more closely.

'You've really gotta do something about that eating disorder, honey,' she says to the skeleton. Then she peers at the lobsters. 'Thinking about a career change? Ever heard of synchronized swimming?'

She looks up at Frank. 'Hey, one of these beauties only has one claw.'

'They drop them sometimes,' he says. 'They can even grow them back, although I've never seen it. Maybe we don't keep them around long enough.'

'Doesn't it hurt them?'

'I don't know,' says Frank. 'I guess if it doesn't hurt them to go into boiling water, it doesn't hurt them to drop a claw.'

No brain, no pain.

Q. What is the best way to hold a lobster?

A. Grasp it carefully around the end of the carapace

where it joins the tail, keeping your distance from the claws.

'Ever heard of sea cucumbers?' says Wilson. He is standing by the tank, watching the lobsters move around.

'No,' says Frank. 'What are they, some kind of seaweed?'

'They're a kind of fishy thing, like sea slugs. But when they're attacked, they can liquefy themselves, pour themselves into some hidey-hole, and then harden up again.'

'Huh,' says Frank.

'Well, there's something we all needed to know,' says Louise.

Someone has attached a Free Willy decal on the lobster tank, and Frank has his eye on Wilson as the prime suspect. It's not that Frank doesn't appreciate the humour of this little act of mock protest, but he is the one who has to scrape the decal off, and it seems to have a particularly strong adhesive. The prime suspect himself is in the produce section at the moment, innocently picking over the potatoes, removing the green ones and putting them in a garbage bin. The produce section is at the front of the store, and to the left of the fish counter, so that he and Frank are within talking distance of each other. Other than this, the physical design of the area has little to recommend it. Frank has pointed out to Kenny previously that it means that customers end up with their fruits and vegetables at the bottom of their carts, while the heavy groceries, like cartons of milk and orange juice and detergent, sit on top of their tomatoes and strawberries. *You gotta understand marketing, says Kenny. The fruits and vegetables are good-looking, so the company wants them up front.*

'So Frank, how come you've been here this long?' Wilson says. 'I mean, twenty, twenty-five years. That's a hell of a long time.' He gives a descending whistle as he lobs a potato into the bin.

'I don't really know,' says Frank slowly. Is it possible to

explain something like this, especially to someone who is only twenty-two himself? Look how time flies? Dang, where did my life go? He suspects that Wilson is really asking something like this: *You seem like a smart enough kind of guy, Frank. What happened to you? And will it happen to me?*

'Well, I got fired from the job I had before,' Frank says finally.

The water sprayers hiss over the lettuces.

It was one of his better jobs, driving a small forklift in a warehouse owned by a chain of hardware stores. Merchandise came into the warehouse from different suppliers, and was shipped out to the retail stores as they placed orders. At first he was clumsy, jerking the gears backward and forward to position the forklift. He often ended up with an older machine as well, because the other men grabbed the better ones quickly at the start of the shift. But he liked the feel of the forklift motor, the powerful whine of the hydraulic lift, and after a while, he could take a pallet full of cases and tuck it into an empty spot on a storage shelf as neatly and quickly as slipping a pancake onto a plate. Space was tight in the warehouse, and he and the other drivers had to zigzag around each other, as if they were doing some kind of mechanical dance.

One afternoon, the shift foreman pulled him over on the loading dock.

Hey kid, you want to make a little on the side?

Like what?

Like a few extra bucks.

Something you have in mind?

The foreman had in mind that a few cases of this and that would disappear from time to time, never very much – you get greedy, he said, you can blow the whole thing – but Frank would change the paperwork so that it would go unnoticed. It meant a promotion for Frank as well, to shipper-receiver, so that he was the one taking the deliveries.

What an idiot he was.

Six months later, he had lost his job and acquired a criminal record.

But working in a grocery store? And for twenty-three years? You try finding another job with a criminal record.

Was that the reason?

Well, of course, there was Doreen again. That was another reason. There was always that reason. For a long time after she left, he couldn't stand even the idea of change, the sickening fluidity of everything. We had a regular life, he could say to Wilson. Cornflakes and instant coffee for breakfast, dividing up the newspaper, I got the Sports, she took the Life section. Shake and Bake chicken for dinner with peas, a salad with radishes and tomatoes, and Thousand Island dressing. A freezer cake for desert, *Jeopardy* on TV after. Errands at the mall, and a movie on Sunday, Mel Gibson or maybe Harrison Ford. The same spot in Wasaga Beach every year with the tent trailer. Every repetition, every round of these things added another comfortable layer on top of the one before it. But then all of these layers which felt so warm and solid to Frank, the easiness of knowing where everything was and when everything would happen, suddenly seemed to overwhelm Doreen with dread that her life had become as fixed and boring as white glue.

You're like a cup of Sanka, Frank. No offence or anything, but what I need is a shot of Johnny Walker.

After she left, with the cat mewing inside the cat carrier, all the accumulated layers of his everyday life seemed to dissolve at once, and the world started spinning like one of the turntable rides at the CNE which whirls around until the riders are pinned to the sides by centrifugal force. All he could think of was trying to hold on, his head buzzing with nausea. He hadn't even wanted to get another toothbrush, let alone another job.

Believe me, he'll say to Wilson, you have no idea until it happens to you.

But twenty-three years?

Well, yes, of course, eventually he thought about getting

another job. Of course he did. He thought about it a lot. Sometimes he longed for something new, something that would send bubbles into his bloodstream, that would provide him with a form of carbonation. Particularly while Vic had been the store manager, he and Louise had talked about quitting almost every week, coming up with parting shots for their resignation letters. *Dear Vic, is it really true you only have one brain cell? Dear Vic, has anyone ever told you you're a supreme, award-winning asshole?* But then Vic was the one who left to go to a franchise store in Sudbury instead, and some of Frank's restlessness passed. And then suddenly, he was too old. Who was going to hire someone in his fifties?

He had assumed that he would have some warning about getting older, and that it would be gradual process. First the warning: *This is it. Get ready. It's about to start.* Then a wrinkle or two, a grey hair, another pound, all of these accumulating at a leisurely pace.

Instead, he had become older in sudden jerks, like a used car hiccuping down the street. One day he smiled into the mirror on a bright afternoon and saw that his skin had splintered into dry lines around each eye. Another day, he noticed that his hair was speckled with grey around his forehead, a forehead which seemed to have crawled backward on his head overnight. A few hours in the sun, and the backs of his hands looked like the skin of a brown lizard.

You don't know what this is like, he'll say to Wilson. Like things are out of control. Like you have no idea how you're going to look or feel every day when you wake up, but you can be pretty sure it isn't going to be an improvement. This is not the kind of thing that makes you feel like running out and getting another job.

That's enough, he thinks. Those are all good reasons, they're good enough, anyway.

What about the depression?

What *about* the depression?

This is not something that he talks about, and he's certainly not going to start with Wilson.

But now it's sitting in front of him, his *clinical* depression. Another surprise, for someone who had bobbed along for years on a cushion of optimism, a cushion stuffed with vague expectations. When the cushion began to thin out, pounded by age and experience, it reminded him of a label he had seen on a life jacket once: *this device loses buoyancy over time.*

Then a grey chill had slowly crept under his skin, setting up house in his organs, hollowing out his bones, sinking into the lining of his lungs. The music playing in the store began driving him crazy. The tapes that scrolled endlessly around, all day, every day, suddenly seemed to be full of gloom and pain, wailing away, the repetition making him wild. Kenny caught him eyeing the speaker up on the wall one day, trying to figure out whether he could reach it to pull out the wire. *Don't do it, Frank. I know how you feel, pal, we all hate that goddamn music, but that's the way it goes.*

The way *what* goes? thought Frank. He was seized with a desire to grab Kenny and shake him, to see if a stream of spongy words would come tumbling out of his mouth – self-starter, pro-active, customer satisfaction, bottom line.

Very gradually, he began to notice things again – the sharpness of a tomato and mayonnaise sandwich, a joke by a street-car driver that caught him by surprise, the smell of a quart basket of purple wine grapes, things that seemed to get their normal colour and taste back. Because he had been so starved by the greyness of the depression, they seemed to have an extra bloom on them that he had never noticed before, to fill up his eyes and nose.

He looks over now and sees that Wilson has given up on the conversation. He has finished with the potatoes, and is mopping down the floor in the produce section, dragging an orange cone behind him that says *Caution – Wet Floor.*

It's not that bad, Frank wants to tell him. There's a lot to be said for things staying the same. Every morning you can wake up knowing what's going to happen that day. There's a comfort in that, he thinks, a restfulness, something you can wrap around yourself like one of those soft flannel shirts. A regular life.

But then he doesn't feel like defending himself to a kid like Wilson any more.

Fish Responsible to the office crackles over the speakers a few months later, interrupting the music. *Fish Responsible to the office.*

When Frank arrives, there are three men in suits sitting there with Kenny, an older man with a face like a scone, a young man with blond hair and shrewd eyes, and a third one who has a bulging stomach, dark hair and glasses.

'This is the loss prevention team from head office,' says Kenny. He is twisting his little finger in his ear.

'We're concerned about your inventory, Frank,' the blond man says, using his first name as if they were friends. His suit is grey, with a white shirt, which has the effect of making him look more severe than he would in a dark suit.

'Why?' Frank says, taken aback. He files inventory sheets every week.

'It's too high.'

'Well, too high,' says Frank. 'That's a relief. Not exactly a real problem, is it? Too low, now that would be a problem.'

'You've got down here you got thirty lobsters when the tank only holds twenty-five. Any discrepancy like that we investigate.'

'I just stack them up,' says Frank. 'But come on down to the fish counter and you can take a look for yourselves.'

'That's what we're going to do. We're going to do a new inventory.'

The three men stand up and take off their jackets and hang them on the back of their chairs. Two of them have short-sleeved shirts on, and the blond one rolls up his sleeves and straightens his tie. Then they pull out some latex gloves, and they all troop down to the fish counter with Frank and stand there, looking at his glistening piles of fish.

'Here you go,' Frank says finally, since nobody else seems to be saying anything.

'Nice setup,' says Scone-face. There is something funny about his hairline, as if his hair has been sewn on.

'Thanks,' Frank says. 'Well, go to it, boys. Let me know if there's anything you need.'

The man with glasses takes out a fresh fish inventory form, and they put on their latex gloves and then they all go to it, weighing and counting. They work in silence, except for grunting out numbers from time to time like '6.3 kilos' or '4.86 kilos' for the man with the inventory form to write down. After about an hour, they move into the back, and go through the freezer and the refrigerator unit. Finally, the blond man says:

'You got anything else?

'Nope,' says Frank. 'What you see is what you get.'

The older man gives him a friendly look.

'Your manager will be talking to you about this,' says the blond man, and the three of them walk back to the office together.

Later that afternoon, Louise drifts casually over to the counter, looking worried. She is studying the scallops carefully.

'So what did the three stooges want?'

'Nothing,' Frank says. 'No big deal.'

She looks up at one of the speakers.

'If I hear that Celine Dion one more time,' she says, 'I'm going to rip her lungs out.'

'I'm sorry, Frank, but that's just the way it is. There's nothing I can do,' Kenny says. They are back in Kenny's office a few days later. The loss prevention team is arranged in various positions around the office, with the blond man half sitting on the desk.

'Christ almighty, Kenny, what the hell are you talking about?' Frank says. Everything sounds blurred, as if he has cotton wrapped around his head.

'Your inventory's out of whack by $8,000, Frank. You reported you got all kinds of stuff and it isn't there.'

'Wastage,' Frank says. 'You know fish? Guess what, boys? It goes bad sometimes.'

'You have to get credits for wastage,' Kenny says. 'I have to sign for it. You don't just dump stuff out. That's just asking for trouble.'

'Maybe you should have mentioned that before,' says Frank.

'That's no excuse,' says the blond man. 'You kept putting it in your inventory sheets. You kept on listing it. Why would you do that if it was wastage?'

'I thought I was supposed to put down everything I received.'

'Oh, come on,' he says. 'I never heard such bullshit in my life.'

'Maybe it hasn't been such a long life yet,' Frank says. The older man almost laughs and then straightens his face.

'Look, Frank, you gotta go,' says Kenny. 'I know you got pride in your work and everything, I know you're good at it, I hear you with the customers and the recipes, but you just can't be out eight thousand bucks. There's just no way. How could you have that much wastage anyway?'

'Why don't you ask head office about the stuff they're sending over? While you're at it, why don't you ask them why they call it the *fresh* fish counter?'

'Hey, hey, now,' says the older man. 'Let's stay calm, everyone.'

'What's going on here?' Frank says, looking intently at Kenny.

'Marco reported you,' he says, 'and once there's a report, we gotta check it out.' He is holding himself rigidly, as if his face is hurting him.

'You tell them why Marco has it in for me?'

'It doesn't matter,' Kenny says. 'It either checks out or it doesn't.'

He stands up. 'You'll get your severance and any vacation we owe you in the mail, Frank. They're going to escort you out now. They'll go with you to get your things.'

Escort me out? Frank thinks. *Escort me out?* He gives Kenny a look, and Kenny looks down at his desk.

The three men walk him down to his locker where he takes out two *Car and Wheels* magazines, a dried-up pen, a pair of shoes, his Donut Delight reward card, a package of crushed soup crackers, a bottle of Tylenol, a roll of tape, some birthday candles from Wilson's birthday, a half-eaten box of chocolate-covered peanuts, a flyer for a new bowling alley across the street, a paycheque stub, a comb and some cough lozenges. He puts these things in a box that Scone-face is holding, and then he closes the rusty locker carefully, as if it might explode. They take his identification card, and his keys to the storeroom, which he has to twist off his spiral key ring. You can send in your uniform tomorrow, they tell him. Then they walk over to the fish counter so that he can get a few things he has under the shelf. The Basic Fish I manual is still sitting there.

Another one of our staff would be pleased to serve you.

He feels his arms and legs moving more loosely than usual, as if his ankles or knees might give way. He tries to concentrate all his energy on making sure that they don't. Left, right, left. His father used to sing an army marching song like that. Left, right, left. I had a good job and I left. First they hired me, then they fired me, then by golly I left. What kind of a song is that? he thinks, and an unreasonable stab of irritation penetrates his daze.

There is a salty, oily smell as they pass the olive table. He sees Louise standing there, a carton at her feet, holding packages of onion bread sticks, her mouth open. Wilson is turning around at the end of Aisle 2 and his lips are moving. Hey

Frank, what's happening? he is saying, looking faintly worried, but the sounds are pouring out of his mouth and then floating away in little puddles.

How should I know? thinks Frank, each word breaking off from the sentence, and outlined separately in his brain. He is suddenly tired, so tired that he can barely walk, and now his muscles feel worse, not just loose, but as if they had melted away, and all that he had left was some bones and ligaments he was trying to drag along, to make them work.

They are coming up to the lobster tank. The lobsters have been moving things around again, and he feels a spasm of rage. You stupid, ugly things, he feels like yelling. The men take his arms, and he shakes them off. Then he realizes that he really is yelling, out loud.

You stupid, stupid things.

The lobsters sit there silently, their banded claws waving a little. The clam shell is slowly opening and closing, and the plastic weeds are pressed up against the side of the glass.

Confidentially, Frank? Between you and me? It wasn't even close.

Hardiness Zones

Two things happen to Leni on a Wednesday in the second week of August while the air is already dry and powdery from the heat. The first thing is that she has a miscarriage, which is something that seems a little garish, even to her. The second is that her neighbour, whose name is Joachim DaSilva, gives her a plant from his garden with the implausible name of *keys-of-heaven*. This strikes her as spooky and hilarious at the same time.

Of course, he doesn't know about the miscarriage, because there is no possible way that he *could* know. If she were going to confide this kind of thing to someone, it would probably not be to a man, and not to a much older man who does not speak her language. The name of the plant startles her, though – this is the spooky part – and she wonders if he has had some instinctive sense about the miscarriage, whether some dusty flicker of intuition has crossed his mind. Then she realizes that it is simply that he is going home to the Azores, and can't take everything with him.

At the moment, they are standing on her porch in the late afternoon sun because he has rung her doorbell. He is holding the root ball of the plant, which is carefully wrapped in a plastic sandwich bag with the name 'keys-of-heaven' written on a piece of masking tape stuck on the front. This information seems to filter into her mind in tiny thought chunks, because she is still woozy from the miscarriage. In fact, at least one of the reasons that she has answered the door is that this involves less thought than not answering it. Another reason is that the miscarriage was seven hours ago, and she is tired of the dreariness of the whole thing. To the extent that she is able to think at this point, which is not very much, she wants to think about something else, something bright or shimmering or silvery or possibly sweet, but in any event, not at all earnest. She is having a hard time summoning this up by herself, so she has opened the door on the off chance that such a thing might be sitting behind it, but instead she finds Joachim DaSilva, standing there in his olive green shirt.

'Senhora,' he says, in a serious way. He hesitates for a moment, and then turns one of her hands palm up and lays the sandwich bag in it. She notices that his fingers are tube-shaped, the skin so hard that it looks like brown paper, each finger with a milky callus at the base.

'For the garden,' he says, the English words coming out of his mouth as if he has been chewing them. His own English is almost nonexistent, so she assumes he has lifted this phrase from someone else. Usually when they talk — if that's what it can be called — they use sign language, not the official sign language but choppy, over-emphatic gestures, like a whacked out game of charades.

English is not necessary, or even desirable, in the area of Toronto where they live, an area where the brick houses have been painted over with turquoise or white or pastel blue or yellow ochre. Their wooden porches have been torn off and replaced with cement and wrought iron curlicues, and on the main streets, bushel baskets of red peppers and eggplants and plum tomatoes sit outside the stores. This Mediterranean make-over is patchy, and some of the original stolid face of the neighborhood shows through it.

Most of the stores, even the bank and the drugstore, have hand-drawn signs: *falamos Portugues*. The fish store has the same sign — *we speak Portuguese* — positioned over piles of squid and dried cod lying blankly in trays. (Amazing, says Toby. They don't look as if they could talk at all.) The cashiers at the supermarket are named Fatima or Luisa, and they shift languages without missing a beat, one minute the barky sounds of English, the next, nasal lines of Portuguese, all at the same time they are turning over boxes of cereal looking for bar codes. Joachim DaSilva is still standing on her porch patiently.

'Thanks.' Leni takes the plant carefully from him, and examines it while they both try to think of something else to say. Then she glances down the street to see if it looks any different after the miscarriage. The air seems more lucid than before, the powderiness gone, as if someone has pushed the contrast button on a television.

The tiny front yards on the street are pockets of crazed colour, heavy orange dahlias under miniature catalpa trees, clumps of salvia jammed together with marigolds and trumpet vines. The intensity of the colours makes the top of her head feel light again, and she tries to smile in what she thinks might be a neighbour-like way at Joachim DaSilva, who is still searching for English words.

'It's hot,' she says finally. She waves her right arm in an awkward arc meaning outside. *'Sim, sim,'* he says, *'esta calor,'* and then he waves his arm gravely as well.

She glances down the street again, towards the corner store a few doors away where a woman in a black dress with flip-flops on her swollen feet is sweeping the sidewalk. A toddler is staggering around the pavement beside her, and the woman stops to take something out of his mouth. A gull that has drifted up from the lakefront screeches.

The corner store makes her think of food, of the shelves inside full of pimento paste, fava beans, olives and potato chips, of the cornbread piled in a cardboard box, the plates of custard tarts, and chourico sausage – two kinds, sweet and hot – on the counter. The store also has:

tapioca pudding mix
tapes of Portuguese singers
quince jam
car deodorizers
Gummi worms
bananas

rat poison

Sao Jorge cheese

Coke, Sprite, Orangina and San Pellegrino water

'*Parto amanha,*' Joachim DaSilva says to her finally, having given up on English, gesturing towards the moving van parked in front of his house. Good, she thinks, and leans against the door frame. I won't have to tell him about the miscarriage.

Why *would* she tell him?

Think about two skinny little gardens next to each other, backing on to a lane. The lane has cracked asphalt, dandelions, chicory, some broken glass, a few scraggly purple flowers, cigarette butts, and rows of wooden garages with peeling paint, some of them upgraded to pink brick with aluminum doors.

Now think about a cinderblock wall almost three feet high, separating the two gardens. The wall is wide, but since it is built on top of the ground instead of being anchored to a footing, it leans to one side.

'God, is that thing ugly or what,' says Toby.

'What's wrong with it?' says Leni. They are in the kitchen of the house attached to one of the gardens, unpacking their worldly goods, which in their case is not very much. The window is open, and a breeze is fluttering the broken venetian blind, making it bang against the window frame.

Leni is standing on a chair, wiping out a cupboard over the sink with an old pink sponge. The air smells like moving day smells, like bare walls and mouldy carpets and dustballs and bleach, because this is their moving day, in fact, their moving-in-together day.

'You're kidding, right?' Toby passes her a stack of plates from a cardboard box. His voice has a diluted Manchester echo in it, something he brought over from England when he was twelve and has been trying to get rid of ever since.

'No,' she says. 'I mean it. Who wants some flimsy fence? This is a real wall. A wall-eyed wall. Maybe we can grow wallflowers next to it. Besides,' she adds, 'he built the wall him-self.'

'Who's he?' says Toby.

Joachim DaSilva has already waved to her from his back-yard in a neighbourly way, although she doesn't know his name yet. He has already told her about the wall, too, pointing to his chest and then miming the placing of the blocks, the slapping and scraping of the mortar, an imaginary trowel making brisk figure eight's.

'Anyway,' she says. 'Let's wait and see.' This sounds good, very all-purpose. Intelligent people wait and see. Wise people wait and see. She can hardly wait to wait and see.

Their own backyard is a makeshift driveway, and part of the ground is covered in gravel and oil stains. Let's dig it up, says Leni later, and so they dig it up, and then they put things in it, things like topsoil, sheep manure, peat moss, bone meal. In some places, they unroll little mats of grass sod. This seems like an odd but engaging trick. (Think of the possibilities, says Leni. Rolled up trees. Just unroll them and plant them. Rolled up buildings, says Toby. Unroll them and stand them up. Saves all those construction costs.)

When the sod is down, Leni plants flowers and shrubs in the flower beds, things she remembers from her father's garden: lilacs, spireas, flowering almonds, mock oranges, asters. Old clean flowers, Ontario flowers with delicate colours.

This is what she plants.

What she grows are weeds.

'They're unbelievable,' Leni says to Sophie one morning.

The weeds have become so vigorous that she is a little unnerved by them. There are stringy weeds, and lacy weeds, and broadleaf weeds with prickles, and one dirty yellow mullein almost four feet high. They spill out of the flower beds into the sod, growing so fast that they seem almost predatory.

'What's the name of that movie where the plants take over?'

says Leni. She and Sophie are sitting at the front desk of the hospital area where they work. The late morning is a slow time, after the rush of people coming in for blood and urine tests from the outpatient clinics. The vinyl seats in the waiting room are empty, an old *Maclean's* magazine with a missing cover lying across one. The walls are painted a pale yellow, which was meant to be cheerful, although it looks dingy under the fluorescent lights. A boy goes by with a boom box on his shoulder. *Baby, sugar, get on down.*

'I don't know,' says Sophie. 'But I know you have to dig the weeds up. You can't just chop them off.' She pushes her glasses up her nose with the back of her wrist, because she is rubbing cream into her hands. (She's a lotion junkie, Leni says to Toby. Lotion, cream, lip balm, all day long.) This means the front desk often smells like artificial strawberry or mango, or plastic vanilla. Sometimes it makes Leni hungry.

A man in a golf shirt appears on the other side of the counter, waving requisition forms. Leni takes his hospital card, flicks up his file on the computer and then stamps the forms.

'Over here,' she says, as she leads him into one of the half-curtained booths where they take blood. She pushes a pillow under the man's freckled arm and ties elastic above his elbow.

'I thought chopping them off would kill them,' she says to Sophie through the green curtain. The man looks up at her nervously. 'Weeds,' she says to him, trying not to laugh.

She wipes the crease of his arm with alcohol, inserts the tip of the syringe and waits for the vial to fill. Then she switches another vial on to the syringe, and then another, the vials clicking together while she sticks labels on them with one hand.

'Don't they need their leaves? I thought they needed them to stay alive,' she says to Sophie. She can't remember exactly why. The leaves make light into water? Water into light? Light into chlorophyll? Isn't that a breath freshener? No bad breath for plants. She takes the elastic off the man's arm, puts a band-aid on it, and gives him a plastic cup with a label. Then she points him towards the bathroom and the tray with the faded sign saying *Urine Samples Here*, and sits down at the desk again.

'They need leaves all right,' says Sophie. 'They need leaves, but they can live for a while on the roots, long enough for the leaves to grow back anyway. If you don't get the roots, you're just wasting your time.'

'Huh,' says Leni. She starts straightening up papers on her half of the long desk, sorting them into different files. The door to the bathroom opens and the man comes out looking around uncertainly, holding his little cup.

'Behind you,' says Leni. She rolls her eyes at Sophie. 'We need a new sign.'

'It's not the sign,' says Sophie. They have had this conversation before. 'It doesn't make any difference. They're just too embarrassed to see anything.'

She takes a tube of hand cream out of her purse.

Leni starts digging up the weeds, pulling up the weeks, yanking out their hairy roots. They seem faintly obscene to her. She also digs up other things, including:

old popsicle wrappers

green lawn edging

pieces of brown glass

plastic lids off coffee cups

some unwound cassette tape and a lot of crumbling brick which seems to rise to the surface as fast as she can get rid of it.

The brick is porous and soft with age, flaking into pieces when she hits it with the shovel. How can there be so much brick in the ground?

'There must have been a brick factory here,' she says to Toby one night, although this seems unlikely.

He is sitting in a worn green chair, reading a journal on eighteenth century law, a pool of light from an old study lamp around him.

There are journals on eighteenth century law? she asked, when they first started sleeping together.

There are journals on everything, he said.

Eighteenth century law doesn't seem like you, she said. Too dry. Or too boring. Or not post-modern enough. Or something like that.

Wrong-o, he said. It's all blood and gore, and nobody understands it. Couldn't be better.

At the moment, he is underlining something in his journal, and writing in the margin. His reddish brown hair is sticking up in the front, because he runs his hands through it when he is reading. He is almost wiry, but not quite, just slightly too solid for wiriness. His feet are wiggling in the trout slippers she brought home for him one day from the dollar store. Fish feet, he had said happily. Perfect for the academic trying to swim upstream.

'Brick factory,' she says more loudly.

'Brick factory, interesting,' he says automatically, his eyes still on the page. He is working as a teaching assistant until a tenure track job comes open, examining older faculty closely for any signs of failing health or interest. In the meantime, he is generating a series of articles, squeezing ideas out of his brain as if he is using some kind of cranial muscles. It takes so much effort that Leni can almost see him expel a new thought from his head with a soft pop.

She waves a hand in front of his face to get his attention.

'Okay, okay,' he says, looking up. 'I heard you. A brick factory. Was there a brick factory here? Could be, I guess. Who knows?'

'Thanks,' she says. 'That's helpful.'

'Well, there you go,' he says. 'I strive to be helpful. Helpful is my middle name.'

He grabs her, pulling her into his lap on top of the journal.

They rearrange parts of themselves to get comfortable, and she pulls the journal out and leans over to put it on the floor.

Then she runs her fingers down the side of his face, looking at the way his tiny reddish beard hairs come up through the skin. This is Sunday night, so he hasn't shaved.

'What?' he says. (What are you looking at? What's up?)

'Let's have a baby,' she says. This startles her almost as much as it startles him, the words marching out of her mouth by themselves. I must want this, she thinks. Next time, however, she would like to have more warning, perhaps just a quick e-mail from the borders of her conscious mind.

'*What?*' he says. (What, are you kidding? What made you think of that?)

'Unless you don't want to,' she says quickly.

'I thought we were talking about bricks,' he says.

'All right, forget it.'

'No, no, I'm just trying to catch up. Don't we have to think about this?'

'What if you can't really think about it? What if it's just some kind of primitive instinct?' Some kind of whispering in your cells. *Baby, sugar, get on down.*

He hesitates for a few seconds. She can see him thinking about not thinking about it.

'So just like that?' he says. 'Instant parents?' He straightens up a little and moves her into a different position on his lap.

'Well, not quite instant,' she says.

He brings his head up to her lips, running his tongue into her mouth.

The thickness of his tongue reminds her of something, so she slides down and undoes his jeans.

'I don't think this is the way babies are made,' he says.

The lilac acquires rusty-looking spots on its leaves, the mock orange refuses to flower and the flowering almond dies. Is it the soil? Too acidic? Too alkaline? Too contaminated with car oil from its makeshift driveway days? Even the nasturtiums, which are supposed to love poor soil, are scraggly, with yellow stems. (Can a flower really love anything? Leni says to Toby. It sounds a little anthropomorphic, he says.) The only thing that grows well – aside from the weeds, of course – is some mint that has crept through the ground under the cinderblock wall from Joachim DaSilva's garden.

On top of this, she is tired of digging up weeds.

Mulch, says the man at the nursery, mulch is what you need, honey. Mulch is the thing. Keeps the weeds down like a charm. We've got some stuff on sale.

He gives her sacks of cocoa bean shells, which she spreads between the plants, filling the air with a sweetish smell. While she does this, Joachim DaSilva watches her with quiet interest. They nod to each other, they are on official nodding terms, but anything else is limited to sign language. Until now.

'*O que e isso?*' he says, pointing to the cocoa bean shells.

'Mulch,' she says, trying to think of a way to mime *keeps down the weeds*. The only Portuguese words she knows are off the notices stapled to telephone poles, their ends fringed in tear-off strips, the paper rippled from the rain. There is something attractive about these notices – their drama (Reward!), their directness (Have You Seen This Cat?) and their candour (Special on Chicken Parts). They seem subversive as well. While the telephone wires above them are humming away with high-tech business faxes, Leni thinks, farther down the poles another level of conversation is in progress, except that this conversation is about concrete things like roofing companies and babysitting services and pets. Things that are actually wanted. Or offered. Or lost.

The notices don't have much of a gardening vocabulary, however.

'*O cacau?*' says Joachim DaSilva, looking puzzled. Leni pats the air down with her hands near the ground to try to indicate the suppression of weeds, but he shakes his head.

This is when she decides to learn Portuguese. She doesn't like the idea of him thinking she is demented, crazy in a neighbourly kind of way, like someone who hoards newspapers.

She went to French immersion schools. She likes languages. How hard could it be?

Can you speak more slowly? Can we go more quickly? Can I change my money? Can I drink the water? How much does this cost? How long does it take to get there? Where is the restaurant? Have you seen my suitcase? Have you seen my wallet? What time do you close? I'll come back tomorrow.

The only thing Leni can find in the library is a phrase book, although it is not particularly useful. She keeps on reading anyway. Portuguese has masculine and feminine nouns. *Salt* is male, *tomatoes* are male, *trees* and *hands* are female. The words for *morning* and *afternoon* are feminine, and the word for *day* is masculine.

Nouns with genders. Very anthropomorphic. Next they'll start talking, she thinks, or ordering a beer.

'What happens when masculine and feminine nouns get together?' she says to Toby.

'Is this a joke?' he says.

She tries out her stiff, new phrases on Joachim DaSilva, and he looks startled, his leathery face creasing. He says something back. She shakes her head. He repeats it more slowly, but she still doesn't understand, and he shrugs and smiles.

'Well, at least that's something,' she says to Toby. 'He's usually so serious.' Although sometimes his seriousness feels restful to Leni – it gives her a brownish-grey quiet feeling, like something old, or the bark of a tree.

He usually has three or four men over in the evenings, and they grill sardines or cod on a rusty barbecue in his yard, and eat them with red wine out of bottles with no labels. Then they sit in the back under a small grape arbour, the grapes still hard and green, and talk until midnight, smoke from the barbecue and their cigarettes filling the air, their dark voices coming through Leni and Toby's kitchen window like round stones bumping against each other.

'I don't understand why he has a garden like a rain forest,' she says to Toby one evening, 'and I can't grow a peony.'

'He's been at it longer,' he says. They are eating dinner, and he is pulling leaves off an artichoke. Leni is momentarily distracted.

'This must be a weed,' she says, studying her own artichoke.

'Weeds are a social construct,' he says, in the voice of the professor who is currently employing him, an older man who is pompous, but emotional enough to be likeable. 'They're all plants. We just divide them up into good and evil.'

Toby treats his food carefully, almost tenderly, she thinks, as she watches him arrange the artichoke leaves on his plate. He is a very deliberate person, and Leni has the impression that he has taken some trouble-making, gingerish element in himself and manually transformed it into a kind of offbeat personal circus, something that is playing all the time. This makes it hard to really see him. Even when they have sex.

'What are you doing?' he says, one night after one of these smooth, cerebral sessions. She has put her legs up against the cold wall.

'Mixing it all together inside,' she says. 'Getting those eggs and sperm together. That's the real sex. What we do is just foreplay, reproductively speaking.' She pictures a horny little sperm, pumping up and down on an egg, even though she knows this is silly.

'Like a fertility milkshake.' He runs a finger up and down one of her legs. It tickles, and she shakes her leg. She can hear a rush of water down a pipe in the wall behind the bed. The room smells of the heavy, itchy smells of sex.

'If I were a plant,' she says, yawning, 'I wouldn't even need you. They can fertilize themselves.'

'Not all of them,' he says in mock indignation.

'A lot of them, I think,' she says, although she doesn't really know. 'Probably more evolved. This is the way the human race will be in another few thousand years.'

'Hah,' he says. 'Don't count on it.' He turns over on his stomach and starts arranging his pillows for sleeping, one against the headboard and the other leaning against that, punched up higher at the front.

'You're pretty cocky,' she says, 'for a stamen.'

'You're sure it isn't a pistil, or a stigma, or something?'

'No,' she says.

Traitors, she thinks. She is surveying the backyard the following spring. Most of the plants, which were supposed to reappear, have expired over the winter.

'What is this, a death wish?' she says to them. 'You're heading for extinction at this rate.'

She gets out the nursery catalogue and starts looking for other plants. Jasmine, monkey flowers, calla lilies. She is half-aware that they are harder to grow, but she is determined – almost pigheadedly determined – to try something else.

But the new plants don't do much better. They develop black spots, or white bugs, or their leaves are eaten into a kind of ugly filigree by insects, or they just shrivel up. Having Joachim DaSilva around to see all this makes her more irritated.

'Maybe you should get help,' says Toby. Get help, like seek therapy, she thinks, or get help, like talk to the nursery again? Find a gardening journal? There are journals on everything.

'There's a phone-in show,' he says. 'I heard it on the car radio. You know, you call in with your gardening questions, and some kind of über-gardener answers them.'

The gardening show features an unwaveringly pleasant man with an English accent. Is it really possible for someone to be so good-natured? she thinks. Is this the result of spending your life gardening? Although maybe his niceness is just an on-air persona. Maybe he becomes peevish and spiteful as soon as he gets off the air.

She calls the number of the show, and an assistant asks her what her question is.

'Why are my plants dying?' she says.

'You'll have to be more specific than that,' the screener says.

'Okay, why did my jasmine, monkey flower and calla lily plants die?'

'Only one question per person,' says the screener.

'All right,' she says in exasperation, 'why did my calla lily die?'

'Fine,' says the screener. 'Please hold, and wait for our signal, and do not, let me repeat, do not, play your radio while you are on the air.'

She holds, and thinks about listening to herself talk on the radio at the same time she is speaking. There is something fascinating about this. Like a new dimension, she thinks, where your words go out from you and come back to you at the same time. Does this mean the same words have two lives, or do the two directions cancel each other out, so that the words never really exist at all?

They have you coming and going, she thinks.

'You're on the air,' says the screener.

'Well,' says the impossibly pleasant man when she asks her question, 'where do you live?'

'In Toronto.' She shifts the telephone receiver a little on her shoulder.

'There's your problem,' he says. 'You're in the wrong hardiness zone for calla lilies.'

'What do you mean?' Does everyone know this? Maybe she is ridiculously ignorant.

'There are nine hardiness zones, at least in Canada there are nine,' he says. 'It has to do with the first and last frost dates, mean temperatures, things like that. Calla lilies need a hardiness zone of at least eight, maybe even nine, and you're in zone six. You need a hardier plant.'

'Such as?' she says.

'We'll send you a list. Stay on the line after you get off the air, and give us your name and address. We'll send you a list of perennials that are at least zone 6, some even hardier.'

The list arrives a few days later. She has no idea what the flowers look like, but the names are hypnotic, like a botanical soap opera.

These are some of the names on the list:

beard-tongue

false indigo (was there a true indigo?)

foamflower

stinking hellebore (really?)

musk mallow

sea lavender

sneezeweed

spotted dead nettle (really again?)

sundrop

obedient plant

solomon's seal

At the end of it someone has added in handwriting: *Cosmos – an energetic self-seeder.* Cosmos is a self-seeder? She starts to laugh. Maybe this is an alternative to the big bang theory, the whole universe starting with cosmos seeds that grew into planets, which then produced more and more, self-seeding whole gauzy galaxies.

She can't find some of the perennials in the nursery, but she plants what is available, her trowel gouging holes in the metallic-smelling soil. The cosmos turns out to be as aggressive as the weeds, filling the bed with pink flowers surfing over a sea of feathery stems. Most of the others refuse to grow, staying exactly as they have been planted, not dying but not sprouting an extra leaf or flower.

Some evenings she hangs over the concrete block wall, watching Joachim DaSilva in his garden, taking off dead flower heads, pulling out weeds, dividing roots. He doesn't seem to mind her there. She notices the wall is starting to lean more.

The ground must be uneven, she thinks. Or maybe the problem is the wall itself, so heavy that even a hair's breadth off plumb would be multiplied by the weight of each cinder block. She skims her Portuguese phrase book. *Can you give me directions? How long is the trip? How long is the wait? Is the road in good condition? Is the car in good condition? I am sick. My child is sick. Where is the hospital? Where is the doctor? This is where it hurts. I don't understand what you are saying. Do you understand me? Where is the bus? Where is the train? Where is the airport?* Nothing about walls.

By then, she has been trying to get pregnant for eight months.

'Maybe we should get tested,' she says to Toby. They are lying on their backs in bed one morning, waiting until they are ready to be vertical. Leni is tired, and her muscles feel as if they are attached to the bed, holding her down. There is a sandblastingly bright sun outside, which is leaking in around the slats of the window blind. She is studying a potato-coloured stain on the ceiling.

'I thought this didn't require planning,' he says. He pulls the top sheet more tightly around them.

'Apparently not,' she says shortly.

'You just want to take my blood,' he says with a Transylvanian accent. 'Go ahead, you've never taken my blood.'

'It's the vampire who has the accent, not the victim.' But she slides a hand between his warm back and the sheet and leaves it there.

'All right, forget it then,' he says airily. 'You had your chance.'

'It's probably nothing,' she says, mostly to reassure herself. 'Anyway, they say try for a year.' Before getting help. Seeking help. Calling into an infertility radio show.

'I knew the minute I got pregnant,' Sophie says. She is sitting at the front desk, checking off boxes on a requisition form in a precise way, her smooth pink nails bunched around the pen. Leni is counting empty vials by putting ticks down in groups of five. 'The second. The exact second. While he was still in me. It was like there was a click, like a ball falling into a slot, like someone yelled Bingo. Both times, I mean with both kids.'

Leni is impressed. She puts a line through a group of ticks and looks over at Sophie, whose narrow shoulders and jelly breasts suddenly seem knowledgeable. Next to her Leni feels like a pencil, her body wooden and mute. Any messages she does get from her body are usually wrong. Her stomach will send out urgent hunger signals, only to feel stolidly resistant when she is actually faced with food. Or she will feel so tired she can barely move, but then will lie in bed, awake as an electric eel. Maybe it shouldn't surprise her then, that she doesn't feel anything, no ball falling into the slot, as she lies with her legs up against the wall, semen leaking on to the sheets.

Finally, she misses her period. This would be exciting, except that she feels so unpregnant. After a few weeks, she gets a pregnancy test – she uses a fake name and sends it down to the lab herself – and it comes back positive. This is less convincing than it should be. Here I am, she thinks, something is actually growing inside me, and I can't even tell. She has assumed she will be elated, has rehearsed in her mind the ballooning excitement she will feel when she gets pregnant, but instead she feels oddly normal, no sign of the hormones which have woken up and started manufacturing their recipes.

One night she tells Joachim DaSilva, just to make it seem more real. '*Bebe*,' she says, out of her phrase book, pointing to her stomach. He seems delighted, breaks out into a stream of thick words, and then shakes her hand carefully.

He shakes Toby's hand too, a few days later.

'Why did he shake my hand?' Toby says suspiciously.

'I told him,' she says.

'I thought we agreed to keep it quiet for now.'

'He doesn't speak English,' she says. 'That's a kind of quiet.

At least as far as we're concerned.'

'Not in this neighborhood,' he says.

Shortly after this, Joachim DaSilva starts taking deliveries of things, mostly furniture, but smaller things as well. Delivery trucks from cut-rate furniture stores stop in front of the house. This is what they unload:

a dark yellow velvet sofa and a matching loveseat

two shiny wood end tables

two blue armchairs with gold fringes along the bottom edges

a long Persian-looking rug and several small ones

a dining room table with an expansion leaf

a black laminate cabinet for a television and CD equipment

and a dining room hutch with a glass door

'You think he won the lottery?' says Toby.

'It seems more methodical than that,' says Leni. 'Like storing nuts for the winter, not like a shopping spree. Although he looks pretty pleased with himself.'

'Ask him. Where's that phrase-book?'

'I don't think it has "What are you buying all that furniture for?"'

'He's probably going home,' says Toby. 'I have an uncle who went back to England like that. The triumphant return, overseas shipping containers full of stuff.'

She thinks of Joachim DaSilva going back to the Azores, telling stories about the exotic ways of Toronto, the unstable climate, the glutinous food, the doughnut shops, the condom stores, bicycle couriers, people who talk to themselves on street corners. His new furniture will demonstrate his success; he has conquered another country and is returning with riches. Vasco Da Gama with armchairs.

It starts with a feeling of uneasiness in her lower back, of being on the brink of something. She doesn't say anything to Toby, because she isn't sure what it is, or that it is anything at all. He leaves for work, and she calls in sick. Then the cramps begin. First there are mild ones, like cracks on a wall, and then these turn into jagged contractions that spread out across her lower body. She starts leafing frantically through her pregnancy books, looking for something to stop them. Drink alcohol? Or don't drink alcohol? Walk around, or does that induce labour? She grabs a herbal book that someone has given her, which recommends:

black haw root bark (or cramp bark)
raspberry leaves
wild yam root
lobelia

She doesn't have any of these things.

The pain drags at her until blood begins to drip out, corkscrews of red ink hanging in the water in the toilet between her legs. Then thick clots began coming, more blood, more broken bottle pain, and then bigger clots, until she is lightheaded and her ears are ringing.

Baby, sugar, get on down. Down the drain. Out with the bathwater. Half birth, half death. A tiny naked fish swimming in amniotic fluid, jack-knifing into the air for a sliver of a second, and then slipping back down into a dark red river.

When the cramps stop, she is so tired she almost falls asleep standing up. She lies down on the lumpy couch and sleeps instantly, a heavy, syrupy sleep in which she is being carried along in eddies and currents, spinning along, a telephone in her hands.

What is your question? says the screener. Please hold, and wait for our signal, and do not, let me repeat, do not, play your radio while you are on the air.

Hello, says the pleasant gardener. Hello, hello.

She tries to clear her throat.

Hello, we might have lost our caller. Are you there, caller?

I'm here, she says, but nothing comes out, her words stretching and swirling away from her.

You'll have to speak up, caller.

Things are getting out of hand, she says.

Well, it's easy for that to happen, he says, especially if there's been a lot of rain. But what's your question?

How much does this cost? My child is sick. Where is the mailbox? she whispers, and then the telephone is swept out of her hands, bobbing into the current and spinning away.

Marching band music. She is groggy, but awake, and the cramps are gone, although her skin hurts. She gets up slowly, and goes over to the window.

There is an annual procession on her street, on a number of the streets around her street. A small bandstand is put up in the parkette, a portable toilet is brought in, and strings of coloured triangles hang along the streets. The coloured triangles look as if they have been borrowed from a used car dealership, as if the houses lined up behind them should have prices scrawled in their windows. *Like new. Mint condition. Fully loaded. The deal of a lifetime. Gently used. Sunroof.*

The procession starts winding slowly down the street, the children first, dressed as adults in old European clothes. They are carrying rabbits and chickens, and four of them are holding a fishnet with dried fish woven into it. One of the rabbits is wriggling, and a girl is hanging on to it desperately. After the children are groups of men in gold-trimmed outfits carrying banners or purple satin pillows, and a cross on a platform with red and yellow plastic roses snaking around it. The air is gritty and still, and the sky looks like dishwater. The sound is coming from a brass band, which is playing lugubrious music. The Used Car Dealers Funeral March, she thinks. In fact, it is the feast of Senhor Santo Cristo, according to a telephone pole notice.

She is still light-headed that evening, when Joachim DaSilva comes by with the *keys-of-heaven* plant. Maybe this is why she is having trouble thinking of something to say, even after she understands that he is leaving. After he points to the moving van, she stares at the root ball in its sandwich bag for a few more seconds, and then looks up. He is still waiting for her to say something more.

'Is it hardy?' she says finally. He looks at her in a sober way, trying to understand.

'Wait a minute,' she says. She goes into the house, and comes back with her phrase book.

'Forte,' she says. 'Is it *forte?'*

'Oh,' he says. *'Mais ou menos.'*

More or less.

She looks up 'good luck'. *Boa sorte!* says the book.

'Boa sorte!' she says to him.

'Obrigado,' he says seriously, as if she had given him something substantial.

Maybe Senhor Santo Cristo will give you a hand, she thinks, or at least a used car. They shake hands, his brown paper fingers and her pencil fingers.

'It's very common,' says Toby. He has one of the pregnancy books in his hand.

'It was early,' he says.

'There could have been birth defects,' he says.

'It's probably better this way,' he says.

He is trying to classify it, to organize it in some rational way, she thinks. It seems more gothic to her, more ancient. A miscarriage. A miscarrier. Someone who can't carry, whose baby slipped out of her hands. *Down the drain. Out with the bathwater. Happy unbirthday to you.*

He holds her, but in a tentative way, as if her body has become alien territory to both of them, more volatile than they thought.

'Let's be optimistic,' he says. But it is too soon to be

optimistic, his timing is off, and this makes her feel stubborn. Why? she thinks. Why be optimistic? There's nothing scientific about this, it's some kind of horrible wet red magic. A hormonal sleight of hand. Now you see it, now you don't.

The day after Joachim DaSilva leaves, Leni notices that his backyard is full of holes. Is he allowed to take plants into another country? Maybe her street is considered part of the Azores, a new colony whose plants are allowed to pass through customs as easily as ghosts going through walls.

The *keys-of-heaven* plant is on the kitchen table, but it is starting to wilt, and condensation is forming on the inside of the sandwich bag. She carries it out to the backyard to plant it. The air is tense and humid. She starts digging with the trowel. As she digs, the trowel hits a piece of brick, and the handle of the trowel bangs painfully against her hand.

A crease of rage shoots through her head, and she throws the trowel against the wall, then she throws the plant against the wall, then she rips up the dried up stalks of the plant next to it, and then she rips up the one next to that. Her forehead is filled with a buzzing fury as she pulls up plants, their leaves powdered with white mildew, or sticky with insect trails, or mottled with brown patches, plants with slugs and spider mites and aphids, their stems spindly or bent with yellow galls. Their roots come out with a thick, tearing sound, the ones that take more effort goading her into a higher pitch of rage.

Suddenly, she stops. Suddenly, she is glutted with her anger, she is queasy with the rawness and richness of it. It reminds her of meat, it is too meaty an emotion for her. She wants to be dehydrated, as dry and quiet as paper, as dusty as flour. She doesn't want to do this any more.

'Jesus, what happened?' says Toby, surveying the backyard. He sits down heavily beside Leni on the back steps. Her hands and forearms are scratched and dirty, and one of her wrists is

84

starting to swell. Toby touches her hair, and then picks a piece of leaf out of it.

'Are you all right?' he says. He looks wary.

This is a cavern of a question, a black hole of a question.

'Are you going to be okay?' he says.

The correct answer to this question is yes. She knows this. She should say yes, it is impolite not to say yes.

'Well, you solved the weed problem.'

'Yes,' she says.

'Just a little bout of insanity?' he says, putting an arm around her and moving his hand up and down on the arm furthest from him.

'Yes,' she says.

Her *yeses* are stacked on top of each other. She wants to rub her skin against his skin, as if he has something that is nourishing there, something that her own skin craves.

'Or sanity,' she says. 'Maybe it was an attack of sanity.'

Now the *yeses* are starting to soften at the edges. She moves a little closer to him.

'We could grow bricks,' she says. 'I'm good at that.'

She watches her words go out and come back to her again.

Do you have souvenirs? Do you have a map? Where is the baggage claim? Is it safe here? Have you seen my suitcase? Have you seen my wallet? Have you seen my child?

The Soft Crack Stage

Talk, talk

Telephone talk.

Blobs of words that fall out of mouths and turn into staccato signals.

Crunchy electrical pulses riding telephone wires.

Syllables unstitching during their nanosecond travel, and fusing together at the other end.

Sounds dissolved into non-sounds, and then reconstituted. Sound into energy. Energy into sound.

Talk, talk.

'If you're so smart,' says Pearl Gertler to Murray Gertler, who happens to be her husband of thirty-eight years, 'if you're so smart, explain this. Go on, go right ahead, Mr Genius.' She is fervently hoping that Murray *can* explain it, but the nerve endings buried in her heavy breasts are starting to ache, which is not a good sign.

Murray is sitting at the town and country dinette set in the middle of the kitchen, and Pearl is standing at the counter where she has the newspaper spread out. The kitchen has beige wallpaper with little brown teapots and carrot bunches flying around on it (a classic kitchen, says their daughter, Ruthie, to her friends – a 1973 edition in mint condition.). This means the kitchen also has a garbage disposal mechanism in the sink, a hand hose for spraying dishes, and an avocado-coloured stove and refrigerator. A small paint-by-number picture of a horse is on the wall near the light switch, something Ruthie did when she was nine, a long time ago.

It's 2001, we can't have a boiling water tap on the sink? Or a nice ice-maker on the fridge? says Pearl, several times a year.

Well, get them put in, says Ruthie.

Tell that to your father, Pearl says.

Ask your mother, she's so weak now, she can't plug in an electric kettle? says Murray.

At the moment, Pearl is pushing a section of the newspaper in front of Murray, who is eating tomato soup carefully to avoid dripping on himself. Despite this, he has a small streak of red on his chin, and a trail of saltine crumbs on the front of his golf shirt, on the little cloth ledge it makes over his round stomach.

Not that he is going golfing today. He didn't have plans anyway, but he certainly isn't going anywhere now. Pearl is pointing to an ad, a small entry under For Sale – Vacation Properties: *Muskoka, sandy beach, 120' shoreline, fully equip. priv. Must sell. 416-486-6788.*

'Look at the telephone number,' she says.

Murray takes the paper, and reads the ad, then shrugs.

'I'm supposed to explain this?' he says. 'Smart is not the same as having ESP. ESP is what you need here. If you want to know what that son of yours is up to.'

He hands the paper back, brushes the cracker crumbs off his shirt and wipes his chin with a paper napkin. Then he blows his nose, a necessary measure because of the hot soup.

'You think it's a divorce?' Pearl says. 'You think that's what's happening?'

That's what she thinks, but she wants someone to tell her there's a perfectly good explanation instead. She's waiting for Murray to say *there's a perfectly good explanation,* to come up with an explanation with nice, well-rounded contours, a substantial explanation, something confident without being flashy.

She touches her apricot-coloured permanent distractedly. Murray sighs, and she feels badly about interrupting the little trance he goes into with a soup bowl in front of him. But this – this is an emergency.

She is still waiting patiently for the explanation.

'So call him, find out, before you work yourself up,' Murray says.

'You call. I can't call. You call.'

In Pearl's experience, Murray will require a considerable amount of work before he will call, a great deal of nudging and persuasion. He has a businessman's queasiness for personal matters, a reluctance to involve himself in things that have a high degree of emotional content. He feels stiff and embarrassed in these situations, and these are not feelings that he tolerates gladly. Besides, Pearl knows that he considers himself above this kind of thing, that he is someone with better things to do, although this is not necessarily the case since his retirement.

'Maybe it's not our business,' he says. 'For once, maybe we should keep our noses out of it. Who knows, maybe they'll tell us when they're good and ready.'

To Pearl, this is incomprehensible, just word fluff, the conversational equivalent of the lint she pulls out of the dryer trap. If something is wrong (and she is sure that it is), she is certainly not going to ignore it, and the first thing she needs to do is find out what's happening.

She is good at this. She spends a great deal of time accumulating and dispensing information about everything and everyone. In fact, she is one of the stewards of a floating body of psychological, sociological and medical knowledge about an extensive group of families, their friends, their acquaintances, their friends' friends and acquaintances, and anyone else who stumbles into their radius. She knows there are people who look down on this, like Murray, but she has no patience for this attitude. As far as she is concerned, her information is as important as the contents of the newspaper or the six o'clock news – *more* important, really, because it is more intimate, more specific. If she needs to know something, say about migraines, she puts this out through her friends, and in a week, she will get better answers than she ever gets from her doctor. If she hears that someone else has migraines, she passes on the answers through a friend. This network is the original listserv.

'It could be anything,' Murray says now, having given up on his soup. 'It could be that Gary just needs a little cash.' But they both know this is a feint. Gary is a partner in a commercial law firm, a man who wears custom suits and has a state of the art wide-screen television, a top of the line gas barbecue, and a fully loaded suv. *Fully loaded,* Pearl thinks. That's Gary.

'Why would he need cash?' Pearl says, just to continue the conversation. Her anxiety is already producing a kind of corrosive cross-hatching just under her skin.

'Or maybe the roof leaks, or he saw a cottage he likes better. On another lake. It could be anything, who knows?'

'Call him,' says Pearl. 'What if they're getting divorced? What if Linda decides to get herself a career, and she moves to Vancouver? Or New York? They do that now – they get divorced and then they send the kids back and forth across the country. What if we never see them except on vacations? And poor Gary, no family, who'll look after him?' She has a dish-towel in her hand, and she is actually wringing it.

Why isn't she collecting this information herself? It's true that Pearl is an expert information collector, but – and this is a big but – there is a difference between the delicate extraction of facts, and taking a blast of bad news about their son directly in the face. That kind of news requires a buffer zone, someone to mediate between her and the raw truth. She needs to get it second hand, or sideways, or doled out in little instalments, so that its poisonous effects can be neutralized.

This is a job she thinks that Murray should do, just the way it is Murray's job to put gas in the car, or register them at hotels on trips while she waits with the luggage in the lobby. In the ongoing negotiation of territory between them, she is taking the position that this job is part of his role, the man's role. The truth is that she is tired of handling all of the information processing herself. He's retired now. Let him help out a little.

Murray pushes himself back from the table, his legs in his tan pants slightly bowlegged. He has a light frame, wide but flat, a concave chest and spindly legs that end incongruously in heavy New Balances.

'Pearl,' he says. 'R-E-L-A-X. We don't know anything yet.'

Pearl plugs in the electric kettle, and gets out two cups, putting a tablespoon of instant coffee in each. Then she gets a jar of powdered coffee creamer from a shelf and adds some to Murray's cup, along with two spoonfuls of sugar from the sugar caddie.

'Relax?' says Pearl. 'While our son is reduced to a sports car and Prozac?'

'Gary is on Prozac?' says Murray.

'Who knows? Who *knows* what he's up to? His marriage is going down the drain, his only chance for happiness, who would sit back and let that happen?'

'You know what jumping to conclusions is, Pearl?' Murray says in irritation. 'You know what it is? That's you. Not just jumping. More like leaping.'

Pearl is now staring out the sliding doors to the patio where the sky is smudged over with uneasy grey clouds. A pigeon with a purple cast on its neck, almost like a birthmark, is darting its head at something on the barbecue cover.

'All right, listen,' says Murray. 'Call Ruthie, maybe Ruthie will know.' His voice has softened a little. He knows she is genuinely upset. Besides, even though she does jump to conclusions, she is also usually right.

'Gary doesn't talk to Ruthie like that.'

'Try it,' says Murray firmly. 'What have you got to lose?'

Pearl realizes that although Murray is still avoiding being involved, calling Ruthie is actually not a bad idea. She pads over to the telephone in her light green velour robe and pushes the speed dial, leaning both her elbows on the counter, a pencil dangling from one hand. While she is listening to the telephone plinking out Ruthie's number, she inspects her nail polish, a pinky-tan colour with a high shine. The skin on her fingers has loosened into folds around her wedding and engagement rings, and she notices again the sag of her freckled forearm around her gold watch with the safety chain. This gives her a small jolt of distaste and alarm, which she automatically converts, into something else, some mixture of stoicism and a flattened, managed form of distress. What, you didn't know you were old?

'He's selling the cottage?' says Ruthie, when she answers, and Pearl explains the reason for her call.

'So he hasn't said anything?'

'Nothing, not a word. Why would he sell the cottage? You think they're breaking up?'

'Who knows, we're not jumping to conclusions here, we're just trying to find out.'

'Well, call me,' says Ruthie, 'if you find out anything.'

'So much for that idea,' says Pearl, as she puts down the receiver. 'We're not going to even see the children before they leave with their mother for Vancouver.'

'What happened to not jumping to conclusions?' says Murray.

'What I tell Ruthie and what I tell you is not the same,' says Pearl.

'No kidding. Anyway, maybe he'll tell us when he's good and ready.'

'You already said that,' says Pearl.

'He's a private person.'

'If that's what you call it.' *Private.* What did that mean with a child, even an adult child?

The kettle starts to shriek, and she yanks out the plug to cut it off. Then she pours the water into the two coffee cups and stirs them.

Murray goes over to the coffee table in the living room, which is separated from the kitchen by a waist-high counter. He picks up a yellow plastic lighter and his package of cigarettes and lights a cigarette, standing up, holding the cigarette like Frank Sinatra.

'A man worried about his heart shouldn't be smoking,' says Pearl automatically, bringing over his cup of coffee and putting it down on a coaster beside his ashtray.

'Look,' Murray says in exasperation. 'If you're really worried about Gary, just call him. What's so hard about it?'

'You call, I can't stand it, I don't want to know.'

'Gary, you there? It's Dad. Pick up if you're there, your mother's having a fit about the cottage ad. What's doing, anyway? Give me a call.' Murray is in the den with the television on mute, watching a Blue Jay pitcher wind up.

'It's me. I'm here. She saw the ad?'

'She reads everything, you should know that. Everything, you name it.' The batter takes a wild swing at the ball, and Murray smacks his forehead in disgust.

'Shit,' says Gary, his voice sounding tired.

'I couldn't have said it better myself,' says Murray. 'What's going on? It'd cut your mother's heart out if she couldn't see the kids.'

'Do you have to be so melodramatic?'

'That's not me talking, that's your mother,' he says, although this isn't entirely true. 'So what's doing?' The batter has struck out, and Murray tries to remember how many millions he extracted in his last contract negotiations.

'Nothing,' says Gary. 'Just a little financial consolidation. We don't use the cottage that much, the drive is too long, all that Friday night traffic on the 400. So why have all that money tied up? We can rent if we want next summer.'

'You got money troubles?' Murray shifts in his seat. The half inning is over, and the field is full of bodies changing places.

'Not troubles. Not troubles. Just consolidating. Getting a little more liquid.'

'More liquid for what?'

'Just more liquid. Look, I have to go, I have to pick Jason up at dance class.'

'He's taking dance? What kind of a thing is that for a boy to take? Sarah, I can see. A girl takes dance.' Murray scratches the top of his head, which the sun has coloured a golden, bread-crust brown, with a few darker age spots. He has a horseshoe-shaped fringe of white hair around the back and sides.

'It's different, now,' says Gary.

'That's it?' says Pearl. 'That's all? Just a little consolidation? That's all you got from him?' She is sitting on the sofa with a bag of low-fat barbecue potato chips in one hand, and a book in the other, the book her book club is reading this month, a historical novel about a woman whom Pearl finds annoyingly passive. She understands that this is a very good book, very lyrical, very enriching, but she can't stop feeling that she wants to yank this woman to her feet, and tell her to pull up her socks and stop mooning around.

'What, you want me to interrogate him? Grill him, maybe, under the hot lights?'

'That's not enough. There's something else going on.' Pearl checks her watch to see whether her oatmeal and honey facial mask should come off yet, and shifts the book on her lap, giving it a little shake, as if this might liven up the heroine, give her some starch.

'Maybe,' says Murray. 'But you can't find out something someone doesn't want to tell you.'

'You must be joking,' says Pearl.

Pearl is planning to make candy. It's not that she has a big sweet tooth. No, she has a little sweet tooth, but that's not why. She is interested in the combination of chemistry and engineer-ing involved, the heating and cooling, the softening and hard-ening, then the pulling or moulding. This seems to her the most difficult, the most technically exotic of culinary skills, and she's ready for it. But she can't decide what kind of candy to make. Since she's never made it before, she doesn't know which recipes are the more difficult ones.

She is sitting on a bar stool at the counter between the living room and the kitchen. She hates these bar stools, the seats are too small and the legs are too long, so that she has to tip herself off them and slide to the floor. However, she continues to use them, because they are supposed to be used, while she leafs through her cookbook, looking for something she can handle. Fondant? The name sounds so old-fashioned that she has the impression that pioneer women made it. Is there some place left in Canada where people are still making fondant? Right after they crochet their doilies. She has only a hazy idea of what fondant is, but the book says the candy is supposed to ripen, and then get dipped afterwards. Ripe candy. That might be a little too tricky.

Newport creams? She has no idea what they are. They sound to her like the American cigarettes Murray's brother smokes when he comes in for a visit from Buffalo.

Then there's nougat, something she has actually eaten before. This is a possibility. Or rock candy? On further investigation, this turns out to be sugar crystals on strings, like the kids used to do for their science experiments. Pearl wants to make something that involves more cooking. Persian balls are out for the same reason. They don't take any cooking at all.

What Pearl really wants to make is something that involves one of the crystallization stages, the heating points that determine how hard the candy will be. The cookbook describes this at some length, but Pearl has the important points in her head.

A sugar syrup is boiled to different temperatures, hotter for harder candy. The stages are tested by dropping a little bit of the syrup into cold water. The first stage in the cookbook is the thread stage, because the boiled syrup makes a thread when it is dropped into the water. Then comes the soft ball stage, where the syrup turns into a squishy ball. The firm ball stage is when the syrup ball is harder. After that, there are other stages.

Pearl studies the diagrams. Crystallization. She likes the idea of the sugar melting into a liquid, and then the liquid gathering itself up and transforming into something harder. And then you can eat it, too. How does this trick work? Who knows?

Of course, it's just candy.

'Gary, it's me. Pick up, I know you're there. I have to talk to you about Sarah's birthday.' This time Pearl is on the upstairs phone, sitting on the bed, looking at her legs stretched out in front of her. She has cotton between her toes as her pedicure dries, and the arm that isn't holding the receiver is hugging her own soft bulk.

'Pearl, it's Linda. Gary isn't here right now.'

'Linda, good, you're there. So what's new? Everything okay with you and Gary?'

'It's just going to be a regular birthday party, games and a video.'

'No Glow in the Dark mini-golf?' This is what they did for Jason's birthday party last year. Pearl found it disorienting at first, a dark warehouse with neon golf balls and clubs, where pink and orange designs were glowing strangely on the walls.

'She doesn't like mini-golf. She just wants games at home. And she wants Barbie clothes for a present. You know, the little sets. She has the disco dress, and the tennis outfit, and the prom clothes, but they have a lot of sets.'

'Barbie as in Barbie doll?'

'Right. They have a Barbie dentist set, and a Barbie veterinarian set, and a bunch of others.'

'The doll has a career?' Pearl feels little filaments of anxiety starting to spread again.

'Why not?'

'What happened to those dolls that went wee-wee when you gave them a little bottle?' She risks touching a toenail, to see if the polish is still tacky.

'She has one of those already. She's bored with it.'

'So now Barbie's going to be a doctor?'

'A dentist. I don't think they have a doctor. Yet, anyway.'

'And how's Jason?'

'Good, he's good. Got a good report card this week.'

'That's because he comes from a good home. You know what they call it now? An intact home. No divorces. No running back and forth.' She knows that this is dangerous ground, but she's fervently hoping that she can get away with at least general statements like this.

'I don't know, Pearl. Lots of kids do okay with that. It just depends.'

'Depends on what?'

'On whether the parents are still friendly. Whether they act civilized and don't criticize the other parent to the kids. That kind of stuff.'

'You've thought about this?'

'Sure. It's everywhere. We have friends. One of Sarah's best friends. The mother lives on this street, the father, two streets over.'

'Oh,' says Pearl.

'And if Gary and I broke up, that's how we'd want it.'

'You're breaking up?' The filaments are starting to claw at her.

'I said *if*.'

'And this *if*, it's a likely *if*, or not a likely *if*?'

'Who knows?' says Linda. 'How can you tell? Nothing is forever these days.'

'But everything's okay right now? I heard you were selling the cottage.'

'Oh, that,' says Linda.

'There's a reason?'

'There goes the other line, listen, we'll see you at the birthday party.'

Pearl sits for a minute, still hugging herself, but now she is

97

rocking a little. Then she takes the cotton out from between her toes and walks downstairs, where she starts wiping the clean counters in the kitchen. She wipes them several times.

Gary is six, a child with bright, black eyes and thick hair. She is pushing him on the swings after school, the swing swooping up and back, up and back. He is anxious again. He reminds her of a deer foal, only darker, something about the combination of unnatural alertness and large eyes.

Not too high, he says.

Slow down, he says.

Don't do that, he says.

She sees that he is gripping the swing chains so tightly, his knuckles are almost white. She wants to take this anxious child and tuck him into a corner of her body, to hold him while she sways back and forth, to wrap him with a soft white calmness that will coat his high-strung nerves. She doesn't have much of this calmness herself, but she has more than he does, and he can have all of hers. She will tell him that he does not have to worry. She will never push him too high. Everything will be all right. Everything will be fine. No worrying, she will say. You're safe, safe from everything. Nothing will hurt you. Everything will be just fine.

But she knows that this is a lie.

Besides, her arms are already full with Ruthie.

'So how was Arizona this year?' says Pearl. She is wearing a light blue pantsuit, matching slingbacks, gold earrings, and a silk print blouse with gold anchors on it. She and Ida, Linda's mother, are standing in a corner of the living room at Sarah's birthday party, holding cups of coffee on saucers. They are watching a group of blindfolded seven-year-olds sitting in a circle, passing around a bowl with a slab of chocolate in it. When the music stops, the girl who has the bowl has to cut off a piece of chocolate with a blunt knife, still wearing a blindfold. The sight of the girl blindly chopping at the hard piece of chocolate, the blunt knife sliding across the surface, is what makes the game funny. Then the music starts again. Linda is handling the cassette player, which has a saccharine children's tape playing.

'Good, good. It's sunny, it's warm, we play golf, we go to the movies, what could be bad? And those American supermarkets, they've got everything. Every kind of low fat, or gourmet, enough frozen dinners to fill a stadium. Diet this, diet that, sometimes diet and gourmet at the same time. It's really something, isn't it, Sam?'

'Really something,' says Sam, Linda's father, who is walking past them, making a wide circle around the little girls so as not to step on any fingers. 'I'm going to the den and see if the game's still on. Murray?'

'This year, they have something new in the supermarkets, or maybe we just never saw them before. Melon balls. Already cut up, perfectly round, not like the kind you make at home. And the flavours of yogurt – mochachino, blueberry cheesecake, you name it.'

'Isn't that interesting.' Pearl shifts her coffee cup to the other hand. Actually, she finds Ida extremely boring.

But it could be worse, she says to Murray after each time they see them. At least they're nice. So what if they don't have too much in the upper story?

'And you?' says Ida. 'You're still doing that yoga? It's not too hard?'

'Three days a week. It's for seniors. We don't do the hard things. No standing on the head.'

There is a shriek, or seven shrieks, as a piece of chocolate goes skittering across the broadloom. Linda settles the kids down again, while Gary reloads the camcorder. Murray disappears after Sam into the den.

Now the game is over, and Sarah is opening her presents. The first one is an answer ball, a black ball with printed answers floating in liquid inside.

'See,' says Linda, 'you ask it a question and then shake it.'
Sarah shakes it and an answer looms into the plastic window.
Linda reads it out loud over Sarah's shoulder. *Better not tell
you now.* The girls shriek. Sarah shakes it again and another
answer looms up.

'Isn't that something?' says Pearl to Ida.

Linda is leaning over the circle of girls.

'No, no,' she says. 'You're supposed to ask it a question first.'

Sarah keeps shaking it. *Answer hazy, try again.* She tries
again. *Signs point to yes.* The girls shriek some more, and
Sarah starts tearing the paper off another present.

'Aren't they dolls?' says Pearl. 'Aren't they the picture?'
The little girls with their shiny hair, their clear eyes and child-
ish skin, all seem extravagantly beautiful to her. Suddenly she
feels overwhelmed with an unexpected squirt of happiness, a
very ordinary kind of happiness, a very domestic kind of happiness, a very melon ball kind of happiness. To be able to watch
these little girls, to sit with the boring but kind Ida, and drink
coffee and chit-chat – what could be better?

'The picture,' says Ida. 'That Sarah. What a business. A
going concern. I mean, you have to admit, we're lucky. Look at
the Finebergs.'

'The Finebergs with the computer consultant son? What's
his name? Mark? Those Finebergs?'

'Steven. Apparently things are not so good there.'

'Why not?' says Pearl, glancing away from the little girls for
a minute to Ida.

If she thought about it, Pearl would admit that some of the
information she collects can be malicious from time to time.
However, interpreting the soundness of the information is part
of the art, something that requires shaving away any distor-
tions until she is down to the kernel, a clear brown nut of fact.
And if she thought about it more, she would say that some people – *some* people – are going to be small-minded and nasty
whatever they're doing.

'Well, Steven it turns out is one of those homos, you know, gay,' says Ida, who is usually a fairly reliable source, maybe because she is so unimaginative.

'But they have kids – two, maybe three, but at least two.'

'He just found out.'

'He just found out?' says Pearl. 'What, he didn't notice before? How could he not notice?'

'Apparently it happens. People like that, they try to ignore it, push it down, and all of a sudden it comes out, like opening a can of soda.'

'So what's he going to do?'

'He's going to the States to live. New York. Or maybe New Jersey, I forget. One of the New's. She'll stay here, her family's here and the kids are going back and forth.'

'Oh.'

'What's the matter?' says Ida.

'You think that could happen to Gary and Linda? I mean, not the gay part, but the break up part?'

'Touch wood, they seem to be okay.'

'What about the cottage?'

'What *about* the cottage?' says Ida.

'They're selling it,' says Pearl.

'My God, why?' Ida sits down heavily on a folding chair, and Pearl sits down beside her.

'You didn't know?'

'What? What don't I know?'

'I'm trying to find out.'

'Trying to find out what?' says Sam, who is back again, with Murray following in his wake. They both have drinks in their hand.

'Nothing,' Pearl and Ida say at the same time. This information isn't ready for dispersal. 'No game on TV?' says Pearl.

'We just caught the end.'

'I bet you got in a lot of golf in Arizona this year,' says Pearl.

'Sure,' says Sam. 'Golf, golf, golf. The only thing is, it's always the same. Same people, same golf, same weather.'

'What's wrong with the same?' says Pearl. She says it just a little too loudly. Ida and Sam look at her. Murray looks away.

'Nothing, nothing, it's just a change is nice, too.'

'You think it runs in the family?' says Pearl to her coffee.

'Sorry, Pearl, I didn't hear that.'

'Nothing.'

The presents are all opened by now, and Sarah charges over to where they are standing.

'Here comes trouble,' says Pearl, setting down her coffee cup, opening her arms and beaming.

'Do you have to do that in here?' says Pearl. Ruthie is in her parents' kitchen, brushing a golden Labrador with a wire brush. On top of the table is a plastic baby carrier with a baby in it, a baby with almost no hair, dressed in a blue terrycloth sleeper, a baby who is in fact sleeping in his sleeper.

'Yes,' says Ruthie, 'if you want to talk to me.'

'I need you to call Gary,' says Pearl, letting it go because she is asking a favour.

'Why?' Ruthie says.

'Because maybe he'll talk to you.'

'It's too intrusive.' Ruthie stops brushing for a minute and pulls dog hair out of the brush.

'He needs the support of his family at a time like this.' Pearl takes the wad of dog hair from her, puts it into the kitchen garbage, and then washes her hands.

'I can't just call him up out of the blue and say, "What are you selling the cottage for?"'

'So don't call him up out of the blue. Think of a reason to call, and then nudge the conversation round to it.'

'I don't know.' Ruthie gets up, goes over to the sink, and fills a bowl with water.

'You're not using one of my good bowls for the dog?' says Pearl.

'It all gets sterilized in the dishwasher.' Ruthie puts the bowl down on the floor, and the dog laps at it sloppily. Then she sits down at the kitchen table, and starts going through the contents of a diaper bag. Some things she tucks back into the bag, like bottle liners, a plastic nipple, two disposable diapers and a baggie of powdered formula. A dried-up tin of Penaten, a gummed teething cookie and an old package of wipes go into the pile she is throwing out.

'You could ask him what he's doing for the summer,' says Pearl.

'Now that's subtle,' says Ruthie. 'He won't see that coming at all.'

'Fine, think of something yourself.'

'I don't have to think of something, because I don't really want to do this.'

'Don't you want to know?'

'Not really. I have my own life.'

'What's that supposed to mean, young lady?' says Pearl, although of course she knows.

'Face it,' says Murray to Ruthie. He has wandered into the kitchen, and has picked up the Penaten tin, turning it over in his hands. 'We're not going to hear the end of this until your mother finds out what's happening.' He is happy to pass the buck, Pearl thinks, to pass along the investigation work to Ruthie, but she is a stung by their temporary alliance. What is with them? They need to know as well. It doesn't seem fair to her to make her out to be so – so, well, intrusive, the way Ruthie says.

'There's an understatement,' says Ruthie to Murray.

'Don't talk like I'm not here,' says Pearl.

'It's me.' Ruthie is in her parents' bedroom with the door closed, sitting on the double bed. The broadloom is ecru (isn't that one of those Australian birds? said Murray when they put it in) and there is an exercise bike in front of the television. One of the white laminate end tables has small jars and tubes of face cream lined up on it, the other has a half-finished roll of antacids and a plastic container of dental floss.

Okay, Ruthie said, I'll call, but absolutely no listening. I mean it.

'What's up?' says Gary.

'I've been assigned by Mum to find out why you're selling the cottage. She thinks you're breaking up.'

'You and Dad both. Why are you whispering like that?'

'I'm not whispering, I'm over at the house now, and I don't really want them to hear every word I'm saying. They're kind of going nuts.'

'They're driving *me* nuts,' says Gary.

'Look, if something's happening, they're going to have to know sooner or later.'

'Later is a lot better than sooner.'

'You mean there is something happening?' Ruthie is winding the telephone cord around her hand.

'You and David never have problems?'

'We're talking about you.'

'We just thought if we could get it all wrapped up first, it's bad enough without them all over us.'

'So it's true, you are breaking up?'

'Separating. It's called separating when you're an adult.'

'Thank you for that little tip. What happened?'

'Nothing *happened*. People grow apart, that's all.'

'Which people, specifically, here?'

'Linda,' he says. 'The kids are both in school all day now, and she took stock of her life and found it wanting. That's what she says. She needs to explore her potential, grow as a person, she feels like she's stuck in a rut.'

'Is there someone else?'

'See, this is exactly why we didn't want people to know yet, this kind of talk.'

'So what's the answer, since people are going to talk anyway.

You might as well get your version out there.'

'Not that it will make any difference, but there's no one else. Nada. This is between me and Linda.'

'There's someone else,' says Pearl. She's holding the baby, who has woken up and is looking around in an intense way, as if he is filming the kitchen in his head. Ruthie has emerged from the bedroom and dutifully reported.

'You don't know that,' says Ruthie. She taps some formula into a bottle liner in a plastic container, adds water, a plastic nipple and then a ring to hold it together, shakes it up and puts it in the microwave. 'Linda wants to grow as a person.'

'Grow how? She can't grow and stay married? What's wrong with a nice course? There are courses you can take all over the place. You can probably take brain surgery at night now. There's someone else.'

'At least they're both staying in town,' says Murray. He is smoking again, standing in the dining room so as to keep the smoke away from the baby, but still hear the conversation.

'Not necessarily,' says Ruthie, who is watching the bottle going around in the microwave.

'Not necessarily?' says Pearl in alarm. 'What's that sup-posed to mean?'

'Just what it says. Maybe they'll both stay, maybe they won't. Right now, he's moving into an apartment, so she can stay in the house with the kids.' The microwave pings, and she takes the bottle out.

'She wants to break up, and he's the one who has to move out?' Pearl takes the bottle from Ruthie, tries it on the back of the hand that's holding the baby and then inserts it tenderly into his mouth, puckering up her own seamed lips and pushing them out in an unconscious sucking demonstration. The baby, who is a human vacuum cleaner and needs no encouragement, starts sucking automatically, eyes still intently surveying the scene. 'Here, sit, you do too much,' Pearl says to Ruthie.

'There's some nice Danish in the bag, there. It might even be diet Danish.'

'It's stability,' says Ruthie, ignoring her. 'It's the whole thing with the kids, make sure they have stability.'

'And what? Her boyfriend moves in?'

'There is no boyfriend,' says Ruthie.

'I'm going to believe this because the husband says so? The same husband who's so smart he's the one moving out, even though his wife wants the separation?'

'Okay, don't believe it, I don't care.'

'When is this big move happening?'

'Soon. They just wanted to get the birthday party over with.'

'My God, poor Gary. I have to call him,' says Pearl distractedly.

'Don't call him,' says Ruthie. 'He was trying to keep you and Dad out of it.'

'Out of it? We're his parents.' Pearl feels stung again, but this time it is in a familiar spot.

'And he's an adult.'

'I could say a lot of things to that,' says Pearl. 'But I won't.'

Gary is in grade five, but he is having trouble at school. Oh, he is bright enough, almost too bright, racing through his textbooks far ahead of the others. But two boys in his class are laughing at him, excluding him, picking on him. Every day, his feelings are hurt all over again. When Pearl thinks about this, she gets a burning ache on the left side of her chest. She wants to strangle these other boys, well, perhaps not strangle them, but a good hard smack, something to scare the pants off them.

I'll watch them, says the teacher in a tired way, at the parent-teacher interview. I'll watch them, and I can break it up if they do it in class, but I can't make him popular, I can't force them to accept him.

How could he be unpopular?

Why is he unpopular? says Pearl, bewildered.

Who knows? says the teacher, who is on her last interview of the evening, and who wants to get home. Sometimes these things happen, says the teacher. Boys are hard on each other. Although he has a sharp tongue, she adds. Maybe a little arrogant about how smart he is. If you could get him to tone that down, it might help. If it's still a problem, we can try putting them in separate classes next year.

Pearl leaves politely, but inside, she is anguished. Someone is hurting Gary, and she can't fix it. She almost starts to cry at a stoplight on the way home in the car. What kind of children are these boys? What kind of school is this, that would allow this to happen?

The school is no good, she will say to Murray that evening. Let's look around. We can afford it, she will say.

Murray will agree, because he leaves the children up to her. And because they can afford it. That's his job, the affording part. That's the easy job.

'The cat's out of the bag,' says Gary. He is calling on his cell phone, walking up and down in his office. He is a pacer at the best of times, and this is not the best of times.

'What?' says Linda. 'What is that noise, are you on the cell?'

'My parents know, so you'd better tell yours.'

'For Chrissakes, Gary, your parents know? I thought we agreed to keep a lid on it for now.'

'They were going nuts, worried. Besides, they more or less had it figured out.' He is staring out the window now where a damp mist is hanging around the office buildings he can see. The sun, glazed with pollution, is pasted up in a corner of the sky.

'I can't believe you told them,' says Linda. 'And why are you using the cell? Aren't you in your office? Isn't there a perfectly good telephone there?'

'For starters, I didn't tell them, I told Ruthie, but my mother's like a heat-seeking missile on something like this.' He sits on a corner of his desk and starts playing with a paper weight, pretending to whip it through the window.

'I'll say.'

'And your mother is better?'

'My mother *is* better, as a matter of fact, and now we're going to have four parents running around in circles, just to add to the stress. And since none of them can keep their mouths shut, we're going to have to tell the kids now. I thought we could at least make the arrangements first.'

'We can tell them tonight.'

'Great, I can't wait,' says Linda.

'Hey, this wasn't my little idea.'

'That's pretty nervy, considering.'

'I'm not the one insisting that someone moves out.'

'Let's not get into it.'

'We have something to tell you,' says Linda. She and Gary are sitting among the remains of dinner, a half-eaten fish stick left on Jason's plate in a puddle of ketchup, Sarah with her head propped up on one arm, drawing slow, loving circles in her melted ice cream and humming.

'Can I have some cake?' says Jason.

'No,' says Sarah, immediately alert. 'It's *my* leftover cake, and I'm saving it.'

'Leave the cake a minute, this is important,' says Gary.

'Daddy and I are going to live in separate houses,' says Linda.

'Why?' says Jason.

'We're going to be friends instead of married for a while. Friends live in different houses.'

'Where are we going to live?'

'You're going to live part of the time here, and part of the time in a new place with Daddy.'

'Are you getting a divorce?' says Jason. He says this as if a *divorce* was an object that you could buy in a department store, something you could pick up on the way home from work.

'Who's going to drive me to school?' says Sarah. She looks worried.

'No, we're not getting a divorce at the moment, we're having a separation. It has nothing to do with you, it's not your fault, it's just a different way for me and Daddy to be friends. And probably I'll be driving you to school.'

'What about our stuff?' Jason says in alarm. 'What about Nintendo?'

'Some things you'll have two of, some things you'll take back and forth,' says Gary.

'Are we going to the same school?'

'Yes,' says Gary. 'Same school, same class, same teacher.'

'Oh,' says Jason, who doesn't like his teacher this year.

'What about Pickle?' says Sarah. 'What. About. Pickle?' She taps her spoon on the place mat with each word.

The gerbil. Gary and Linda look at each other.

'We'll work it out,' says Gary. 'Don't worry, Pickle'll be okay, he won't be lonely.'

'She,' says Linda. 'Any other questions?'

'Can I have some cake now?' says Jason.

'Linda, I heard, are you all right?' says Pearl. She is opening a box of egg noodles and dumping them into a pot of boiling water, the phone cradled on one shoulder. Murray is doing a crossword puzzle, and pretending not to listen.

'More or less,' says Linda.

'Do the kids know?'

'Yes,' says Linda.

'And your parents, how about your parents, last time I talked to your mother she didn't know.'

'Well, she knows now,' says Linda wearily.

'Are you sure about this? Really sure?' says Pearl.

'We're sure.'

'Well, you can always change your mind, don't let pride stand in the way.'

'I won't,' says Linda.

'You know, like if you get out there and find it's not all a bed of roses, and Gary starts to look good in comparison.' Pearl knows she is going too far, but she is desperate to say these things, to ensure that Linda knows what she knows, has thought about what she has thought about.

'Fine,' says Linda tersely.

'You don't want to let some good-looking face distract you.'

'Thanks, but I'm not the –'

'What?'

'Forget it. Pearl, I'm only going to say this once. There is no good-looking face in my life. None.'

'Well, I just want to say that you're still the mother of our grandchildren, no divorce there, you're still part of the family.' Pearl can't believe these clichés are falling out of her mouth, she sounds like some sentimental movie of the week, but she needs some way to say these things.

'Thanks.'

'Don't be a stranger, okay?'

'Thanks. Listen, I have to go.'

Pearl hangs up the phone, and a wave of misery comes over her. She knows that she has made a mess of this, that she was blundering around, and it makes her feel like wailing out loud for a moment, which is absurd. She gets hold of this squalid feeling, pulls it up briskly, and quickly reshapes it into something tidier.

'I don't know what to think,' she says to Murray. 'She has the kids, she could have a little job. What does she want, anyway?' She would like to understand Linda, but she finds this almost as disturbing as the separation.

She drains the noodles, adds margarine and poppy seeds and sets down a plate on the table.

'We shouldn't be taking sides,' says Murray, and he means it.

'I'm not taking sides. I'm thinking.' She sets out a little plate of tomato slices, green olives and celery sticks. 'Maybe she's got the right idea,' she says, trying this on for size.

'Let's not get carried away here,' says Murray.

Linda takes a few deep breaths. 'I'm getting caller identification if it's the last goddamn thing I do,' she says out loud to the telephone.

Pearl is still looking for candy recipes, for something with a chemical reaction that doesn't look too hard. Tonight she's thinking about pulled mints. This recipe calls for boiling the syrup to the hard ball stage. *Hard ball.* This is what Gary says when he's talking about his deals. One tough candy, those mints must be.

She turns the pages of the cookbook. Horehound candy. What a name. She can't picture herself offering this to anyone. A little horehound candy, Ida? Then there's divinity fudge. Maybe a little too much the opposite. Pearl is getting a headache, and decides to go to bed. No rush on the candy. The book will be there tomorrow.

Murray is already in bed, snoring quietly, the television still on. Pearl clicks it off, and gets in beside him, the warm envelope of bed, the lump of his sleeping body, his cotton pyjamas and old man smell, all wrapping around her. She wouldn't admit this to anyone, but this is one of the things she likes best about being married. She wiggles her heavy body into place, and then falls asleep in half a minute.

Sometime during the night she has a dream, a liquid dream that fills up her head so that she feels woozy, even in the dream. She is in the Glow in the Dark mini-golf course, inside the warehouse. Instead of Jason and his birthday party friends, she is playing with Gary. They pick up their fluorescent clubs and balls, and the little pencil and score sheet. Pearl is afraid that she is going to trip on something, break an ankle.

You're holding the club wrong, Gary says. See, try it like this.

She tries to imitate him.

No, no, says Gary. You can't get any control over the ball that way.

She hits the ball anyway, and the ball goes ricocheting around the course, zinging into walls and bouncing around as if it was motorized.

I told you, says Gary. He is angry at her.

The next hole, there is a miniature house over the hole. It looks familiar to her, and she realizes that it's Gary and Linda's house. She turns to Gary, but he is suddenly the size of the little house. He is shouting at her from the ground.

What? she says. What?

He is still shouting.

I can't hear you, she says.

She bends over to get closer to him.

You're still holding the club wrong, he says.

'Pearl, I can't believe it, Gary and Linda? They were such a cute couple,' says Dottie Fineberg, who has called Pearl to offer support.

'You said it,' says Pearl. 'At least they're staying in town.'

'So I understand. At least, so far.'

'What are you talking about?' says Pearl. Dottie is also a friend of Ida's.

'Ida says Linda's thinking about her options at this point. She feels she gave up one career already, so now she's being careful.'

'A dental hygienist is a career?'

'A career is a career,' says Dottie. 'You have to wonder, though, in these situations.'

'Wonder like how?'

'Wonder like whether there's someone else, a third party.'

'For Gary? Don't make me laugh,' says Pearl. 'For Linda, now that's a different story.'

'You know something?'

'I don't know anything, I just wonder why a woman suddenly up and decides a marriage is over. Out of the blue.'

'Ida says Linda swears up and down she isn't seeing anyone,
and she can't believe that in this day and age, people are still
jumping to the same conclusions.'

'Maybe because they're usually right,' says Pearl.

'It depends. It just depends. Marriages can break up for
other reasons. It's possible.'

'Of course it's *possible*,' says Pearl. 'It's just not that likely.'

Gary is twenty-four, starting law school, and he is transpar-
ently pleased with himself. This is not an appealing quality, but
he is still so young that Pearl thinks he will outgrow it. Or the
novelty will wear off for him. They're so brittle, these kids,
their personalities seem to harden in an outline first, just a
sketch of their internal structures, something to be filled in
later by experience.

At least, she thinks this is what will happen. She notices that
Ruthie already seems sturdier, more filled in than Gary. In fact,
Gary is growing from the outside in, first the shell, and then the
inside layers, while Ruthie is developing from the inside out.

Now, isn't that interesting? Which way is the right way?
Isn't that fascinating? Isn't that disturbing?

But here she is, worrying again. She must have caught this
from Gary. Stop it, she says to herself. You have two healthy
children, good children, *sound* children. You could knock them
on the side of their heads, like melons, and you would get a
clear tone back. Just stop it.

'You've reached the Gertler residence, we're not available to
take your call right now, please leave a message for Linda,
Jason or Sarah, and we'll call you back.'

'Hi, Linda, it's Pearl. Look, I just wanted to say – I don't
know. I don't know what I want to say. Call me.'

Pearl wishes she'd never started this message. What does

she want Linda to call her for? She doesn't know. She needs an answer ball. *Concentrate and ask again. My sources say no. Better not tell you now.*

'Make him give it to me.' Sarah is wailing in Pearl's kitchen, pointing to Jason who is sitting on the broadloom in the living room, hunched over his Game Boy. It's Friday night, and Gary has brought the kids over for dinner, which is finished.

'It's *mine*,' Jason says, not taking his eyes off the game.

'How about a little cookie?' Pearl says to Sarah. 'Just you and me, we'll tuck ourselves in on the sofa, put the nice mohair throw over us, snug as a bug in a rug, and we'll watch that Emeril.'

'She's not going to be interested in a cooking show,' says Gary. He's sitting at the dinner table with a cup of decaffeinated coffee in front of him. Murray has a little indigestion, and is lying down in the bedroom.

'Why not? He's a real card,' Pearl says to Sarah.

'What kind of cookie?' says Sarah.

'I have to make a call,' says Gary, heading for the den.

Pearl settles Sarah down on the sofa and turns on the television in the living room.

'I'll be there in a minute, dolly,' Pearl says. 'I just have to go to the little girls' room.'

On the way back, she is passing by the den, and she hears Gary talking.

'Hi, honey,' Gary says to someone.

Pearl is instantly tense, as if everything, not just her hair, but her ears, everything were standing on end.

'At my parents,' he says after a pause.

There is another pause.

'Go ahead, talk,' says Gary. 'The coast is clear.'

Pearl suddenly realizes she is eavesdropping, and goes back into the living room where she sits down heavily on the sofa.

Sarah and Jason are fighting over the television now.

'Cut that out,' says Pearl, automatically. 'Your father will be here soon.'

Both of them stop and look at her strangely.

'He's already here,' says Jason.

'Oh, right,' says Pearl. 'I forgot.'

There is a thought that has been swimming around in Pearl's brain for a few days now. She has caught a glimpse of it a few times, she knows it's important, but she can't bring it up to the surface. It's a dark, slimy thought, like an eel, and she keeps seeing the tip of its black tail, before it dives down again into her brain.

This time, though, she grabs it as it comes up to the surface and holds on tightly. The eel expands into an extraordinarily ugly and painful thought that blots out everything else. Pearl can hardly stand this thought, but now it has taken hold and instead of slipping away, she can't get rid of it.

Now the thought is squatting in her mind, right in the middle, so that all the other thoughts have to scurry around it. She is arguing with the thought, pointing out that it can't be true, showing over and over again that it's impossible, but it's just growing bigger.

This is the thought:

Maybe Gary – Pearl's silky-skinned baby, her chatty toddler, her dark-haired, deer foal of a six-year-old, her earnest school project maker, her lightly pimpled, overgroomed teenager, her cocky law student, her shiny adult with the custom suits and the DVD player, her out and out blinding success of a lawyer-with-a-beautiful-family son – maybe he is finished growing up. This is him. This is who is he is. No excuses left.

And maybe he isn't so great. Maybe he is weak. Maybe he is arrogant. Maybe he is not very truthful. Maybe he is willing to let people blame his wife for something that is really his fault.

Maybe Gary has grown up to be a real jerk.

* * *

Pearl has decided on her candy. She is going to make toffee. In fact, she is going to make coffee toffee – what a name! Maybe she will have Linda and the kids over when it is ready. And Ruthie and the baby. Even the dog. And Ida and Sam. She will say to them casually, after dinner: How about some coffee toffee? No, that sounds ridiculous. How about some candy? I made it myself. Ida will say in astonishment, You made it yourself? As if this was brain surgery. Or even dental hygiene. Pearl will pass the plate to Linda. Go ahead, she'll say to Linda. Take some. Hardly any calories. You deserve it.

She will boil up sugar, water and coffee until it starts the crystallization process. However, she will only let the liquid harden so far. She will only boil it to the soft crack stage. What is the soft crack stage? It's the next stage after the hard ball stage. It's the stage when if you put the hot syrup into cold water, it separates into harder strands. But they're still pliable. They're still a little soft. That's the soft crack stage. That's how you can tell the difference between the soft crack stage and the hard crack stage, which is the next stage up.

At the hard crack stage, they break.

The Cardinal Humours

When Eduardo de Mejia left Barcelona on an overcast, grey-yellow day in the fall of 1873, he left behind his wife and his two sons, and he took with him trunks and barrels of medicaments, syrups, dried herbs, bitter decoctions, tonics, infusions and paregorics, and sixty-three glass vials of tinctures. In one barrel he also packed his pill-making equipment and his distilling apparatus, carefully wrapped in coarse cloth and padded with straw. Then he sailed to Havana to open a *farmacia*, a trip which was more horrible than he could have imagined, a trip he survived because he was able to use his medicaments to control the violent dysentery he and most of the other passengers contracted.

He made this voyage because he was desperate to find a place where he could practise his calling as an apothecary, and where he could allow his fierce curiosity free rein to explore the limits of the botanical world to yield up curative substances, something which had proved to be next to impossible in Barcelona for reasons which had accumulated over the course of a number of years, despite his many efforts. Among other things, one of the doctors in his area had started selling his own medicines on the side and was encouraging his medical colleagues to do likewise, a course of action which the apothecary considered both overreaching and unprofessional. His wife Pilar, who came from a family of merchants, was also of the opinion that his *farmacia* had been badly located for business, on a small *calle* on the west side of the city which was away from the main commercial thoroughfare. They both understood that the apothecary was not a particularly astute businessman because he was too absorbed in the scientific side of his work, and that although he was able enough, even gifted, in the diagnostic arts, he needed particularly favourable business conditions to compensate for his ongoing preoccupations.

Eduardo de Mejia had been told by a priest who was a friend and confidant of an uncle in Pilar's family that Havana was desperately lacking in both *farmacias* and doctors, a state of affairs that sounded promising. The depleted condition of his finances did not suggest many alternatives, and Havana seemed to offer both the business climate that was necessary for his success, and something more indefinable as well. To the apothecary, who was weary of the formality and stuffiness of Barcelona, Cuba appeared to be an upstart of a country, and its youth and brashness intrigued him in much the same way as the rapid growth of a medicinal plant, or the combination of two chemical solutions to create a third.

That is, he wanted to see what was going to happen next.

Pilar, who was less adventurous, or perhaps justifiably suspicious that she had more to lose by moving to the New World and that she would find it hard to do without many of the conventional but pleasant features of her life in Barcelona, agreed to join him with the boys once he had established himself to her satisfaction. The apothecary did this with dispatch, locating on a busy *calle* near a cathedral because despite his lack of natural business acumen, he was able to learn from his previous mistakes. He arranged his medicaments in rows of green glass jars and china canisters along shelves in his new *farmacia*, where they covered most of the walls and looked, to him at least, almost beautiful in their calm potency. This impressive display, his propitious location, his extensive diagnostic skills, and a genuine interest in the well-being of his customers, or at least their corporeal forms, all contributed to a quickly growing and faithful clientele.

Nevertheless, Pilar did not come as she had promised, and although the apothecary was piercingly lonely, he found it difficult to press her on this matter because he was apprehensive about the effects of such a terrible voyage on his family. He kept thinking about his sons, particularly his younger one, Jorge, who was six years old and had silky black hair and eyes like the brown seeds of an apple, but who was also thin and given to fevers, so that the apothecary was deeply concerned that he might not survive the trip. Sometimes the apothecary would wake in the early hours of the morning, rigid with fear, from dreams in which Jorge had been reduced to a skin-covered skeleton by dysentery, or was covered with purple blisters, while he searched the ship frantically for his medicaments which had all disappeared. So although he wrote letters to Pilar in encouraging and endearing terms, letters that were carried to Barcelona in ships full of leaking barrels of molasses and bales of dried tobacco, he did not exercise his authority to order them to join him. This was also because he recognized, as Pilar had realized almost immediately, that a husband who is an ocean away had very little real power over a wife with a modest, but independent income by virtue of having been born into a family of some economic means.

Eduardo de Mejia continued to hope that travel conditions would improve, and that Pilar would be tempted by his letters, in which he wrote at some length of an island where canes were milled into drifts of sugar, and fermented into rum.

This is a country, mi amado, which is heavy with guavas and coffee and papayas, which is fibrous with sisal plants. A country where the fronds of bulging palm trees slash in the warm wind, and where the sea, clear and gelatinous with salt, moans and rises and melts and foams like a giant animal, leaving milky lines on the sand.

He was quite proud of these passages which he felt were poetic in style, but they did not have the desired effect on Pilar.

Travel conditions did improve, but very slowly, and over many years. In the meantime, his sons grew older and became youths, and then young men, and eventually married, and finally Pilar, who had been an indifferent correspondent from the beginning, stopped writing altogether.

Eduardo de Mejia began to suspect that his wife might have arranged to have him declared legally dead, so that she could marry again. This suspicion was not merely the product of his imagination, although he was generally inclined to sombre thoughts, but rather emanated from a rumour to this effect, which had floated across the Atlantic with a warehouse clerk who was the son of a business associate in Barcelona. Nevertheless, he thought of himself as an honourable man, and he did not feel he was free to marry again until he knew that this was the case for a certainty. At the same time, he was reluctant to make inquiries to confirm the state of affairs, for reasons he did not entirely understand.

It was not as if there were no other prospects available to him. He was a man of average height, but he had a head of heavy straight hair, closely-lidded grey eyes with large dark pupils, and a mobile mouth. His physical characteristics and the stature of his profession meant that he had already been the subject of a number of delicate inquiries and approaches from men with families which included well-born and unmarried women, particularly those women who were over twenty, but who had not yet settled upon suitable husbands. Religion was not something that stood in his way either, as his own form of piety was shaped by his worldly views, and Havana society, such as it was, took a more liberal perspective on these matters than society in Barcelona.

Because he was a thoughtful man, he sometimes wondered to himself whether his own lack of interest in these personal affairs originated in his reluctance to make himself vulnerable again to the dreary longing that he had felt for Pilar, and even more so for his sons, their spinning excitement, their elaborate stories, and their hairtrigger tears, together with the warm-bloodedness and even the abundant irritations of domestic life. His family had been a tiny country with its own intricate geography in which he had unaccountably lost his citizenship. Perhaps some part of him had decided on his behalf, without benefit of deliberate thought, that it was safer and preferable to avoid anything that could penetrate the carapace he had slowly built up over this longing. Whatever the reason, by the time he reached his mid-forties, he was prepared to admit to himself that his sentiments were as dried up as the Seville orange peels he kept in one of his jars for headaches.

This did not mean that he was isolated, since he had a comfortable circle of friends, mostly men whom he had encountered in the course of business dealings. These included a young lawyer with an excitable temperament who had his offices next to the *farmacia*, a shipping agent with subtle manners he had met while arranging for the shipment of certain narcotic compounds, and a banker with pockmarked skin who kept a catalogue of arcane knowledge in his head on everything from mineral salts to the historical usage of currency, which more than compensated for his pedestrian opinions.

There were others, of course, but his need for companionship was not extravagant, because his primary devotion was to his books: the *Materia Medica*, the *Botanica Naturae*, and the *Scientia Herbarium*. He had a consuming fascination with the study of apothecary arts, and he spent hundreds of hours attempting to unravel both the puzzles of the body and the actions of medicinal compounds, and to place these things in beneficial juxtaposition. In the absence of his family, he cultivated a luxuriant intellectual life, which had its own deep satisfactions.

His loneliness became little more than a chronic ache, an annoyance, something that required judicious management from time to time, but nothing more than that. He was curiously unaware of the fact that although his intellectual endeavours were driven by the tireless search for curatives for his customers, the one ailment that he had not sought to remedy was his own.

'Surely this is a relatively benign condition,' said Tomas

Escobar, indignantly, although of course, as a lawyer, his habit was one of perpetual indignation. He was standing in the *farmacia* in the summer of 1885, pocketing a small envelope of valerian while he handed some coins to the apothecary.

'The man wants babies,' said the lawyer. 'This can hardly be considered in the class of a criminal act. He doesn't hurt them. Why put a man who wants babies in jail?'

Eduardo de Mejia closed the brass drawer of the cash register with the heel of his right palm, and moved back to the mahogany counter. The *farmacia* was cool and quiet, the rows of green glass jars tinting the light. Along the top row were the poisons, which he kept in cobalt blue bottles to remind himself of their dangers. The dust and fish smells and shouts from the street outside expired in the mosaic foyer before they reached the main room. There were no windows, only the light from the foyer, but the ceiling was very high, and all the surfaces in the room were hard, including the glazed wood counters, the tiled floor, the brass weighing scales, the empty flasks for the formulas he prepared for the various ailments of his customers. The only things in the room that were not hard or shiny were the medicaments, the herbs, the pills rolled in sugar, and the acrid tonics, which were carefully stoppered so as not to lose their potency. All the hard surfaces and the high ceiling in the room made it feel airy despite the dim light, because there was nothing to absorb or deaden the air.

'He can have as many babies as he wants,' said the apothecary, 'as long as they are his own.' He put the glass top on the jar of valerian, and swept a few flakes of the herb from the counter into his cupped hand. Then he took down a leather-covered book, wiped his pen nib on a piece of paper and wrote in a precise, angular script: June 15, 1885: *T. Escobar, – insomnia –* 1 packet Valerian.

'I assume that we're talking about Señor Guillermo,' he added while he was writing.

The lawyer leaned over to rest his elbows on the counter

where he was standing, his fingers interlaced, his thumbs tapping together. 'He took another baby from its carriage, right in front of the nursemaid,' he said. 'He stopped to admire the baby in the cathedral square, picked it up, and simply walked off with it. The nursemaid ran after him, imploring him and screaming at him until he walked into his house and shut the door.'

'What happened to the baby?'

'When the *policia* arrived, they found the man in his courtyard, under a sea grape tree, singing a song, the baby in his arms. The magistrate is proceeding this time.'

'The man is clearly deranged,' said the apothecary, shutting the book and replacing it on a long shelf filled with identical books. 'He owns a coffee company, there is no reason why he cannot find himself another wife. His wife has been dead for years. If he found someone with good hips, a young woman, he could have his own babies to his heart's content.'

'Well, my job is to extricate him from these proceedings, whether he is deranged or not. Which leads me to my present request.'

'Yes?' said the apothecary, a little warily.

'Do you have some kind of *medicamento* that would help him, that would inhibit these impulses? If I can convince the magistrate that he has been restored to reason, maybe he will dismiss the case.'

'I have an elixir for hysterics, to make them calm. You might try that.'

'He is very calm already, almost too calm.'

'Well,' said the apothecary, taking out his handkerchief and wiping his nose, 'this may take some thought.'

'I don't like to see a man like this go to jail.'

'I don't recall any of your clients that you wished to see in jail,' said the apothecary drily. 'Leave it with me for a while, let me consider the problem, and I will see if I can come up with something.'

'*Excellente*,' said Tomas Escobar, relief almost physically framing him in the dim light of the *farmacia*.

'Do not expect too much,' said Eduardo de Mejia. 'I doubt there is a cure for a hunger like this.'

The apothecary closed up the *farmacia* at noon, and walked back to his house for the midday meal. He kept constant habits as a matter of course, attending at the *farmacia* every day and at regular hours, almost regardless of the prospect of customers. The *farmacia* provided both a stimulant to his thoughts and a solace to him, things that were beyond mercantile considerations.

That afternoon, the Cuban sun was hot, burning through his formal black coat, even though a muscular wind was whipping off the harbour. The clouds above him looked as if a giant hand had flung a bolt of cottonsilk across the sky. A daytime moon hung to one side, like a white bubble.

He was greeted by his housekeeper, Maria Elena, a woman with a long neck, pale lips and eyes the colour of the coca syrup he kept in the *farmacia*. He relied on her, the work that she did and his household needs having grown together over the years so that they fitted together almost perfectly, although whether this was because of her skill in addressing his needs, or because his needs had gradually become shaped to the way she performed her household tasks, he could not say.

She had shown some interest in his work, and so he had instructed her with respect to some basic salves, which she used for the burns and cuts acquired by the other servants in the course of their labours. He had occasionally considered the possibility of taking on an apprentice, and once caught himself wondering idly about her capacity for understanding the more complex formulae, before hastily dismissing the thought as absurd.

Today he ate lightly, although he drank more than usual. Maria Elena waited on him, as he did not like to have too many servants about, and she slid plates of *arroz con pollo*, bread, and sweet egg custard onto the table, and filled and refilled his glass with red wine. Her clothes rustled with an agreeable papery sound as she moved.

When he was finished, he retired to his bedroom, where he took off his coat, unbuttoned his stiff collar, and stretched out on his bed. His head was buzzing a little with the wine and he was damp with perspiration. This made him grateful for the light breeze that was coming through the window, gently pushing and stirring the gauzy muslin curtains. A gecko was darting along one wall, and he watched it while he thought about Señor Guillermo.

What would alleviate this kind of ungovernable passion? In addition to the elixir for hysterics, he had herbs for clearing the mind, but these were for people feeling cloth-headed, not for those with unruly impulses. He had glass vials of tinctures to calm sexual urges (and others to stimulate them) but these seemed too specific to be helpful in regard to other impulses.

He shifted his position on the bed, and thought about the cardinal humours of the body.

The first humour: blood.

The second humour: phlegm.

The third humour: choler.

The fourth humour: melancholy.

Would an imbalance in one of these produce the desire to take a baby? It seemed unlikely. Possibly this urge stemmed from the glands themselves, or even the mucous membranes.

His mind drifted from one physic to another, feverfew, belladonna, laudanum, bloodroot, golden seal, hops, skullcap. Some of them he had tried himself, to test the effect or to measure correct dosages. For the most part, though, he was forced to rely upon the reports from his customers, particularly for those ailments that concerned the maladies of women. The glassy quiet of the *farmacia* and their urgent necessity created an atmosphere of professional intimacy, where they talked to him about things that they would never otherwise have mentioned, at least to a man, the cramping in their bodies every month, the heavy flow of blood, the sadness that descended abruptly like an iron coat, the cracked nipples from their voracious infants.

His thoughts gradually became looser and more intermittent until he was asleep, an uneasy sleep from which he woke an hour later, feeling groggy. He washed his face in tepid water from the basin, while Maria Elena made him black coffee. This he drank in one gulp, and then he looked up to see her watching him. She dropped her eyes, framed by their sparse lashes, and then took his coffee cup and left the room.

He walked back along the narrow streets to the *farmacia*, and sat down in the back room with the boiler and the distilling apparatus with the *Materia Medica* open before him. The afternoon was not generally a busy time, although business would pick up later with people on their way home coming in for stomach remedies, headache powders and lumbago pills. In this quiet period, something he looked forward to every day, he usually pursued his studies or wrestled with some problem of a customer, although he often slipped into a kind of lassitude at this time as well. All the corporeal dislocations and afflictions presented to him by his clients occasionally weighed heavily upon him, the thousand ways in which the body became internally knotted and disordered, especially since the means he had to address these ailments, to coax the body back to its natural state, were more limited than he would have wished. As well, he was often hectored by a sense of absurdity about the whole endeavour. Nevertheless, under his care his clients often improved, their body liquors beginning to spurt again, their gout crystals dissolving, their goitres shrinking, and their heart muscles induced to thump in a regular cadence.

'I do not envy you,' said Tomas Escobar said to him once. 'How do you withstand the constant exposure to such distasteful problems?'

He had come into the *farmacia* in time to overhear the end of a whispered confession relating to a digestive disorder.

'These?' said the apothecary. 'These are the easy ones. Too much fruit, too much wine, a sour stomach, they can be quickly restored to health. And then they are grateful, and you have justified your existence to God for one more day.'

'God,' snorted the young lawyer, who was something of a freethinker, although more from natural impatience than philosophical study. 'Do not talk to me about God. As far as I can tell, He is taking a very long siesta. Either that or He is punishing my clients for crimes which do not fall within the range of human understanding, crimes that only the celestial eye can detect.'

'Punishment is the essential condition,' said the apothecary. 'There is no point in attempting to understand it. You would be better off to keep an eye on those whom God helps, study that instead.'

'Equally mysterious,' said the lawyer.

The apothecary had been invited to dinner that evening at the home of the shipping agent, who had some years ago secured the services of a profligate but accomplished cook. The guests, who included the pockmarked banker, a coffee grower and Tomas Escobar, had eaten a garlic and crayfish *paella* with Marsala wine to accompany it. They were sitting now in the agent's courtyard watching the light fade, surrounded by planted boxes of red, hairy-tongued hibiscus. The sky had been washed pale orange overhead as the sun receded, and there were a still a few small puffs of clouds in it.

'I hear that our *abogado* has been retained to act for Señor Guillermo,' said the agent, as he reached over to refill Tomas Escobar's glass with the dark wine. There was a general murmur of recognition.

'You will earn your fee there,' said the banker.

'He is certainly puzzling,' said Tomas.

'What a strange affliction for a man,' said the agent, lighting a thick cigar from the candelabra on the table after passing around a small tray of them. 'Now if Señor Guillermo were a woman, one might understand it. Perhaps a woman who had lost a child, her womb calling out for the curl of a small body, her breasts weeping milk.'

'Do you think that only women possess that kind of longing?' said the apothecary.

'You say that as if you think otherwise,' said the agent.

'I wonder,' said the apothecary. 'Perhaps in the same way that women have a tiny parody of the male organ between their legs, men have a tiny womb secreted somewhere within their muscles or organs. After all, men have breasts as well.'

'Well, you are the man who would know about such things,' said the banker. 'As for me, my view is that paternal love is a different thing altogether from the love of a mother. It is a more dignified and elevated feeling, not the untidy emotion that mothers have.'

'I am not sure that I agree,' said the agent. 'Take Tomas, for example, look at the way he lets his little boy crawl all over him in the square when they are out for a stroll. It is difficult to imagine a man more besotted.'

Tomas Escobar looked both embarrassed and pleased.

'It is not a matter of the degree of emotion,' said the banker quickly, so that they would not have to hear a speech from Tomas. 'It is the fact that it proceeds from the head in a man, from his intellect rather than his body. With women, it is merely an instinct, one that they have in common with animals. Señor Guillermo's disorder is one of the mind.'

'Are you sure that matters can be so easily divided between the body and the mind?' said the apothecary, who thought, not for the first time, that the banker possessed the most conventional and banal of views. 'After all, they are connected by many things, the sinews, the vertebrae, the blood vessels, the humours. I find it difficult to tell, for example, when I see someone who is sad, and also has an inflammation of the heart, whether it is the sadness that is causing the inflammation, or the inflammation that is causing the sadness.' He took out his handkerchief, and rubbed his nose.

'Well, in that case,' said the agent, 'perhaps you have something that can help Señor Guillermo, something that by healing his body will also ameliorate the condition of his mind. I know him, he is a good man. We must take care that he does not spend too much time in the clutches of our young friend here.'

'I have already consulted Eduardo,' said Tomas huffily, until he saw that the agent was tweaking him, as well as asking a question.

The apothecary was playing with the cork from the wine bottle, turning it from end to end in his hands.

'The problem is that any remedies that I have considered will dull all his urges and impulses, all his passions, not merely his desire to take babies,' he said.

'Interesting,' said the agent, rotating his cigar against the side of his plate to shape the ash. 'And have you offered Señor Guillermo this choice?'

'No,' said the apothecary, taken aback. 'I assumed that such a state of mind would not be appealing.'

'It might be more appealing than jail,' said the coffee grower.

'But people cannot live without their desires, their itches,' said the apothecary. 'Perhaps even their inflammations.'

'What about when those desires are distorted, like Señor Guillermo's?'

'Very perplexing,' said the apothecary slowly. He drank some wine and then rubbed his forehead. 'But these are also the things which make people who they are. Bones which have mended crookedly, adhesions in the organs, the seams of old wounds, these are what distinguish us from each other. If we did not have scars, we would be blank, like a sheaf of white paper.'

'A bleak view, no?' said the agent, leaning back in his chair. 'Surely we are not just a mass of our scars? What about the little felicities of life, the moments of satisfaction or sweetness? They must leave marks as well.'

'Of course,' said the apothecary. 'Those are the reasons why we have scars, instead of open wounds.'

The apothecary spent much of the next day reading through the *Botanica Naturae*, and poring through his own notes that he had made over the years. Although he was deeply absorbed, as usual, by the hundred secret rhythms of the body, by the end of the day he had found nothing useful.

'I think I will have to examine Señor Guillermo, to try and diagnose his condition,' he said to Tomas Escobar, who had dropped in for a glass of rum from the bottle that the apothecary kept in the cupboard with his lancets and fleams. 'So far, I have been unable to produce a remedy, and I believe this is because I do not really understand enough about the problem.'

'Of course,' said the lawyer. 'I will make the arrangements and let you know.'

Señor Alejandro Guillermo received them in his drawing room, which was painted a deep blue, with dark wood trim carved in the shape of curled vines. His hair was white and wiry, although it was closely clipped, and a short white beard pointed down from his lined face, where a mole rested on one sallow cheek. He was sitting stiffly, both hands on a walking stick between his knees which he used to stand up when they were shown into the room. A servant brought in sherry and cut-glass goblets, and Tomas Escobar introduced the apothecary and explained the purpose of their visit.

'An apothecary,' Señor Guillermo said. 'I must admit that I do not feel the need for a cure myself, but I have promised to go along with Tomas and his stratagems.'

He smiled at Tomas, a slow, patient smile, and motioned them to sit.

'But surely you are in legal trouble,' said the apothecary, who was curious. 'In fact, your liberty is at stake. Does that not suggest that a solution to this intemperate passion is necessary?'

'If everything proceeded from a problem with the law,' said Señor Guillermo, 'we would be in trouble indeed. But, please, make your examinations, ask your questions. Do not let me stand in your way.'

The apothecary listened to his chest, extended his arms and watched how they fell, pressed at various points on his back and scrutinized his palms. He also put his fingers on the older man's wrist and felt the pulse. He noted that the man's eyes were yellowed, with an explosion of tiny red veins in one. His tongue was grainy and white, and there was an oily wax in his ear canals.

'Please pardon this liberty,' the apothecary said, as he stuck a small pin into Señor Guillermo's hand, and squeezed out a drop of blood. This he rolled between his own thumb and finger, sniffing it, and then tasting it.

Then he asked the older man a series of questions, listening gravely to the answers. Finally, he said: 'I think we are done.'

The apothecary and the lawyer walked down the *calle* together, stepping over the refuse in the narrow stone streets, the smell of the refuse mixing with the brackish smell of the sea.

'Well?' said Tomas Escobar.

'I suspect that his disorder stems from some kind of grief,' said the apothecary. 'There is no yellow bile that would signal the predominance of the choleric, but he is obviously too feeling a person to be phlegmatic. I think an excess of sanguinity can also be ruled out, which leaves the melancholic.'

'And does all this mean that you have something that will help him?'

'I need time to think,' said the apothecary.

They walked along in an amiable silence until the street came out on a grassy area, where they sat down under a ceiba tree. It was hot, even under the tree, and the apothecary could smell the scent of a white ginger bush nearby. A bee buzzed, hovering around the ginger, while the apothecary thought. The lawyer lit a cigar and examined it closely.

There was hypericum for anxious melancholy, thought the apothecary, but it deadened everything. There was licorice root for angry grief, but it was not particularly effective. There was devil's claw, or marsh mallow for the sadness that stemmed from inflammation. There was coca, for grief from exhaustion, to lift the spirits.

Have you lost a child yourself, then, to disease or mishap? he had asked Señor Guillermo.

Not that I am aware, said the man.

If one is not aware of it, then it is not a loss, the apothecary thought, but he did not say this.

Perhaps he could induce the flow of grief, he thought now, much as he might lance a boil. If the grief was drained, the urge might be weakened. However, he was not sure that Señor Guillermo would allow such emotion to escape his reserve, and in any event, the apothecary was of the view that once the humours were out of balance, they must be addressed physically.

Well, Señor Apothecary, he said to himself, what is your conclusion?

That this is a man in good health for his age.

That this is a man who appears sane in every way but one.

That what this man needs is not a *medicamento*.

What he needs is a child.

'A child?' said Tomas Escobar. 'That is your conclusion? A child? After all that thought? I could have reached that conclusion by myself.'

'Yes, but you would not have been able to rule out everything else first, as I have done,' said Eduardo de Mejia.

'But if he is deranged in this way, would he not be a danger to a baby?'

'I do not think so. And he has a housekeeper and other household staff to look after it.'

'This is all very well,' said Tomas, 'but I cannot provide him with a baby. I am his *abogado*, not a midwife.'

'There is no shortage of babies in the world.'

'But would he take on any baby, without it being his own issue, or even his own station?'

'He seems to be taking them now,' said the apothecary.

There was a flash of heat lightning.

Maria Elena dropped the wine bottle on the floor. The bottle shattered, and a red stain began creeping around the pieces of glass.

'Madre de Dios,' she said, as much to herself as to the apothecary, whose wine she had been pouring.

There was another flash of heat lightning, and she jumped again. She smelled like lavender and fear.

'It is nothing,' said the apothecary. 'It is of no consequence.'

'You are brilliant,' said Tomas Escobar, a week later.

'In your eyes, I am brilliant, except when I am an idiot,' said the apothecary.

'Then you should enjoy this while it lasts,' said Tomas cheerfully. 'Señor Guillermo has agreed, I have spoken to the magistrate, and we have even found a baby. His cousin's niece made an unfortunate liaison, and was sent to Matanzas to keep her condition quiet. She has now been delivered of a boy which the family would very much like to have disappear, or at least disappear as her child.'

'Well,' said the apothecary, taking out his handkerchief.

'You do not seem very pleased.'

'You are pleased enough for both of us,' said the apothecary.

On the way home that evening, Eduardo de Mejia noticed that the wind had become stronger, pulling and pushing at him in a way that was arrogant and exhilarating at the same time. He decided to take the path by the harbour, where the ocean was rearing and dropping in an agitated manner. The wind smelled of salt here, and the apothecary wondered, not for the first time, what the effect of living entirely surrounded by an enormous body of salt water might be upon the human constitution, which itself required both salt and water for survival. Was there some tidal rhythm in the human body as well, some ancient salt-water memory that was restored, or perhaps even depleted by proximity to the ocean?

He was preoccupied with his thoughts, so that he did not see the four men coming towards him, staggering with drink, until they were quite close. One stopped to urinate against a wall, while the other three cheered him along. The apothecary wondered if they were sailors. As he stepped around them, one of them grabbed his arm.

'Not so fast, Señor Gentleman,' said the man, who was tall, with shoulders that had been rounded by muscle. He was wearing a dirty white shirt, and had a narrow head, with a sore at the corner of his mouth.

The apothecary shook him off.

'Remove your hand,' he said disgustedly. 'Go home, you are inebriated.'

'Hear that?' said the man with the sore. 'We're inebriated.'

He drew out the last word in an exaggerated manner.

'So that's what it is,' said one of the other man, snickering and bumping into his companions.

'There's a toll for this path,' said the first man. In his drunken state, each word emerged laboriously out of his mouth, as if his tongue had become clumsy.

'Do not be ridiculous,' said the apothecary, although he was starting to become a little uneasy. He realized that he had left the *farmacia* later than usual, and that it was now almost dark. 'Here, let me pass, or there will be consequences.'

'Nice coat,' said the man. 'Isn't that a nice coat?'

He fingered the cloth of the apothecary's coat while one of his companions nodded gravely, and the other two convulsed in laughter.

The apothecary struck his hand away.

'This is outrageous,' he said, and tried to push past the men. The one with the sore spun him around and hit him on the side of the head.

The apothecary was stunned by the blow, as much by the shock of it as by the pain. He stumbled to one side, and the man hit him again, this time in the midriff. The apothecary doubled up, his flattened lungs scraping for air, and the man hit him again, on the other side of his head.

'Stop,' the apothecary whispered, wheezing. Although he was not a weak man, he had been taken by surprise, and he did not think that he could fight four of them at once.

'What was that?' said the man. He hit him again, this time in the face, and the apothecary heard his nose crack, and felt a warm trickle on his upper lip.

'I have something for you,' said the apothecary, a little louder.

'Yes?' said the man, his fist still balled up.

'In my *farmacia*, I have something better than rum, something that will send pleasure running through your veins.'

'Eh?' said the man, who had been expecting money. He shook his head as if there was an insect buzzing in his ear.

'Come with me,' the apothecary said, wiping the blood from his lip with his hand.

He could see the man slowly turning this idea over in his mind, his senses dulled with drink.

'Why not?' the man said finally to his companions. 'If he's lying to us, we will rob his *farmacia*, take the money. In fact, we will rob it anyway,' he added.

He grabbed the apothecary's arm again, gestured to the other men, and they walked in this way back to the *farmacia*, or rather the men lurched and swore and made incoherent jokes, and the apothecary tried to both keep his balance, and avoid having his arm wrenched out of its socket. Occasionally the man holding the apothecary would fall against him, and envelop him in a vapor of rum, the sour smell of urine, and another cloying smell, which made the apothecary suspect that he worked on a sugar boat. The streets had emptied for the dinner hour, and there was no one to notice this strange parade.

When they arrived at the *farmacia*, the apothecary unlocked the door with his free hand, and they went inside.

'Now we'll see,' said the first man, who planted himself in front of the door, folding his arms across his chest.

The apothecary took down a glass jar of white powder, and mixed up a solution.

'Take this,' he said, 'and you will feel like you have never felt before.'

'How do we know it isn't poison?' said one of the other men.

'I will take it as well,' said the apothecary.

This seemed to satisfy them. The apothecary took a mouthful of the solution first, and then the others drank. Within a minute or so, the four men were arranged on the floor, looking dazed.

The apothecary spat out his mouthful, and stepped over the stupefied men.

'Sleep well,' he said to them.

'Señor,' Maria Elena said in alarm, as he stepped into his house a few minutes later. There was dried blood under his nose and glued into his hair, and a blue-black bruise was coming up on his face.

'It is not serious.'

On his instructions, she washed the cut on his head with diluted vinegar. She worked carefully, only faltering when he winced from the sting of the vinegar. He stopped her several times to take a drink of sherry, as he found he was shivering.

'A blanket,' he said finally, as he could not stop his

movements. She brought him a light green quilt trimmed with gold braid and wrapped it around him, and then began dabbing a salve of his own composition on his cut and bruises. The apothecary found himself suddenly and profoundly exhausted. He roused himself with an effort.

'Now, you must straighten my nose, or it will mend improperly.'

'Señor, please,' she said. 'This is beyond my abilities. You need a medico.'

'Nonsense,' he said, although he hesitated a little.

He gave her directions, and they went through them in detail. Then he gulped down more sherry, grabbed the armrests of his chair, and said: '*Now.*'

Maria Elena visibly gathered herself, pinched the end of the bone and the cartilage in his nose with her muscular fingers as he had instructed, and pulled it towards her. The apothecary cried out, and tears sprang to his eyes.

'*Perdon*, Señor,' she said in anguish, and reached out in an involuntary movement to touch the side of his face with the palm of her hand. The apothecary sat there motionless, his eyes closed. Through the pain ringing through his head, the burning warmth of the sherry, and the fog of his exhaustion, he could only think of one thing; he could not bear to have her move her hand.

Without conscious thought, he put his own hand on top of hers to hold it in place. Her hand was wet and warm, and he pressed her palm into the skin of his face. He could feel the small bones of her fingers, which smelled like the salve, a musky combination of olive oil and cloves and manzanilla.

The ticking of the ormulu clock stitched the silence of the room. His pain, which had been pushed into the background by her hand on his skin, began to subside, but still he did not move. They sat there, so close that he could feel her breath, and waited. Suddenly he was overcome again with a heavy fatigue, and fell asleep in the chair.

He slept restlessly for an hour, stirring and mumbling, until a stab of pain brought him awake again. Maria Elena was still sitting patiently by his chair. Her hand was in his own, although both had slipped off his face. He raised her hand and turned it over slowly, as if he were looking for something on it, and then straightened himself and stood up.

'That will be all,' he said.

'Are they dead?' said Tomas Escobar. It was the following evening, and the apothecary and his friends were celebrating his escape, at the home of the shipping agent.

'Certainly not,' said the apothecary. 'I am not a murderer, even of criminals. After all, without such men, what would happen to your business?'

The others laughed. He realized that his escape had delighted them, not only because they were fond of him, but also because it was heartening to them that a man such as himself could outwit such a dangerous situation.

He wished that he could feel the same way. Although he gave every impression of enjoying this impromptu celebration in his honour, in reality he was taking pains to ensure that no one would know how deeply shaken he had been by the incident. In part, he felt such distress was unmanly, but he was also puzzled by the intensity of it, when all danger was now past. He felt as if the major lobes of his brain had refolded themselves in a different configuration, and that he had lost all orientation as a result.

'What was it then, that you administered to them?' said the shipping agent.

'Only a narcotic,' said the apothecary. 'It dulls pain in smaller doses, but it induces stupor in larger amounts.'

'How did you know of this?' said the banker in admiration.

'I would not be an apothecary if I did not know of such things. In fact,' he added, 'the Greek word *farmacon* means both medicine and poison.'

'And the men?'

'The men are in *prision*,' said the apothecary. 'Indeed, per-haps Tomas will be approached to be their lawyer.'

'They can rot in *prision* as far as I am concerned,' said Tomas, and the others laughed again at this uncharacteristic sentiment.

They drank the shipping agent's excellent wine and made much of the apothecary, and little of his enemies, the shipping agent's sardonic remarks provoking them to frequent outbursts of laughter, which came all the more easily since it was greased by relief.

'Shall we move indoors?' said the shipping agent after an hour, slapping at an insect.

Rather than feeling comforted by the attention of his friends, the apothecary's feeling of disorientation was increas-ing. There was something about their solidity that seemed to highlight his own confusion and disarray, rather than compen-sating for it.

Even more remarkable was that a picture of the night before kept floating into his mind, a picture of himself sitting in his chair with Maria Elena's hand on his face, each time accompa-nied by an aching in his chest and eyes.

He shook himself. Next he would be stealing babies, he thought. He got up from the table.

'Gentlemen,' he said to his friends. 'By all means, continue with the party indoors. I must go and attend to some matters.'

'No, no, stay a while longer,' said Tomas. 'It is not every day that we can celebrate such an adventure as this.'

'Yes,' said the shipping agent. 'You are the guest of honour tonight. What business can be so pressing?'

'I must go,' repeated the apothecary, this time more urgently. He did not wish to disappoint his friends, but he was becoming too distressed, and he was afraid that he would not be able to hide it, especially if he drank any more.

After further backslapping and toasting, he was permitted

to leave. He walked swiftly back in the direction of both the *farmacia* and his home, his agitation increasing. The darkness seemed thin and mean, and the stars were a spray of old white particles across the sky.

As he walked, his anxiety grew stronger. He started at the clang of a gate closing in the distance, and glanced over his shoulder at the shadows slipping around him.

I am a man of study and science, he reminded himself, but his chest was pounding. He reached the street of his house, but did not turn down it right away. Instead, he paused. He was torn between whether to go home, or go on to his *farmacia*. The idea of sitting in his chair again, of Maria Elena's presence, was overwhelmingly, almost unbearably powerful, but he was disgusted by it at the same time. This seemed to point to the *farmacia*, but he was also tormented by the thought that a *medicamento* for his condition was unworthy, another sign of his own weakness.

He stood in the street for a few minutes, touching the bandage around his head with the fingertips of his left hand, as the night wind moved restlessly through the fronds of the palm trees. Abruptly, he started towards the *farmacia*, less from a conscious decision than because of the need for movement. He walked more quickly now, almost running. His hands were shaking a little, and perspiration was rising on his upper lip.

At the *farmacia*, he locked the door behind himself, and then stood there until his eyes became accustomed to the dark, and he was able to make out the shapes of the jars of medicaments. Their smells combined into one smell, a smell that was at once dusty, sweet, pungent, bitter, weedy and metallic. He ran his hands along the jars, and fingered the small bottles of poisonous remedies.

Then he took the jar of white power, which was still sitting on the counter from the night before, and carried it into the back room, to his regular spot with his chair and books. He drew a small beaker of water from the tank, stirred some of the white powder into it, and poured it into a glass. After this, he lowered himself into his chair, and by force of habit, opened up his *Materia Medica*, even though he could not see the words.

Instead, he watched the silence collect around him, his fingertips resting on the book in his lap. Then he touched the glass, which felt hard and cool. He had a salt taste in his mouth.

There were footsteps outside the *farmacia*, and a group of people walked by, a snatch of their conversation lingering after them.

Still he did not move, except to put one hand across his eyes, and hold them, very tightly.

Plural

Luckily for us, there was an official explanation for why everything in the house was off-kilter. This was the explanation: trains ran along an old track behind the house, and the noise and rumbling made the dishes rattle and the pictures on the wall shift. Lamps or vases or anything that wasn't in a cupboard had to be pushed far back on the tables or shelves. Otherwise the train vibrations would make them migrate slowly to the edges, and eventually they would fall off and crash.

We were careless, so this happened a lot.

Straightening the pictures was useless because another train would come along the tracks behind the house in an hour or two, and they would all shift again. What's the frigging point? our mother said to people. She wanted to explain that none of this was really her fault.

She would work the trains into the conversation the first time people came over, near the beginning to get it out of the way, after they had taken off their coats but before they were settled in with coffee or beer or were feeling for their cigarettes. In fact, she could slide it in while they were still looking around, the men rubbing their gripped hands together to warm them up, the women trying to sneak a look at their hair in the hall mirror and puff it up at the sides without anyone noticing, their bodies still outlined in cold air. Hey, look at that, nice little place you got here.

Nothing special, go ahead, sit down, she would say, as she moved the front door mat that said Welcome to Our Humble Home back into place with her toe, holding a coat in each hand, and pushing the inside door closed with her elbow. Then she would say something about the trains and give a quick laugh, not a funny laugh, but a way of getting them to join in and agree how useless it would be to straighten things. If she were really in luck, a train would come long then to prove her point, roaring and shaking the ground so that it sounded like it was about to burst right through the back door and into the kitchen. They would start to look nervous, and then she would tell them that you can get used to anything.

Yeah, no kidding, they would say, thinking of all the things they had gotten used to, all the things they were putting up with even now. You got *that* right.

Our mother was thin and blonde and wired and bored, and she had a flyaway haircut that looked as if she had been standing in a stiff breeze waiting for her life to arrive. It was obvious that there had been an inexplicable delay in this regard, and everything about her was dry as a result – her chalky lips, her skin, her brittle fingernails. She was only thin from the waist up – further down, her hips and thighs bulged out in her pale blue jeans, which made her look globular.

But she's clever, I said to a girlfriend once.

She was clever, naturally clever, and most of it went into the way she talked, choppy little sentences that were sometimes funny, and sometimes bitter, and sometimes both. She might actually have been smart, instead of just clever, but it was difficult to tell because she had dropped out of school after grade eleven. 'Not because I was pregnant,' she said, wanting to make this clear, she would never have made such a stupid, cow-like mistake, 'but because I wanted to get pregnant.'

On this point, at least, she turned out to be wildly successful.

Although she would never admit it, she liked the trains. They ran along a ridge of blue-black cinders, with wide ditches on both sides that were clogged with hollow-stemmed weeds and purple phlox that had drifted out of other people's backyards. Asters and fleabane and yellow loosestrife and a lot of other plants with ragged, tough leaves, or suspicious orange berries also grew there. The tracks were an unclaimed area in the city, wilder than a street, scrubbier than a ravine, more overgrown than a vacant lot, a left-handed place that was not on the regular map, a relief from the obedient shrubs and trees of the street which ran parallel to it. Translucent snail shells and river pebbles were mixed in with the dirt at the bottom of the ditches, because the tracks were laid over an old stream bed. Our backyard was separated from them only by a rusty wire fence and some Chinese elms, and this suited our mother. The truth was that she didn't mind things being out of place, and she enjoyed all the roaring and shaking.

'Cheap thrills,' she would say, as the vibrations started, steadying her coffee cup in one hand and her menthol cigarette in the ashtray with the other, her elbows and forearms holding down the newspaper she had spread out on the table. She read her horoscope, the comics and the movie section, in that order. Then she read all the columns, Dear Abby, Recipe Corner, Adopt-a-Child, Gardening Beat, Craft Creations. Sometimes she would tear out things and put them up on the fridge with the lumpy magnets we had made out of playdough at daycare. *Luscious Low-Fat Lemon Cake. Crochet an Autumn Throw. Easy Easter centrepieces.*

The ragged newspaper pieces got yellow and curled up at the edges since she never made any of them, although she seemed to think of herself as someone who might crochet an autumn throw at any minute, or come up with a stunning centrepiece or whip up a cake. She was always on the verge of being domestic, just a hair's breadth away, but she never quite managed to get around to it.

Of course, it might be that looking after us used up any domesticity she had. She often complained about us, anyway, starting with the beginning.

'No warning,' she said. 'Nothing, not a clue. Not a goddamn clue.'

'You couldn't tell?' I said.

'Nope.' She lit a cigarette and inhaled, then let the smoke

out in a rush. 'I was big all right, big as a house. Like a whale.
Like a sperm whale. Get it? A sperm whale. At the end, I
couldn't even get out of a chair without someone pulling me up.
But I couldn't tell. How could I tell? It was my first time.'

'How about the doctor, didn't the doctor know?'

'Well, if he did, he didn't bother telling me.'

'So how did you find out?' I asked, even though I had heard
the story before.

'I was just lying there,' she said, flicking her cigarette with
her thumbnail. 'I was just lying there dead tired, and everything down there hurt like hell, and the doctor said "Here
comes another one," and I thought, ha ha, very funny. And then
out came another one.'

Think of two blobs of cells stuck to the inside of a humid red
muscle, the cells growing, duplicating themselves over and over
in some fleshy code, organs, spinal cords, soft bones, getting
larger and larger. Becoming two bodies, curled into fetal question marks.

Did we grow into each other, fitted together like spoons? Or
were we squashed front to front in a kind of amniotic clutch?

Could we hear the thumping of each other's arteries? Were
we drinking the same amniotic fluid? Could we *taste* each
other?

Think of four arms and legs in such a small space, moving
slowly in watery arcs and then, as the space becomes more
cramped, tangled and struggling against each other. Could we
tell which were our own arms and legs? Did we know that there
was an *other* in there?

Ready or not, here we come.

You go first.

Was Kevin more ready? Or maybe I was just further from
the bottom the day we received our eviction orders.

'It's the hormones that do it,' our mother said. 'Some kind of
message they send out.' Like what? Like fire alarms?

Evacuate. Get out. Move to the exits. Do not use the elevators. Or maybe we just wanted out, our new lungs craving the feel of air.

Ready or not. We were premature. First one, then three minutes and seven seconds later, another one, covered in bloody sludge, ha ha, very funny, two wrinkled underweight preemies, barely human and straight into incubators.

In our birth pictures our eyes are slits
and our faces are masks
and we look like alien babies.

After a month they brought us home, out of our glass cages, but still with the mossy black hair of newborns. We were so small, she said, they put us in a carriage together.

'Scrawny little things, you looked like chickens,' our grandfather said. 'A carriage? A shoebox, the both of you fit in a shoebox.'

Did we remember each other? Were we glad to see each other?

'Well, you sucked each other's thumbs,' our mother said.

Then people came to see us. Her friends, or people they knew from work, the discount store where she was a cashier, or Lecco Extruders, where he made plastic gas tanks for cars. Hey, Al, we really should drop something by for those kids. People were fascinated by this reproductive trick, the sheer fertility of it, and then the strangeness of the double babies. (Like I'd had a goddamn litter or something, instead of just twins, said our mother).

Even in an era of quintuplets and sextuplets, twins still rated at least a visit and a plastic container of macaroni and cheese with bacon bits for the freezer. The visitors also brought baby clothes in sets of two, not exactly alike – you gotta make sure they have their own personalities, they said knowledgeably – but with the same design in different colours, blue and green, or yellow and blue.

'I never dressed you the same,' our mother said. 'I didn't want you looking like something out of Ripley's Believe it or Not.'

'That's bullshit,' Kevin said to me once when we were older. 'You look at all those pictures, we've got the same stuff on in all of them.'

There were a lot of those pictures. Twins are very photogenic, something about there being two of everything. Double vision, the whole thing improbable. That faint whiff of clone.

This wasn't enough for our father, who left several months after we came home.

'I forgot something,' he said to our mother, one day in April when a heat wave was under way, having apparently lost its footing in the calendar, sliding back from July into the early spring. The bright sun was melting the snow at such a rapid rate that water was pouring off roofs, overflowing rain gutters, streaming down the sides of streets into the storm sewers. He was in the kitchen, making himself a ham sandwich, and she assumed he was referring to the mustard.

'We need eggs, too,' she said, as he grabbed his jacket and the car keys, and left. He left behind his open sandwich, a knife and an open jar of mayonnaise beside it, a piece of orange cheese curling up at the edges, and the kitchen radio tuned to an all-talk station. And us.

The sandwich sat on the counter for three days.

She had an old wallet photo of him at someone's birthday party, sitting at a table in a bar with a bottle of beer in one hand. A triangular face with a loopy grin, cheekbones like small round muscles, and anxious eyes. There was a shine on his face from sweat, and he had the half-incomplete look of someone drunk, as if his brain had its shirt undone. He was good-looking, but in a temporary way.

'Good-looking,' said our grandfather bitterly. He thought this had gotten his son off the hook, had saved his son from having to be anything else, like brave or strong or loyal.

I think our father was ambushed, though, that both of them were ambushed by the constant crying and the mess from two babies, the bottles, the diapers, the iron weight of our demands. I think that despite her pregnancy plans, our mother turned out to have only a small amount of motherliness, a little premeasured test-tube of the stuff, and that it was stretched paper-thin by all the feeding and changing and lack of sleep. I think our father had planned to be fond of us (or at least one baby), had intended to love us, but one melting snow day, his nerve broke. His usual ace in the hole, his looks, wouldn't have impressed us, and maybe he didn't really have anything else to give us.

This might have been true, anyway.

To our mother's great relief, there was a daycare in an old psychiatric hospital near us, and although it was intended for the children of the nurses and orderlies who worked at the hospital, they took some local children to fill up vacancies. It was housed in a wing of the hospital itself, a cluster of massive old buildings that were surrounded by parking lots, and trees that dropped clumps of yellow seedlings and pale green keys onto the car windshields.

We were a novelty – in fact, this was the start of our real career as a novelty. Either we were being fussed over, or we were deliberately not being fussed over by people who felt they were above all the rubbernecking, who were determined to treat us as normal. But even this wasn't normal, because their deliberation coloured everything they did, as if they were constantly averting their eyes from our twinness. There was no 'normal' available. One of the daycare workers in particular was fascinated by us, a woman in overalls who seemed big and white and flabby compared to our mother. She sweated a lot, a tomato juice smell under her arms as she reached over our heads to help us with something.

When it was raining, they took us for walks inside the psychiatric hospital, instead of outside on the grounds. There was

a code door between the main part of the hospital and the daycare, and sometimes patients would be waiting by the door
when we came through, shifting rhythmically from one foot to
the other, saying the same snatches of words over and over.
They didn't seem to be there because they wanted to get into
the daycare, or even because they knew there was a daycare
there, but simply because it was a door of some kind. Although
sometimes they would shift their attention from the door to the
little parade of children, and flutter around us as we walked
through the hospital.

Often the daycare workers would halt us in a recreation area
filled with slack-faced people sitting at tables, smoking. They
would distribute orange quarters to us, the smell of the orange
rinds mixing with the smoke catching in our throats, our hands
sticky with juice. Then a daycare worker would sing songs with
us, and one or two of the patients would join in, tuneless voices
with their words slurred by medication.

Sy and I went to the circus.

Sy got hit with a bowling pin.

We got even with the circus.

We bought tickets and didn't go in.

We didn't understand the joke in the song, but it didn't matter, because neither did they.

This was when we started to realize that not everyone was a
twin, when we started to think we were something different. In
fact, we might have become pleased with ourselves, except that
one result of our father leaving was that our mother was always
looking for some sign of irresponsibility that went with our
genitals, a fatal abandon-your-wife-and-children gene sleeping
in the soft pouches between our legs like a time bomb. Particularly as we got older, the expectation that we were likely to fail
her, or at least fail someone, hung around in a small, persistent
way.

So we began to think we were special, but likely to be defec-
tive.

Another result of our father leaving was that our grandfather moved in with us.

His own wife, Myrna, had been hit by a tank truck carrying heating oil on St. Clair Avenue a few years before, the oil leaking through a valve and making iridescent puddles around one side of her body where she was lying in the street. He told us her head had been cocked to one side with her eyes open, and the blood coming out of her mouth. 'As if she had just asked the wrong question,' he said.

This worried us a lot. Clearly the wrong question could be extremely dangerous, but we couldn't figure out how to tell which ones were safe.

He wasn't there when the accident happened, but he heard all about it from the driver afterwards, who was sent by the oil company to visit him with a flower arrangement of carnations and lilies, and a legal release to be signed. The driver knocked gingerly on his door at first, and then when it became clear that our grandfather wasn't going to kill him ('don't get me wrong, I thought of it,' he said to us) the driver became almost hysterical himself, spilling out details.

'In his uniform and everything, his nose running like a tap,' our grandfather said, rubbing his own freckled upper lip. He paused in the story, and looked out the window for a minute while we waited patiently.

'She had good teeth,' he said finally. 'No fillings. Nice and straight. You don't see too many people with teeth like that.'

Our mother put up with him because he helped to support us with his Ontario Hydro pension, and because he wasn't bad company. All he ever wanted from her was dinner and clean clothes. His sex life at the time consisted of masturbating in the dark in theatres, something he did with such skill that it was almost unnoticeable, except for a tiny groan at the end, which he tried to time so that it was during a loud part of the movie. He wasn't a flasher – when he realized that we had seen him do this once, he stopped taking us with him. His main fault as far as our mother was concerned was that he passed a lot of gas. 'Christ almighty,' our mother complained, fanning the air.

'It's a sad ass that can't rejoice,' he said defensively.

He and our mother played cards in the evening, endless games of gin rummy or crazy eights for matchsticks. Our bedroom was at the top of the stairs, and so we could hear the *whrrr* of the cards being shuffled.

'Jesus, what a hand,' he said in disgust. 'A real pisser of a hand.' There was a moment of silence, when we knew he was sneaking a look at her to see if she had bought this.

'Yeah, right,' she said. 'And me sitting here on a gold mine.'

There was the quiet slap of the cards for a while, and then a grunt from him.

'Christ in a convertible.'

More card sounds. Then he cleared his throat, which meant that he was picking up and discarding.

'All right, that's it. I'm cooked, I've had it,' he said.

'Yeah?' We could hear the click of her lighter as she lit a cigarette. The smell of the lighter fluid, and then the tobacco smoke, drifted up the stairs. 'I'll believe it when I see it. You got my sevens, don't you?'

'Nope.' He was rearranging his cards. 'I've got nothing here, nothing.'

There was another pause as one of them took a card, studied it and then discarded it with a flat snap. Another pause. Another card down.

'Not that you would tell me if you did,' she said. 'I bet you're up to your ass in clubs.'

'I swear to God.'

A few more minutes went by. We could hear the faint suck and exhale of her smoking.

'Right church, wrong pew,' he said, as he studied the card he had picked up.

'Sure,' she said. 'I believe that.' Her chair creaked as she shifted her weight.

More soft slapping of cards, and then the hiss of a beer bottle being opened.

Another grunt. 'Finished. I'm finished,' he said. 'I'm a dead man.'

The beer bottle clinked on the table.

'You think I'm a moron?' she said, but more confidently, even cheerfully.

A few more slaps and more clinking.

'Gin,' he announced, allowing triumph to leak into his voice.

'Why, you lucky goddamn duck,' she said, completely surprised.

Are you identical?

This is the first question people ask twins. Then they ask: which one is older?

Occasionally, they reverse the order of the questions.

This is followed by a quick inspection, a fleeting glance from face to face.

What are they looking for? To verify the answers, see if they're true? To catalogue the differences? The similarities?

I can tell you apart, they say triumphantly, as if your twinness is a personal challenge to them. I can tell which one is which. One of your eyes is a little bigger. Your mouth is a little smaller. I can tell.

We can tell, too. Usually.

Twins always have another name, as well as their individual names. They're called 'the twins', one unit, or sometimes 'the Stewart twins' if there is more than one set around.

School is when this really starts in earnest, when teachers, children, janitors, bus drivers, other mothers start asking and inspecting. We understood that these inspections were part of the deal. We understood that we were a kind of public property, a cross between being a little freakish, and a ready-made psychological experiment. In fact, most of what we knew about twins actually came from other people.

Twins have a secret language. We were told this so often we thought that maybe we'd had one, and had just forgotten about it.

Twins get sick at the same time. This was true. 'Haven't they ever heard of germs?' our mother said irritably.

In some places, twins are a curse and are killed at birth. This made us feel shocked and dangerous at the same time. We decided to stay away from those places, wherever they were. It didn't occur to us that this might be an odd thing for people to say to children. Of course, we had a grandfather who liked to tell us about his wife's death scene.

The last question had nothing to do with being twins.

Where's your father?

It was the first time we understood that someone was missing.

'Where *is* he?' we said accusingly to our mother one day, as if she had somehow misplaced him. She was cutting out a recipe for marmalade from the newspaper. We were still anxious about asking the wrong questions, but we needed something to say to people.

'Christ, I don't know,' she said, as she kept on cutting. 'If I did, I'd be looking for money, I can tell you that.'

From this we took it that he had money, possibly ours. We had been puzzled for some time about why everyone seemed to have money except us, our mother, our grandfather, purses, pockets jingling with nickels, dimes, quarters, pennies, loonies.

But why had he taken our money? Didn't he have his own?

The house was old, and it was so drafty that we carried around in our heads a weather map of where all the cold and warm spots were. There was a laundry chute from the second floor to the basement, and we spent hours dropping miniature cars on strings down the chute and hauling them up again, or passing notes back and forth with words written in lemon juice. The words slowly appeared in brown when we held them to a light bulb, and since we were using swear words, we thought this was hilarious. The chute also gave the house a secret core, as if the normal right angles of walls and floors had been outsmarted.

'Let's go down it,' said Kevin one day. We were stunned with the brilliance of this idea, amazed that we had never thought of it before. Then we came up with a plan, which we felt was fool-proof. One of us would go down tied to a rope, and the other would hold the rope so that he wouldn't go too fast. We would rub the one going down with soap, so that he wouldn't go too slowly. And we would pile the dirty laundry at the bottom, just in case.

'I'm smaller,' said Kevin, 'and it was my idea.'

He stood on a blue-painted chair and climbed in while I braced myself with the rope around the newel post at the top of the stairs. His feet and legs disappeared quickly, but then he stopped, stuck just under his arms. He couldn't go down because the chute was too small. I pulled on the bristly rope until my hands were red, but I couldn't pull him out because he was too heavy – he was only barely smaller than I was. He couldn't push himself out because he was stuck under the arms, so he couldn't get them into the right place, and there was nothing under his feet. Our perfect plan started to disintegrate into grubby little pieces.

It began to dawn on us that I was going to have to get help, and the help was likely to be irritable about this. We thought this over earnestly for several minutes, but we couldn't think of anything else to do.

'You're not mad, are you?' I asked hopefully as our mother yanked Kevin out of the chute.

She looked at us as if she couldn't decide.

After the first couple of years of school, the principal put us in separate classes. We were bewildered by this idea. We were not quite a unit anymore, no longer entirely fused, but we still operated in tandem, connected by thousands of tiny fibres.

'It'll do you good,' our mother said brusquely. We thought about this for several days.

What we thought was: *why?*

The first day of this new arrangement, I felt suddenly self-consciousness. I sat at my desk at school, looking at my legs and hands, which seemed enormous. I tried not to move, hoping people wouldn't notice I had become a giant. I wanted to roll into a ball, tucking my huge feet in. The day stretched out as I sat there, holding my balloon head.

After school, I found Kevin on the edge of the playground, digging a hole in the sand under the climber with another kid.

'Let's go,' I said.

Kevin kept on digging.

'Ricardo has some explosion powder,' he said. 'We're going to explode the sand.'

I looked at Ricardo, who nodded his head up and down vigorously.

'In my pocket,' he said. 'Right here.' He patted the outside of the pocket of his pants.

'So what?' I said scornfully. 'We gotta go.'

'I want to watch,' said Kevin. He looked down at his hole.

It was dark and damp under the climber, which had a platform and a red slide attached to it. I could see pieces of sky through the slats of the platform. It was grey, with darker grey wrinkled lines in it, like elephant skin.

'Bye,' I said to the sky pieces. On the way home, I checked over my shoulder a few times to see if he was coming.

Later when he got home, I was lying on my bed, running one of the little cars back and forth along the wall. He stood in the doorway to our room with his jacket on. 'It was fake explosion powder,' he said. 'It didn't even work.'

I turned over, so that my back was towards him and my face was to the wall.

* * *

We had the same dream, and we had it more than once, although not in the same night, and not at the same time. This was the dream.

The laundry chute had become a secret passage, a dusty, dirty staircase that led from the basement up to the roof. The sides of the staircase were old stud walls, stuffed with newspapers and torn fibreglass insulation. Some of the studs had writing on them, a word or two, and an arrow to an electrical cord or a thin copper pipe. The air in the staircase was still and dark, and smelled like dry rot.

Sometimes in the dream I was climbing the stairs over and over, and other times I was hiding in the staircase, soaked with fear, holding my breath. In Kevin's dream, he would reach the top of the staircase, and then have to race down again, pursued by the vague, dangerous people who inhabit dreams. So it wasn't exactly the same dream, but it was the same dream place.

We kept this quiet, as we knew that it would only bring out our least favourite of the twin stories, the eerie twins stories. ('And so even though they were separated at birth, they both named their children Michael and Jennifer, they both had Toyota Corollas, they both suffered from migraines, and they both liked blueberry pie.') So what? we wanted to say. Big deal. How many people like blueberry pie? But the real reason we didn't like these stories was that they emphasized the freakishness of twins.

This didn't explain how we could have dreamt about the same place. Even we were puzzled.

Maybe one of us had dreamt it first, and described it to the other?

Maybe.

We got older. We avoided doing the same things as much as possible. Isn't that *interesting*, people said or sometimes, isn't *that* interesting. I joined the swim team, swimming lengths until I was stupefied by exhaustion, the coach, who was also the math teacher, pushing us relentlessly.

'You think it's all speed? It's stamina, you bastards need stamina. You got the stamina of Jell-O. Worse than Jell-O. Dog shit. You got the stamina of dog shit.'

We dove off blocks at the start of our races, although these were horizontal dives, a way to cover some of the pool length in the air, to get a head start before we hit the water. We would swing our arms back, and then forwards to launch ourselves into the air, arcing over the pool lane, staying up an improbable extra second before skimming into the chlorinated water.

Kevin played hockey, where he was a wild, sloppy forward. He rarely got goals, but he was a popular player because he always seemed to be just on the brink of getting one, or narrowly missing one. This made the high school crowds hopeful, stamping their feet and calling his name as he coasted lazily out onto the ice, grinning and raising his stick to them. He was often gloomy himself, but in an oddly buoyant way, as if he expected the worst, but wouldn't actually mind when it happened.

'What's eating him, anyway?' my mother said to me once.

'What?' I said. I hated her talking to me about him. It seemed invasive, because it wasn't just about him – our selves were still joint territory. And if there was something wrong with him, I wouldn't have known. Every part of him was so familiar, as familiar as my own fingers, that it didn't occur to me that he should be anything else.

Or maybe it was more than that. If there was something wrong with him, I was convinced that it would be my fault, or at least my responsibility to fix it. There was only a finite amount of personhood between us, and if he was missing something, it must be because I had taken it.

How do you like competing against your brother? they asked, when we stumbled into the same sport by accident, like track and field. We understood from the way people asked this that it should feel bad, or at least complicated. For once, they

were right. In some part of me, some old deep part, like cartilage or organ lining, I was afraid that if I beat Kevin at the
sprints, he would evaporate, his body becoming gradually
transparent. Or worse, that I might disappear instead. I knew
this was ridiculous, but I couldn't shake it off.

I began to hate him moving into anything that I thought was
mine. In fact, I resented him being around me at all, and
started fiercely guarding my separate world. We became the
wrong ends of magnets, our force fields repelling each other.

We had become sick of our quasi-celebrity as well, and
started being sarcastic with our public. Are you identical? No,
we're mechanical. No, we're convertible. No, we're just smarter
than you.

But are you close? they said.

Close? What does that mean when you have the same DNA?

'You've got a zit on your chin,' says Kevin.

'Thank God the zit police are here,' I say to the kitchen
stove. I'm heating up yellow pea soup from a can. We're stuck
in the stale, empty days between Christmas and New Year's
Day, and my mother is over at the discount store, marking
down tinsel and tree ornaments and wrapping paper. My
grandfather is dozing on the couch in a faded flannel shirt, his
mouth half open, a strand of spit between his lips.

Kevin takes a couple of pieces of bread and sticks them in
the toaster.

'We're going ice-fishing tomorrow,' he says casually, leaning
against the counter.

'Who's we?' I say. I open the dishwasher, looking for a clean
bowl.

'Me and Scott. His parents have a cottage on Kempenfelt
Bay, up near Barrie, and they've got a hut.'

'What about rods?'

'He's got extras,' he says. 'He's got all kinds of shit, rods,
lures, the whole thing. Plus he's got a case of beer.'

I pour the pea soup into the bowl, and put the pot in the sink. 'You don't even like fish,' I say. 'You hate it.'

'Who says we're going to catch any? Besides, we can give it to someone.' His toast pops up, and he takes the jam out of the refrigerator.

'This is just so you can get plastered.'

He looks up with a half-smirk, grape jam sliding off his knife. 'Something wrong with that?'

I know he's telling me this because he needs a ride. I'm the one with the car, a rusted out Mazda with a loose clutch pedal and a distributor that has to be dried out when it rains.

Ice-fishing.

I've never been ice-fishing. I've never been fishing, any kind of fishing. And I'm interested in the beer. I'm not much of a drinker yet, and I'm looking for practice.

All right.

This is how we end up driving west along the bottom of Toronto, while a greyish-pink sun climbs over the edge of the lake. Scott is up at the cottage already, and we're going to meet him there. It's snowing lightly, but the snow is melting right away, making the highway a shiny black. A string of cheap motels lines the lake side of the highway, and the other side is a forest of pixel board signs. 7:08 a.m. There's never been a better time to buy. 30% less fat. Minus four degrees. Canada's best selection. Take it out for a test drive. A whole new way of thinking. Wake up to the taste. 4.1% financing. Always fresh.

'Got a map?' says Kevin. I'm driving.

'Pretty hard to miss Barrie,' I say.

'Right,' says Kevin, looking in the glove compartment, which has a broken catch. All he finds is an old parking ticket, which he uses to wipe the foggy condensation from our breath off the inside of the windshield, as the defroster wheezes uselessly. This job done, he hikes his seat back, and stretches out his legs. Then he crosses his arms and tucks his hands into his armpits with the thumbs out, and closes his eyes. We turn north onto Highway 427, and then hop over to the 400.

'Let me know when you want me to drive,' he says a little while later, not meaning it.

'Sure,' I say, not meaning it either.

We stop after an hour at a restaurant attached to a gas station so that we can eat breakfast. The Formica table has a game on it, a small wooden triangle with golf tees in holes. The scoring is on the side in red letters:

One tee left = Genius.

Two tees left = Adequate Brain Cells.

Three tees left = One Brick Short of a Load.

Four tees left = Don't Know Enough to Come In Out of the Rain.

We play while we wait for our food, greasy fried eggs with brown edges, bacon, home fries, white toast and butter, a piece of pale lettuce and a tomato slice. I have two tees left and Kevin has one.

'Well, at least we're not One Brick Short of a Load,' I say, as we get back into the car holding cardboard cups of boiling hot coffee.

'I need more proof than that,' says Kevin.

I tear a plastic triangle out of my coffee cup lid, and then burn my tongue on the coffee. Brown fields with patches of snow over the whorled grass slip by.

By the time we pull up in front of the cottage, the sun is pouring out of the sky, and the air is cold and damp and white-smelling. As we get out of the car, our legs stiff, eyes blinking in the light, Scott comes out of the cottage and leans over, with his forearms on the porch railing.

'Call your mother,' he says. 'She said right away.'

We look at each other.

'You call,' says Kevin.

We stomp the snow off our feet on a boot mat inside. The receiver on the telephone is cold.

'A stroke,' she says. 'Thirty-seven goddamn years old. The

funeral's at noon, they just got a hold of us. Your grandfather is going, so what the hell, I'm going to drive him. It's in Hamilton, that's where he was living. In a rooming house. After all these years, he still had your grandfather listed in his wallet as the person to call in an emergency.'

'Give me one good reason why we should go,' says Kevin. 'One good reason.'

'I want to see what he looks like,' I say. I'm not sure we should go either, but if he's against it, I know where I stand.

'You want to see a dead guy?'

'He's your dad,' says Scott, a little shocked.

'Not like a real dad,' I say. 'He took off when we were babies.' I don't want him to think we're assholes. He has a point, though.

'This could be our last chance,' I say to Kevin. 'Well, I guess it *is* our last chance. To see him. I mean, maybe seeing him dead's better than nothing.'

'The ice isn't in great shape, anyway,' says Scott. 'Been too warm.'

'Come on,' I say. 'Don't you want to know? This is a one-time thing. We can always go fishing.'

'We can take the beer in the car,' says Scott.

'Now you're talking,' says Kevin, relieved to find a good excuse.

We get back into the car, this time with Scott sitting in the back with the case of twenty-four, and start bumping down the lane that goes to the highway.

'Let's crack that beer,' says Kevin. I don't know whether he actually wants one, or just wants to show this is why he came.

'Be my guest,' says Scott.

'I *am* your guest,' says Kevin, 'at least as far as the beer goes.' He crooks one of his arms back through the space between the front seats so Scott can put a bottle in his hand.

I take a bottle, too. I need something, and maybe the beer

is what I need. I'm astounded by the idea that we actually have a real living and breathing father, not just some family ghost frozen into a picture at a birthday party. Except that he isn't living and breathing any more. This father only appeared for a second, and only for the purposes of disappearing again. Permanently. As if we somehow missed the bus he was on, not just the bus, but missed the boat, missed the train, missed the plane. The ending to something that had never even begun. Every time I try to think about this, my brain cells implode.

After a couple of bottles, I fall in love with driving, the highway hanging in front of me like a white snake, the liquid speed of the car, the whole landscape so brilliant that I have to squint, my head singing with the beer. I'm so exhilarated with this that I never want to do anything else, until I remember where we're going and why. I try to push the thought away, but the farthest I can get it is a corner of my mind, where it sits like a ball of barbed wire.

'Let me out, I'm gonna throw up,' says Kevin suddenly. He's been making steady inroads on the beer. We're about halfway there.

'Shit,' I say, 'we don't have a whole lot of time.'

'You want it in the car?' says Kevin.

I pull over right before a bridge. Kevin staggers into the brush beside the bridge and throws up. He comes back to the car a few minutes later, still drunk, but cheerful.

'You should see this,' he says, 'it's really something.' He has his arms stretched out, as if he is trying to hold something enormous in them, his face turned up to the white sun.

I get out and look around. Scott is already out, lighting a cigarette, a bottle in one hand. We're on a limestone bridge, hanging over a set of railroad tracks. The embankment is covered with dead grass, underbrush, some dark red branches and a piece of tire tread. Someone has spray-painted 'Bill H. sucks the bone' on the side of the bridge in straggly letters. The bare branches of a tree farther down the road look whiskery against the sky. A small flock of birds is flying over the tree in a ragged formation.

I don't know why Kevin is so excited, but he's drunker than I am, and I'm drunk enough.

When I turn around, he is climbing up on the limestone wall on one side of the bridge.

'Christ, get down, you idiot,' I say. 'You're going to kill yourself.' The wall is only about three feet high, but it's a twenty-foot drop on the other side to the tracks.

'He's right,' says Scott.

'You're chicken heads,' says Kevin kindly. He seems hugely happy.

'You're pissed out of your mind,' I say, moving towards him to pull him down. My own legs aren't working that well.

'Don't get near me,' he says. 'You touch me, and I'll lose my balance.' He teeters a little to demonstrate.

'Okay, ha ha, it's a great little joke, now get down,' I say. My words are coming out too fast and running into each other. I can see Scott rubbing a hand across his forehead.

'So the dad is dead,' says Kevin. 'Dead, dead, dead.' He starts singing as he begins walking along the wall, arms outstretched for balance. 'Ding, dong, the dad is dead.'

I'm following behind him, trying to stay close enough to grab him if he falls. This doesn't seem likely to work, but I can't think of anything else to do. The thought of him going over is making the tendons on the backs of my legs ache. The word 'dead' is going around and around in my head, and now it's become flat and woody.

Kevin slows down, humming.

'Too bad,' he says. 'I had a few little questions I wanted to ask him.' He starts walking more carefully, looking down at his feet.

'Like – where've you been for seventeen years?' he says. His words are furry, and he does a little shuffle with his feet, ending with one of his arms raised up in the air. 'There's a good question. Or why'd you leave? There's *another* good question,' he says, congratulating himself. He is reaching the end of the bridge, so he turns around and starts walking towards us again.

'I guess this means he's not coming back,' he says abruptly.

'Well, not if he's dead,' I say. My nose is cold, and I take off one of my gloves to wipe it.

'Good point,' says Scott. He gestures with his beer bottle. 'That's a very good point.' I forgot he was there. 'I think it's going to rain,' he says in a detached way, peering at the sky and putting the bottle to his lips.

'Hear that?' he says. 'There it is again. Thunder.'

'That's not thunder,' I say. I put my glove back on.

'What a bastard,' Kevin says hopelessly. 'What kind of a prick would leave us?'

'You're asking me?' I say. 'What are you asking me for?'

'Well, he's dead,' says Kevin, as if he is explaining something reasonable.

'Oh, right,' I say. Inside, I can feel a small burst, like an abscess coming to a head, a small pocket of father bitterness leaking out. The rumbling is getting louder.

'Fuck him,' I say, suddenly furious.

'Yeah, *fuck* him,' says Kevin, trying it out. 'You got it,' he says admiringly. 'C'mon up,' he adds, motioning extravagantly with his hand.

I'm drunk enough that this makes sense to me, so I grab the wall, and hoist myself up. The wall is rough and cold.

'Fuck him,' we bellow at the top of our lungs, our words bouncing along the tracks, the hoarse sound coming up from our chests and through our throats, and then we're slapping each other's hands, shaking our fists, waving our arms, and yelling.

When we stop for breath, the rumbling is even louder.

'You should get down,' says Scott in an off-handed way.

'Why?' says Kevin.

'Because,' he says. 'It's dangerous.'

'Maybe you're right,' says Kevin in surprise, as if this has just occurred to him.

The sudden self-awareness makes him freeze, and with the stiffness, he starts to lose his balance. He does it slowly, like a mirror breaking in slow motion, and as he starts to go over I grab him, except that my arms are working in slow motion as well, and I can only get hold of the sleeve of his jacket and his arm, but I hang on, and he grabs back, and we both go over, the sun still blinding, Scott's face going by with his mouth shouting something, the noise of the train blocking out everything else, twisting slowly sideways in the air as if we're wrestling, and then landing with a bone-jarring crash in the brush at the side of the tracks, as the train roars by.

'You're still here,' says Kevin in a conversational way, a few minutes later. We're lying in a pile in some gorse, and the air is gritty from the train. The side of his face is bleeding and one of my legs hurts like hell, a sharp, grating ache. My mouth has a sugary taste in it from the beer. Out of the corner of my eye, I can see Scott stumbling down the embankment.

Kevin tries to sit up, struggling with a bush that has snagged his jacket. The jacket is ripped, a long gash down one arm, and the sight of it catches me by surprise, and pulls out of me an old feeling, as if itchy blood were still flowing along some capillary between us. This only lasts a second, and then it's swamped by a different kind of feeling, a stone-cold loneliness so desperate that maybe you can only feel it about a person who was beside you when you were growing organs and glands and nerves, a person who was with you when your brain cells were expanding in grey cauliflower clumps, and when the skin on your fingers was turning into fingerprints.

A person you were joined to in a shotgun marriage before you were born.

'Something's sticking into me,' says Kevin. He is sitting up, and pushing some branches away from him.

'Same here,' I say.

Ipso Facto

Garnet Miller is a small, jittery man who complains a lot, and at the moment he is complaining to Evan, whining away like a human mosquito in Evan's ear. Evan has the telephone receiver propped up on one of his shoulders, and he is getting a thin cramp in his lower neck. This is because Garnet has a considerable amount to say, and most of it is uncomplimentary. Evan takes the receiver off his shoulder, bends his head over to the other side to stretch his neck, and then looks at the receiver in his hand for a second, a piece of grey plastic which is continuing to talk on its own.

Of course, Garnet has a good excuse for going on and on. He is down at 52 Division, making the most of his constitutional rights after being caught in a random drunk driving check, and he is talking to his lawyer, or at least his lawyer's articling student. Evan is in his office, which is a little cubbyhole painted an exhausting white, and carpeted with commercial grade red-brown broadloom. While he listens to Garnet, he is looking out the window, where snow is starting to drift down aimlessly.

Surprisingly, Garnet is not drunk for a change, at least as far as Evan can tell over the telephone. Garnet's problem is that when he reached into his glove compartment to get his licence and registration, the police noticed a bundle of money in it from a KFC outlet on Jarvis Street, which had been held up two days earlier.

'Just my usual goddamn luck,' Garnet says to Evan, who has now shifted the receiver to his other ear, and is rubbing the first one.

'There's luck and then there's luck,' Evan says. If it had been him, he thinks he would have remembered to take the KFC band off the bundle of money. Or to put it somewhere other than the glove compartment.

'Yeah, well, hindsight's easy, hotshot,' says Garnet. 'Now just get Alec the hell down here.'

Evan puts the receiver down with relief, and stretches his neck again. He has been chewing cinnamon gum, but the taste is gone, so he takes the gum out of his mouth, wraps it in a scrap of paper and pitches it into his wastebasket. Then he shrugs himself into a sports jacket, pulls a sheet of his notes off his pad, and walks down the hall in search of Alec.

Alec is one of the two partners in the law firm where Evan is articling, a small firm on the first floor of a house with patterned tin ceilings and a forsythia bush outside which turns a deep yellow in the spring (but not now, the beginning of November), a firm which is on the brink of getting a cappuccino machine to replace the coffee-maker.

Alec is in his office, playing with his new electronic organizer, and waiting for murder cases to come in.

'Look, court dates, addresses, everything goes in it,' he says happily to Evan. His office is much bigger than Evan's, but most of the space is taken up by a heavy oak table standing in for a desk. The cheap finish on the table is crackled with age, and it looks like it belongs in the janitor's room at an elementary school. A Kandinsky print is hanging on the wall, a spray of coloured lines and shapes, which has dust along the top edge of the frame. It seems out of place, as if Alec decided one day that he needed a picture, hung it up and then forgot about it.

'But what's the difference between that and a datebook?' says Evan, looking at the organizer.

'About five hundred dollars,' says Alec. 'So what's up?'

Evan hands him the sheet of notes, and relays his conversation with Garnet.

'Lesson number one,' Alec says. 'If he was smart, he wouldn't be a thief.'

'Aren't we supposed to be on his side?' says Evan doubtfully.

'This *is* being on his side,' says Alec. 'You should hear what the prosecutors say about him.' He closes the organizer and stretches his arms over his head. 'What the hell, I guess I better get down there, he's probably going nuts, and I need to get out of here anyway, I'm falling asleep.' He stands up and checks his inside jacket pocket to make sure he has a pen, and then pats his pants to find his car keys.

Evan hands him a pad of paper. Even after three months as an articling student, he still doesn't really understand the mixture of contempt and grudging attachment Alec feels for his clients. Alec talks about them as if they were annoying but hapless relatives who keep on stumbling into trouble, necessitating irritated rescue attempts on his part.

Evan follows Alec into the waiting room, which is the original living room of the house. It has a plaster ceiling instead of a tin one, and the plaster has been swirled like the icing on a cupcake. Along the top of the window, there is a strip of stained glass in a dark red and green thistle pattern.

Alec reaches for his coat on the coatrack with one hand, and picks up his briefcase with the other. He does this in one long swoop with two dips in it, passing the briefcase from hand to hand as he slides into the coat. His movements have the certainty of constant repetition, and they make him look almost graceful for a second, which is an achievement, Evan thinks, because he isn't a graceful man.

This is what Alec looks like: tall, in his fifties, with a large, egg-shaped stomach – like a pregnant woman, he says to Evan in a rare self-deprecating moment – and his stomach does have that kind of surface tension, although the bulge is smaller. He has sloped shoulders, and his feet are long and narrow. They look like the feet of someone else, someone more fastidious than a middle-aged criminal lawyer.

The door bangs behind Alec. Lisa, the secretary, is not at her desk in the waiting room, so Evan heads back to his own office. He opens up a file of photocopied case decisions he has to read and summarize for Guy Colangelo, the other lawyer in the firm, and tries to set his mind to *absorb*, as if this were a point on a dial. The first decision is densely written, and his eyes are dry and tired. After five pages, he starts to feel as if someone has poured glue into his brain cells. Evan extricates his long legs from under the desk, puts them on top, and tilts back his chair. The snow outside is dropping in wet clumps now, and he can hear the scraping and clanking of a snow shovel nearby. These alert snow-shovelling citizens are impressive, these people who get down to it right away, except that he can't help picturing them spending their winters waiting eagerly by the door, poised with their shovels at the ready so they can leap out at the first sign of snow. And the idea of shovelling snow that is still falling seems valiant, but futile.

Futility makes him think of Garnet. *I almost had him*, Garnet said on the telephone. He had tried to convince the cop who pulled him over that he was the payroll supervisor from the KFC human resources department. *Fuck, I almost had him. Half a minute, maybe forty seconds, I seen him thinking about it, I'm holding my goddamn breath, and then finally he says, no way. No way, payroll is all cheques or direct deposit.*

Hard to believe anyone would have fallen for this for longer than a minute, Evan thinks. A payroll supervisor who keeps a roll of company cash in his glove compartment? *I almost had him.* Maybe this is why Alec is so hard on his clients, at least when they are out of earshot, although his insults are milder, more intimate than the kind of ferocious sarcasm he reserves for other people, like prosecutors, jail guards, bailiffs.

What a birdbrain, he'll say after talking to someone like Garnet. An idiot, Guy will agree, having represented the same person in family court. They know the clients well because some of them have been coming to the firm for years, at least as far as Evan can tell from their files. The two lawyers have shepherded enough people to populate a small town through their first juvenile appearances, then their minor charges, and later through their assaults and armed robberies, the lawyers and clients locked into a kind of reluctant, intermittent relationship.

Garnet must be their prize birdbrain, Evan thinks, shifting a little and rocking back further in his chair. He knows that Garnet is a regular customer, a string of minor charges, although their relationship has started to deteriorate lately as a result of the cutbacks in legal aid.

The reason Evan knows all this is because Alec is a talker, and by now he has heard about most of his clients, or at least the repeat customers. Alec talks all the time and about everything, a running play-by-play of his life, with colour commentary whenever there is a gap in events. He gets away with this partly because he's good at it, whole loops of words slipping out of his mouth so easily and naturally that he must have been almost forced to become a lawyer.

His fluency helps to make up for the fact that he is not a very efficient lawyer, at least in Evan's view. He has watched Alec submerging himself in his cases, grabbing handfuls of facts and law and flailing around with them like a poor swimmer. After a while, he lines up the evidence and the legal principles into some kind of order. Then he makes up arguments, spiky arguments, sprawling arguments, arguments curled inside other arguments. They distract him, and Evan sees him grab scraps of paper to write them down. If there are no scraps of paper, he writes on the covers of books, Canadian Bar Association notices, flyers for 2-4-1 Pizza, anything to trap these arguments before they slip away.

Then he uses all of them in his closing addresses, without discrimination or order, a miscellaneous collection of thoughts rattling around like spoons in a tin box.

So this is one problem, Evan thinks, bringing his chair back down with a thud and reaching again for the cases he is supposed to be reading.

The other is that most of Alec's clients have been caught red-handed.

* * *

Law school, 1998. By the time Evan arrived at law school, he assumed that he was an expert on educational boredom, a veteran of droning teachers under fluorescent lights, of the stale air in rooms with bulletin boards and industrial clocks and yellow laminated desks.

He was wrong. Law school was the pinnacle of boredom, a decathlon of tedium, a boredom so acute and stifling that it almost had a shape of its own. In his civil procedure class, he watched a man in a beige pullover at the front of the room serve up hundreds of dull facts until they were overrunning the classroom like centipedes, and he decided to quit, over and over again, until even that was boring.

He never actually said 'I quit' out loud though, or went to the registrar's office to sign the papers, or even stopped attending class, at least for longer than a week or two. There was a counter pressure to the massive weight of boredom, an unreasonable conviction that there was more to law than this.

For one thing, he could hear it.

Or he could hear *them,* faint sounds and rhythms underneath the doctrines he was reading. He could hear the deep tobacco sounds from old cases, and the sounds of pink-lidded statutes skittering across glass. He could hear the salt-marshy sounds of discretionary powers, and the sounds of chilly constitutional principles with whistling choruses. He could hear brash criminal defences groaning in their sleep, and green regulations rustling together. All he had to do was to get through law school, graduate, and make it to his articling job, where he would find the real law, the three-dimensional law, this law that he could walk inside and breathe.

Of course you're deranged, said a girlfriend kindly.

While he studied, he had to physically stop himself from getting up from the desk every ten minutes, wrapping his legs around the legs of his chair, holding on to the edge of the desk. He pictured himself sitting in a small grey cotton cell without windows, hanging on to a basket full of legal phrases, sentences snaking out over the rim. He sat there and studied until he felt that there was nothing left of himself except a ropey stubbornness.

And then he was done.

Alec is back in an hour and a half. When Evan hears his voice in the waiting room, he comes out to hear about Garnet, grateful for the interruption. Alec is throwing his coat onto the coat rack and setting his briefcase down, the same choreography but in reverse. He has this down to a science, Evan thinks, his time perfectly calibrated to the legal aid fee.

'Christ, I forgot what a whiner he is,' Alec says. He rubs his hands, which are red from the cold, and stamps the snow off his shoes. Then he goes over to the pile of mail on Lisa's desk, and starts leafing through it. Lisa, who is back at her desk, rolls her eyes at Evan. He knows she hates it when Alec goes through the mail, because he opens anything that looks interesting or like a cheque – pretty much the same thing, according to her – and he takes it into his office. This means that she can't date-stamp the letters or make sure they are in the right file, sacred secretarial functions.

She is in her twenties, with feathery dark hair cut close to her head, small brown eyes that have finished rolling now, white skin with olive undertones, a wide nose with a white scar on it, and three earrings in one ear. Her upper lip looks slightly flattened, as if she had banged it into something. She has stubby fingernails that are painted purple, and there is a kind of sleekness about her, like an otter.

The reason Evan knows about the mail problem is that Lisa talks too, although nothing like Alec. Maybe working for Alec has made her garrulous in self-defence, a necessary step to avoid being drowned in his flood of words. Or maybe the reason is Evan himself. He often attracts people's confidences, anxious women on airplanes who talk in torn voices about their stale marriages, tired men on buses who worry about their gay sons, teenagers whose parents are divorcing, remarrying, moving, having more babies, in the throes of some kind of familial perpetual motion. He doesn't encourage this – quite the opposite – because most of what they say is dreary and uninteresting. It's something about the way you look, said his girlfriend, when he was complaining about this flood of confidences. What? he said, half alarmed, inspecting the pale hard skin on his arms, pushing back his straight brown hair.

As if you grew up playing contact sports, while your mother washed your clothes over and over in fabric softener, she said. This was close enough to the truth to make Evan wince.

At the moment, Alec is skimming one of the interesting letters that he has taken from Lisa's desk, sliding a mug under the spout in the coffee machine, still talking at the same time.

'The guy never shuts up,' he says about Garnet, 'and only about one minute of it is any goddamn use. Most of it is just bitch, bitch, bitch.' He tucks the letter under one arm so that he can put sugar in his coffee. Then he jerks his head in the direction of his office, and he and Evan go in and sit down.

'At least he's good at complaining,' says Evan. Garnet sounded convincing on the phone, like a man who had really been hard done by.

'Yeah, that'll help a lot. Or maybe he can get the judge to listen to his bone-headed views on the law, which he knows exactly sweet dick all about.' Alec makes a disgusted noise somewhere between the back of his nose and the back of his mouth.

Evan knows he hates having to listen to clients. Alec is not really an intake person, his valves are perpetually set to output. The problem is that he has to extract every scrap of information from the client that might help, all the pieces of what happened.

Or even what *might* have happened.

Evan thinks about Garnet walking into the KFC outlet, his

cowboy boots clicking on the floor. In his mind he can almost smell the cooked smell of the fryer exhaust, the vinegary sweet cole slaw. He sees Garnet drumming his fingers on the plastic hood over the potato salad, pretending to study the lighted menu along the top of the wall, pictures of chicken dinners so warm and bright that they look as if customers could order a family to go with them. *I'll take the big bucket and a set of relatives.* A teenager behind the counter, his brown hair pulled back in a ponytail, a hairnet under a baseball cap with KFC written on it, a few pimples on his chin. Garnet offering him a cigarette. *Go ahead, I'm not going to tell anyone, who the hell's gonna see you anyway, it's almost midnight for Chrissakes.*

This is all Evan can imagine, because he still doesn't know exactly what Garnet is alleged to have done.

Alleged. What a word, the sheer legalness of it, a useful word for someone who is almost a lawyer, someone who has only a year of articling left to go. Every time Evan thinks of this, he gets little trickles of elation down his arms and back, and his lungs feel like they are banging together with excitement. This makes up for the times he thinks about representing clients in court, the thought alone making him so nervous he feels like chewing off his own fingers. But he went to law school, he waded through all that boredom to become a trial lawyer, not to highlight useful cases in yellow marker. The trial lawyer that he has in mind is a vague combination of Atticus Finch and Zorro.

'I'm taking you with me on Grabowski tomorrow,' Alec says, as Evan tunes back in. 'You did the research, hell, you probably know the case law better than I do, and you can see another trial.'

That's one reason, Evan thinks. Another reason is that Alec needs an audience, one that can be relied upon to be complimentary.

Alec punches some numbers into the telephone, then starts skimming a sheaf of notes Evan has provided him from interviews with witnesses on the Grabowski case.

'Why didn't you ask him about the car?' Alec says to Evan in exasperation, while he listens to his voice mail messages. 'You think it's easy to get a hold of these guys? What about his wife, you talk to her yet? Where's the research on the preliminary issue? Jesus, what a mess.'

Evan is almost used to this now, although he was stung the first time Alec raked him over.

'He does it to everyone,' Lisa said to him in the photocopying room, not unkindly, but a little wearily. 'Don't let it get to you. You know what they say, think about him in his underwear.'

Something about this banal advice is oddly touching. Evan tries to follow it, but his imagination, which is usually good, fails him. Alec in briefs with frayed elastic? In coloured boxers? His fleshy, oval stomach hanging over the edge? Evan can't see it.

It does make him think differently about Lisa, though.

'I'll take your clients any day,' says Evan the next morning to Guy, a bulky blond man whose features look almost randomly assembled, narrow grey eyes and a small bump of a nose stuck on a long, amiable face. They are sitting in Guy's office this time, which is piled with files and papers, unstable towers of documents lined up on the floor, pink telephone message slips scattered over everything. Crayon pictures done by his children are taped up on the wall. Guy looks as dishevelled as his office, his suit jacket collar folded under on one side, but he doesn't have the kind of frenetic air that sometimes goes with dishevelment. Instead, he is a mild, self-contented man, almost entirely lacking Alec's acidic drive.

'You can have them,' says Guy, who is trying to find a file on the overcrowded desk 'They're all yours. Although I guess they don't usually end up in jail, at least there's that.' His cases are low-end child support claims, undefended divorces, custody and wardships. He half lifts a stack of papers with one hand so that he can peer at the name tabs of the files underneath. 'Most of them, anyway,' he adds, grabbing the top of the stack of papers as it starts to slide off.

Evan has already noticed that sometimes the same person will be charged with both a criminal offence and defaulting on child support payments, not necessarily in that order. When this happens, Alec defends him on the criminal charge, and Guy goes to family court with him. You have to know how to work the file, Alec says to Evan, work every angle so that you're billing everything there is on it. Evan finds the cynicism of this unsettling.

'Relax,' Guy says now, when Evan repeats it to him. 'He has no idea what he's talking about. He reads all this stuff on law office management techniques, and then starts spouting it. The truth is that he wouldn't know a law office management technique if it bit him on the butt.'

The truth? The truth is that neither of them would know the truth if it bit them on the butt, thinks Evan. Up until now he has thought of facts as if they were hard, knowable things, like marbles. Did something happen or not? Was it raining at the time? Alec in particular seems to consider facts to be more variable, capable of forming an infinite number of configurations. Alec doesn't talk about what happened in a case, but what different witnesses will *say* happened, and there are as many versions of this as there are witnesses. He treats all these versions equally, measuring them fairly and dispassionately with respect to how believable they are, and whether they help his case. Different slices of reality, fanned out like a hand of playing cards, to be selected or discarded. The thought makes Evan feel irritable and restless.

'Time to get your ass in gear,' Alec says to him from the doorway of Guy's office. 'Grabowski's meeting us in Courtroom 44.'

Grabowski turns out to be a bloated-looking man with

floury skin and full lips. 'Goddamn it,' says Alec as they walk into the courtroom. Grabowski turns around, startled, anxious lines around his eyes, which are very light blue, so light they look like jellied water.

'No, no, it's okay,' says Alec, 'we just pulled a judge who's into the law. Don't worry, I've got it covered.' He starts rapidly flipping through Evan's research as the bailiff calls the first cases.

The courtroom is old and elaborate, with a mosaic tile ceiling, carved wood trim and high casement windows. At the floor level, however, the proceedings are seedier, a disjointed series of two minute case appearances in which defendants wander up hesitantly when their names are called to stand beside a lawyer and set dates for trial, or plead guilty. There is a lethargy that seems to have settled over everyone, the accused, judges, prosecutors, defence lawyers, as if they are doing a run-through of their lines for a mediocre play which they know will never open. The defence lawyers and prosecutors address the court in perfunctory scraps of more formal speech, while the accused twist their hats in their hands, or hook their thumbs in their pants pockets, or cross their arms in front of their chests and rock on their heels. In the audience, people in dirty white sweaters or faded windbreakers or iridescent shirts shift restlessly on the wooden benches, waiting their turn.

Grabowski goes to the washroom at the first break, before his case is called.

'Looks tired, doesn't he?' Alec says to Evan. 'He says he's not sleeping at night because of the charges.' This seems oddly solicitous. Maybe this is one of the reasons his clients like him, Evan thinks.

'Watch this.' Alec leans over when the judge comes back in. 'He's going to find some stupid point of law to play with, I guarantee it.'

Evan studies the judge, a serious man with a sagging, grey face and unfashionable aviator-style wire glasses. He might simply be bored, Evan thinks defensively, although why he is on the judge's side, he doesn't know. It must be a tough job, though. If it were him, he thinks he would be dying a slow intellectual death from the parade of drunk drivers and prostitutes.

Grabowski starts nervously as his case is called, and they move up to the front of the court. As Alec has predicted, the judge seizes on a legal point in his argument, and starts challenging him. Alec seems to have the answers, most of them right, or close to right, anyway, even though he has spent approximately ten minutes going though the file, as far as Evan can tell.

In fact, Alec is obviously enjoying himself to the limit, despite his lack of preparation, or even because of it. Evan can almost see cold seams of adrenaline leaking into Alec's veins. His usual disorganization is less apparent because the argument has turned into a debate between the judge and him, the two of them snapping points back and forth while the prosecutor, a pedestrian lawyer – a cop before he went to law school, according to Alec – sulks at his counsel table.

This is the kind of situation in which Evan almost loves Alec, or at least the idea of Alec, his rock-like poise, his sarcasm, his voice with its gritty chords, its syncopated rhythms of mockery and persuasion. He seems – what does he seem? thinks Evan, in a rare flush of admiration. He seems almost *brave* – a cranky, vain kind of bravery.

Evan turns to the tired Grabowski, and finds that he has almost dozed off.

Afterwards, on the way back to the office, Alec is delighted with himself, gloating in a way most people keep safely hidden in their heads.

'Another virtuoso performance,' he says to Evan, only half-kidding. Then he starts reviewing the trial, minute by minute, filling up the thin story with what he was thinking, what he predicted, what he was trying to do and how it worked, why he said this instead of that.

What does he do when he doesn't have someone with him? Evan wonders. Talk to himself? Is he afraid he'll vanish if he isn't talking? Or maybe talking gives him some kind of purchase, some kind of traction on the slippery surfaces of his work.

Alec is still rehashing the highlights of his argument.

'So justice was served?' says Evan. He intends this to be ironic, just a way of getting a word in edgewise, but suddenly, he really wants to know.

'Get serious,' says Alec.

'At least they haven't found the scissors,' Alec says a few weeks later.

Garnet had scissors? thinks Evan. He doesn't say it out loud, though. He worries that Alec has told him about the scissors, but that he wasn't listening. He finds it hard to listen to Alec every minute, to follow the slew of words without taking a break here and there.

'Huh,' says Evan, in what he hopes is a noncommittal voice. 'What about the KFC band on the money?'

'I told you,' says Alec. 'If he was a brain surgeon, he'd probably be working as a brain surgeon.'

'But what are you going to do about it?'

'Something,' says Alec. Evan knows this means that Alec hasn't figured out what to do with it yet, how to get rid of this inconvenient fact, or at least camouflage it, this fact which keeps skewing whatever version of the case Alec is working on. He has seen Alec do this before, keep the worst facts segregated off by themselves until he can work up the nerve to deal with them. In Garnet's case, Evan thinks, he will have to take all of them, the warm night, the kid behind the cash register with the hairnet and the cigarette, the scissors (whatever he did with them), and the money, and heave the whole collection into the air, hoping they come down in a new design, rearranged so that they don't point so stubbornly at Garnet.

'Eyewitness evidence is notoriously unreliable,' says Alec. 'Fortunately for us.'

'Why?' says Evan. 'I mean, why is it unreliable?'

'People's memories don't work like video cameras.'

'Why not?' says Evan. This feels like the proper mentor-articling student relationship, where the mentor delivers knowledge in stylish, restaurant-sized servings.

'People remember things in a way that makes sense to them, whether or not it's accurate. They eliminate the details that don't fit their preconceptions, and add in others.'

'You mean, it's more like believing is seeing, than seeing is believing?'

'Exactly,' says Alec.

Evan waits for a few seconds, but they seem to have come to the end of this particular knowledge serving.

'Garnet's having a hard time in jail,' he says, to fill up the space. Evan has had another call from him. He is in custody, his bail hearing with Alec having gone badly. (What can you expect with his record – a string of Fail to Appears – and no surety, said Alec after the hearing. Or that goddamn prick of a judge, said Garnet.)

In the telephone call, Garnet sounded like he was almost scared, although he didn't say this. He complained about the number of people in his cell, about the overcrowding at the Metro Detention Centre, and Evan realized that in spite of his record, Garnet hadn't actually spent much time in jail. One of his cell-mates was talking about making a bomb (out of what? toilet paper? soap? Garnet said to Evan with anxious scorn). The bomb maker also sat up at night in the bunk bed over Garnet's, rocking himself when they lowered the lights and crooning *all the little red birds on the side of the earth*, over and over. The other cell-mate had bad gas. Garnet was upset when Evan laughed at this. You think that's funny? Wait until it sends Mr Little Red Birds over the edge.

'The thing is,' says Alec, 'the kid at the KFC place will be able to identify him and there's a limit to what you can do with that eyewitnesses-are-unreliable number. I mean, Garnet sounds like a liar when he says he wasn't there.'

That's because he probably is one, thinks Evan. In his mind, he can see Garnet again, waiting in the parking lot, watching the gulls from the lake pick at the scraps in the garbage can, waiting until the kid behind the cash register goes out to the back for more frozen french fries. Then he throws his cigarette away, and pushes open the glass door, quietly vaulting the counter, prying open the computerized register and pulling out the money, some loose bills and then under the bill tray, a tight little bundle with a label around it.

'Of course, he says he didn't do it, but that's what he always says,' Alec says, tapping his pen against the edge of his desk. 'Actually, he really half thinks he *hasn't* done it, whatever it is, that he's never guilty of anything. As far as he's concerned, his life just keeps ganging up on him without any warning. He convinces himself of some story, and then we get ambushed at the trial by the evidence.'

Almost perfectly sealed up in his own little transparent sac of reality, Evan thinks. But then maybe he's not so different from anyone else. If facts really are in the eye of the beholder.

'Some of our clients have made poor choices,' says Lisa, who is leafing through a computer supplies catalogue. She and Evan are the only people in the waiting room at the moment, so she is sitting in one of the chairs, and Evan is sitting at her desk, feet up again. The morning sun is coming through the stained glass strip in a way that makes small coloured shapes on the desk, and he is idly moving his right foot in and out of one of the colours. There is a frost pattern on one side of the window, a set of crystalline formations that are starting to melt. The new snow beyond it looks damp and bright, different from hoary mid-winter snow.

Lisa is a talk show fan and has a whole vocabulary to go

with it, a kind of shorthand psychology that hasn't been dumbed down so much as flattened, and packaged into little empty parcels. *Forgiveness. Moving on. Getting over it.*

This stuff probably even works, Evan thinks gloomily. A few months ago he would have been inclined to be condescending about it, but now he is attached to Lisa in a simple, sticky way, his feelings having hooked on to her so quietly and easily that he almost didn't notice it happening. This means that he is willing to see merit in anything she says, to extend to her a huge, soggy, tender benefit of the doubt. When he comes in and sees her typing at her computer in the morning, crumbs from a half-eaten piece of toast and boysenberry jam at the corners of her smooth mouth, he feels a kind of heaviness in his forehead which makes him want to hold on to something.

It could be partly gratitude, he thinks, trying to talk himself out of these feelings, or at least lower their octane level. Lisa is the source of important information, such as the previous criminal records of clients, where to park near the downtown law library, how to work the photocopier, or what an affidavit looks like. Anyone would start to feel affectionately toward someone who was constantly rescuing them.

He knows this is not really it, though. She also exudes a kind of warm, soundless hum that reaches into his bones and makes them ache. She must have some of the same electrical ions as a pear, he thinks. Or a glassy note from an instrument, something like an oboe.

A short movie involving the two of them has been growing in his head, ballooning gradually into existence. The script and background change from showing to showing, but there is a physical undercurrent running through it that remains the same. Lust, gratitude, affection – not all that different, really, he thinks. Some of the same ingredients. Easy to move from one to the other, or to become overwhelmed with a syrupy, addictive combination of all of them.

She takes interior decorating classes at night, something she is sensitive about. It's an underrated profession, she said stiffly, when he started to laugh. Now he knows better, and he tries to take a serious, or at least a polite, interest in conversations about colour accents, room lines and perspective. Her next assignment is to design a living room.

She closes the computer supplies catalogue with a whump, and brings out two fabric swatches from a bag at her ankle.

'Extra marks if I get it in early, but I can't get the couch right.'

One of the fabric swatches has green vines on a navy blue background, the other is a satiny cream with green stripes.

'If it was you,' she says. 'Which one?'

He gets up and comes over to sit down in the chair beside her, and then dutifully examines the swatches, turning them over in his hands.

'It's the same green, you know,' she says. They look different to him. She puts the pieces side by side and folds them so that a green vine is next to a green stripe. They look the same now.

'See, it's an optical illusion,' she says. 'It's the background that does it. Change the background, you change everything.'

'Huh,' he says. 'So how did you get into this stuff?' He is just making conversation while he examines the hairs on her forearms. The light from the window has turned them into filaments that are so soft they are making his groin warm.

'You're kidding, right?' She looks up from the swatches. 'You think I want to stay here for the rest of my life?'

Evan gets a knife-sharp vision of a grey corridor stretching out before her, opening mail, typing and listening to Alec's corrosive criticism.

Lisa's other interests are less sedate.

'You know her husband takes sex pictures,' says Alec casually one day. They are walking over to the courthouse, a cold wind sniping at their faces. The grey sky is spread with clouds that are ribbed, so that they look like white corduroy. Alec takes long strides with a little snap at the end of them, his arms swinging in counterpoint, his stomach swaying. 'He's a professional photographer, but he has this side specialty, you can dress up as your fantasy and he'll take pictures of you.'

Evan is once again startled by the cultural variety of Toronto.

'I dropped by his studio once,' Alec says, slowing down to pull his coat collar up around his neck, trying to put a glove on with one hand by trapping it against his side. His briefcase is in his other hand. 'Just for the hell of it, to see. He's got portraits of people in strange sex outfits all over the walls, ordinary people, could be your aunt or uncle, overweight, bad haircuts, too much makeup. It wasn't even that titillating, to tell you the truth, just kind of pathetic.' He pulls the glove the rest of the way on with his teeth.

Maybe that's not the point, thinks Evan. Maybe they're creating new versions of themselves. The photographs are just evidence, a hard copy.

'Here's a friendly warning,' Alec says. By now they have almost reached the courthouse. 'She tries to sleep with the law student each year.'

Evan gets a sudden, hopeful cramp in his chest.

'What do you mean, *tries?*' he says.

'I want to do a case,' Evan says to Alec, a few weeks later. 'Something on my own, I mean.'

He is spending so much time doing legal research that he is starting to think that some of the hundreds of volumes of case reports are becoming familiar. They fall open at certain spots, coffee stains on pages with particularly important cases. The names of the cases pop out at him, names that seem incongruous in relation to their legal problems. Regina v. Woolenshuft – not a German philosophy professor but an indecent exposure defendant. D'Angelo v. D'Angelo – a vicious child custody dispute. Regina v. Goodfellow – attempted murder. Regina v. Majesky?

Shoplifting. How do these people become cases, Evan thinks, their lives spread-eagled on pages to provide the facts for some point of law?

'Sure, sure,' says Alec. 'I'll give you a few files to go in and set the dates for trials. In fact, I've got one tomorrow you can do. That's how we usually get the students on their feet. When you get used to that, we'll find you something else.'

The next day, Evan introduces himself to the client in the hall of the courthouse.

'Who the fuck are you?' says the client, who is charged with assault with a weapon. 'Where's Alec?'

Evan explains.

'Yeah?' says the client. 'A goddamn student, how d'ya like that? How old are you, anyway? Sixteen?'

Evan explains some more, adding that he is twenty-four. The client is in his fifties, grey hair in a thin ponytail, a musty smell around him as if he has been living in an attic, or perhaps a basement. The bailiff comes out into the hall and reads a list.

'That'll be us,' says the client as his name is read out. 'C'mon, junior.'

Evan walks up to the front of the court with the client, through the little wooden gate and bows to the judge. He is suddenly short of breath, and his voice sounds thick and strange.

'Evan Creighton,' he says to the judge, 'representing the accused.' He bows the way he has seen Alec do it. Just a little bend, Alec said, if your case is decent. If you've got a loser, might as well kiss the goddamn floor. You don't have anything else.

Even though Evan can hardly get the words out, he is fiercely delighted by the idea that he is actually representing someone. After a brief exchange, a date is set. Then they walk out again, Evan fumbling with the gate on the way.

'Not bad,' says the client generously. 'Although you'd have to be a moron to fuck that up.'

* * *

'You think I'm ready for this?' says Evan dubiously. He now has several weeks of date setting under his belt, and Alec wants him to do a trial.

'You're ready,' says Alec. 'It's just a small claims court case, it's only six hundred dollars, but it'll give you some practice.'

Garnet – the regular customer – is being sued by a car repair garage which replaced the alternator and did some body work on the left side of his car. Because he was a little short of funds at the time, he went to collect his car at night, removing it discreetly from the garage lot with a second key that he had.

'Classic Garnet,' says Alec.

Of course, the garage had his licence number, his name and his address, with the result that the owner had a small claims court case filed for the cost of the repairs within a week.

'What did you *think* would happen?' says Evan to Garnet, later that day. Garnet has finally obtained bail, so they are talking at the office. Or outside the office, because Garnet is a smoker. They are standing in front of the door, and Evan is trying to write on a pad, something that is not easy with cold fingers and without a table. The snow has roofed the parking meters, the bushes and the cars parked on the street, and there are soft white clumps spread over a tree. One of the cars is running, sending a plume of exhaust into the air, and a woman in an orange ski jacket is wiping the snow off the windshield with a brush. Even from where Evan is standing, the snow looks wet and heavy as it slides onto the hood of the car, and then over the front.

'I wasn't really thinking about it,' says Garnet.

'No kidding,' says Evan. Garnet is so close to being good-looking that Evan has been surreptitiously glancing at his face to figure out why he is merely close. His teeth, Evan thinks, a little too yellow. And his lips are slightly sunken, so that he will look gnarled in a few years.

'The goddam alternator still didn't work, I had to take it someplace else,' says Garnet in an offended tone. He takes a quick drag on his cigarette, so tight that it looks like he's biting a piece of the filter off. Then he exhales smoke and white breath together. The woman has stopped wiping off snow and is now rummaging around in the car trunk.

Evan puts his right hand in his left armpit to warm it up, and wonders how he is going to be able to spin these facts into something credible.

'I wouldn't worry about it too much,' says Alec the next day. 'He's judgement-proof anyway.'

'What?' says Evan.

'He doesn't have any money or property,' says Alec. 'They can get a hundred court judgements against him, and they're not going to see a dime.'

Evan realizes this is why he is being allowed to do the case.

On the day of the trial, he feels tense and alert, all his senses turned up several degrees. Garnet seems a little unsteady, but Evan puts this down to nervousness. They walk into the court-room, where a court reporter is talking into a transcribing mask.

'You didn't tell me there would be a breathalyzer,' Garnet says to Evan in a panic, the words riding out on a little whiffle of stale beer.

'Keep your hair on,' says Evan, 'it's just the reporting equipment.' He himself is almost rigid with anxiety, now that he realizes his one and only witness is drunk.

'Settle,' says Alec in amusement, when Evan calls him from a pay phone in the hall. 'Set up a payment plan where he'll pay them so much a month. Tell them it's better than nothing, which is what they'll see if they get a judgement against him.'

Evan proposes this outside the courtroom, but the garage owner, who doesn't have a lawyer, is indignant.

'We did the goddamn work, we should get paid.'

By this time, Evan is desperately attached to the idea of set-tlement. He tries reasoning with the garage owner some more.

'Big shit,' says the garage owner. 'I'll see his ass in jail then if he doesn't have any money.'

Evan reflects that this is likely to be the case, one way or another.

Since the owner refuses to settle, the trial proceeds. A mechanic testifies about the work done on the car, which Evan barely understands. He spent his teenage years on hockey and football teams, rather than inside car hoods. His cross-examination is spotty and ineffective, only reinforcing the mechanic's testimony, instead of weakening it.

Then Garnet gets on the stand. He is surprisingly knowledgeable about cars, describing the alternator problem in detail, and he has just enough alcohol in him to make him articulate, rather than incoherent. 'Why the hell – excuse my French, Your Honour – should I have to pay, when they didn't do the repairs? I mean, I had to pay someone else to do it all over again.'

Garnet is doing what he does best, Evan realizes – complaining. And when he's complaining, he's convincing. At least for a few minutes, and this is all it takes in small claims court.

Evan manages to make a respectable closing argument, assembling the various elements of the case into a scenario in which Garnet is the long-suffering victim of the garage's incompetence. The judge looks sceptical, but awards only one hundred and fifty dollars of the six hundred against Garnet.

Evan is so excited that his head feels like it is filled with helium. He has won a case! For a client!

Garnet is morose. 'Where the fuck am I going to get a hundred and fifty bucks. Rob a bank?'

Evan wonders if this could be considered a form of working the file.

Evan wakes up a little after midnight, feeling as if he has sand in his bloodstream. Greyish-white light from a street light is coming in through the blind, drawing rectangular slits in the darkness on the wall of his bedroom. He lies in bed thinking about Garnet's trial, his criminal trial, which is coming up in a few weeks. Then the light from the window turns to blue, and Evan gets up and pulls apart the slats of the blind so that he can see outside. The street is filled with snow ruts from car tires, overlapping each other and weaving together around corners. A snowplow is sitting there, stopped, a blue light revolving on top. It backs up, making a slow beeping noise, and then proceeds down the street, pushing the snow into low crumbling walls on both sides.

Evan is cold, so he gets back into bed and dozes off again, his sleeping thoughts continuing on from his waking thoughts in a seamless flow. He sees Alec sitting at the counsel table in court, taking notes, with Garnet whispering furiously in his ear. The KFC teenager is on the stand, with a new haircut for court, wearing a borrowed suit, pleased to be the centre of attention but anxious not to say the wrong thing. The judge, an older man, his prostate bothering him again, is already visibly counting the minutes until the mid-morning break. The prosecutor, a frazzled-looking woman in a badly fitting dress-for-success suit, is taking the witness through his story.

I'm coming out of the back room, says the teenager. I'm coming out of the back room with a box of frozen fries, I stop to give it a boost with my knee and get a better hold of it, I don't notice him at first, and then there he is, standing by the register. We stand there for a second, and then the guy grabs a pair of scissors from the shelf under the counter and pushes me up against the wall, he's got the scissors up at my neck, the box is falling, and he's screaming at me, *get out of here, get out of here*, even though he's got me pinned to the wall and I can't move a muscle, and then he starts screaming *you tell them you didn't see who it was*, over and over. *You tell them you didn't see me.*

'The deadline's tomorrow,' says Alec, who is winding a scarf around his neck, on his way out the door. Lisa is staring at her computer, and Evan is standing behind her with a cup of coffee

in his hand. (What about that cappuccino machine? he says to
Alec. You and Guy, says Alec disgustedly.) Evan and Lisa are
working on a brief for one of Alec's appeals, with Evan compos-
ing and Lisa typing.

'We're getting there,' says Evan.

'Finish it up tonight,' says Alec cheerfully, 'and you can do
the photocopying tomorrow.'

He pulls on his coat, and leaves in a gust of cold air.

'He's in a good mood,' says Lisa.

'He won today,' says Evan. The darkness outside is giving
the lighted room a false intimacy, an unearned sense of warmth
and closeness. This is usually the kind of situation where people start confiding in him, offering up their well-worn anxieties
for a second opinion.

'What the hell is this?' says Lisa.

She is peering at the changes Evan has scribbled on a draft.
There are two parts to the brief, the facts of the case and the
legal argument. They are working on the legal argument first,
even though the facts section is first in the document.
Shouldn't we work on the facts first? Evan says to Alec. No,
says Alec. You're not paying attention.

'Okay, here,' Evan says to Lisa. 'I'll read it to you.' He puts
down his coffee, and picks up the paper. They both watch the
print scrolling by on the computer screen until she finds the
right spot, and then he dictates the changes. As he talks, he sees
her hands pattering briskly over the keyboard, his words track-
ing out across the screen. Then they find the next spot, and he
reads some more. His bone-aching feeling is stronger than ever,
and he can smell her from where he is standing, a clear smell,
like old carrots and water.

After a few minutes of this, she stops and rolls her head from
side to side. The bone-aching feeling turns into a kind of blind
elemental pull, which makes him want to rub his face against
her shirt. As she rolls her head around, the elasticity of her neck
surprises him, and he puts out a hand involuntarily, as if to

steady her head. The skin on her neck feels slightly grainy. She stiffens, and he starts telling her a story about Alec in court that day, something funny he said in cross-examination. She starts to laugh, a blob of sound that comes up from her throat, her back softening in a momentary conspiracy with him against Alec. His fingers seem to have expanded, the tips widening and the skin on them thinning out so that he can feel every tiny bump on her neck.

He searches desperately for another story about Alec. All he can think of is Alec's warning about her. *She tries to sleep with the student each year.* Maybe they can laugh at this, he half thinks, his brain feeling spongy. *Can you believe he said that?* Even as the words are coming out of his mouth, though, he realizes this is a mistake. The words become fixed in the air by his sudden self-consciousness. What an idiot, he thinks savagely. A prize birdbrain.

'He's yanking your chain,' says Lisa after a second, but she twists away from his hand and her face is tight.

'It's not true?' Evan says. He feels a stab of bleakness as he watches his movie start to fade, the shadows and depths flattening out until it looks like a drawing on a sheet of paper.

'He wishes,' she says shortly. 'It's all in his head. He likes to think it's a regular soap opera around here.'

Stranded in different versions of reality, Evan thinks. He watches his fingers shrink back down to their normal, football-holding size.

'Hey,' Lisa says, looking at him curiously. 'Don't worry about it. It's not that big a deal, he's an asshole, that's all.'

She pulls his sleeve. 'Come on, let's get this thing done. Just the facts left and then we're out of here. An hour, tops.'

'You think so?' says Evan.

'Sure,' she says. 'The facts are the easy part.'

Choke

This is the first part of the story. After this, there is a second part.

The first part of the story starts with a question.

The question is: does it matter how someone dies?

I say this out loud to Joe: Does it matter how someone dies?

The words loop up like the black plush ropes for theatre lines:

Does it *mat*ter how *some*one *dies?*

– No? says Joe. He is getting ready for work, sliding into his clothes with abrupt movements, and he is not interested. I am sitting up in bed, pulling at the blankets which are twisted together, one orange and one light green, colours which belong to melting sherbet, not blankets. Outside the window, nickel-grey clouds are covering most of the early morning sky. They are hanging so low that the sky looks as if it is about to sit down.

– I'm talking about the person who dies, the deceased. Does it matter to him? I say.

Joe has tuned out again. He is thinking about work, so pre-occupied that the air around his body seems serious as well. He slips his wallet into the back pocket of his pants, and a handful of change into the front. The light is on in the room, even though it is morning, because the sky is so dark.

While he is thinking about work, I am thinking of quick deaths, heroin overdoses, people who fall from ladders, people who are hit by cars, people who jump from overpasses. These are different from slow deaths, from lingering deaths, which are not related to my question. My question is: as long as the death is quick, does the person who dies care about how it happens?

– For instance, I say to Joe, what if a person chokes to death on a piece of potato?

– What's your point? says Joe.

– My point, I say (and believe me, I've thought about this, I say), is that there wouldn't be time to care, to feel embarrassed in the seconds before a death like that. My point is that all a person would feel is panic.

I don't say this:

In my opinion, choking to death on a piece of potato is an absurd way to die. It is a slapstick death, a freak cartoon of a death.

I don't say this:

The deceased may not care, but his family and friends do. Beneath the frozen shock, beneath the acid grief, they feel an undercurrent of shame. Then they feel ashamed of their shame. A piece of potato? *A piece of potato?* Why not a heart attack? they think inadvertently, and then they are appalled at themselves for thinking like this. After all, what's the difference?

Dead is dead.

– Dead is dead, I say to Joe.

– What brought this on? says Joe.

There are benefits to dying by choking.

For example, there is no drawn-out illness.

There is no hospital half-life.

There are no chemotherapy cocktails.

All the messy, day-to-day drudgery of suffering is eliminated.

But there are drawbacks to dying by choking.

It is so unexpected. Surprise! He's dead!

It is difficult to believe. Dead?! Dead?!

It is sudden, which means that the most ordinary moments are slapped up against the most fatal. A few thin seconds between banality and eternity.

Listen to this. This is the conversation that my mother and father had before they went to the restaurant that night.

– What time do we have to be there? said my father. They were in their small bedroom, which smelled of citronella to keep the moths away. He was rubbing the skin on his jaw.

– Yes, you should shave, said my mother. She had a very faint accent, not really an accent at all, but her D's were heavier, her words more nipped in at the edges and more glottal, traces of the French-speaking town near Hearst where she grew up.

She was standing by the dresser, turning over the tangle of underwear in her top drawer to look for nylons without runs. A slanting shaft of light from the early evening sun had settled on the top of the dresser, quietly pooling around the pile of change, the old sales slips, and the earrings.

– We talked about seven-thirty, but they're usually late. Make it quarter to eight, said my mother.

– A tie? he said.

– I doubt it.

She pulled out a pair of nylons, and then sat down at a small make-up mirror with the nylons in her lap.

First, she switched on the round light bulbs around the edges of the mirror and examined her face for a second or two, turning it one way and then the other. Then she spread a milky beige fluid on her face in a colour that was so close to her own, it looked like liquid skin. After that, she sketched in her eyebrows in short strokes with a pencil, and carefully drew eyeliner across the lids. Then she rubbed a cotton swab across a cake of brown eyeshadow and brushed it onto her eyelids, and combed her eyelashes with black mascara. She worked carefully and dispassionately, as if it were someone else's face.

Did all this make her good-looking?

Probably not, although, she was not *bad*-looking, either.

She had a small, kite-shaped face, walnut-coloured eyes, and dark, springy hair. Her skin was very smooth, but a heavy smooth, not a delicate smooth.

Her name was Adele, and she was on her second husband, although the first marriage was so brief, it hardly counted. (He was just the starter husband, said my brother Denis sadly.) He was the one she married because she was pregnant with Denis, the one she was able to move up from when my father came along.

The last step in her routine was to outline her lips in plum-coloured pencil, and then fill them in with lipstick.

Can you imagine her doing all this if she had known that her husband was going to choke to death on a piece of potato and die in an hour and seventeen minutes?

She would have been better off learning the Heimlich manoeuvre.

My father was taking vitamins. Vitamins! Banal, yes, but also something that implies a future, that positively reeks of a life expectancy, any life expectancy. People don't take vitamins if they think they're going to die.

After he took his vitamins, he disappeared into the bathroom with a washcloth and towel, and came out a few minutes later with a spray can of deodorant in his hand. Then he put on clean socks, and he did shave, going back into the bathroom and breaking into a new package of disposable razors and drawing careful strokes on his cheeks. After that, he sat down stiffly on the bed – he was not particularly tall, but he had long, hard bones – turned on the television, and began watching part of a documentary on cicadas. This was how he synchronized his dressing with hers, so that they were both finished at the same time.

– What's this place like, anyway? he said.

– I don't know, they suggested it, she said. She was frowning at one side of her hair in the mirror.

Stephen and Alison were the people who suggested it, the kind of friends they could telephone on Saturday morning and say *what are you doing tonight?* without feeling embarrassed because they didn't have plans for Saturday night.

Too bad Stephen and Alison weren't busier.

– We need more toothpaste, said my mother to herself, plugging in the blow dryer. The sun had finished setting, and the light outside was turning a grey-violet colour.

My father, bored with the cicadas, was flicking through the channels.

You see how ordinary this was?

And even in the restaurant, a minute before my father started to choke, Stephen was telling them how he almost bought a new car. My mother was listening to Stephen and wishing she had not worn a short-sleeved dress, because there was a gust of cold air every time the restaurant door opened. The restaurant was Italian, small, yellow-stuccoed, known for its garlic bread, a place which had a spike in customers afterwards. Death is good for business.

Stephen was telling them how he had started looking for a new car, not for any particular reason but simply because he wanted it, and how he began picking up brochures, dropping into dealerships, talking to salesmen, building up a kind of momentum – Alison rolled her eyes at my mother at that point – until he sat down and worked out the finances. Those goddamn interest rates. Well, that was the end of that idea, he said, all the air just went out of his little daydream like a tire – and here he gave a little hiss to show them – and then they noticed that my father's face was turning purple, and his arms were moving in an agitated way.

– Your father's name? said a school secretary. It was a month after the funeral, and I was in the school office, a cramped space with green and white spider plants growing on every desk and counter. The secretary was filling out a form so that I could play the clarinet in the school orchestra.

– He's dead, I said, astonished by this again as the words came out of my mouth.

She noticed my lack of practice.

– I'm sorry, she said awkwardly.

Now, of course, I'm good at it. I can say quite casually: oh, he died. When I was thirteen.

What? No, it wasn't really a big thing.

* * *

This is what my father looked like:

He had pale skin that was the colour of celery root, pale hair, pale eyebrows. This gave him an unfinished look, as if his colour allotment had run out by the time it reached the full height of his head.

He was very quiet.

Not a calm quiet.

Not a bitter quiet.

Not a wise quiet.

Just quiet.

He used this quiet like a woolly barrier. All his emotions were filtered through it, so that what emerged were measured, neutral feelings. Often he sat for hours in a chair in the living room, a glass of whisky in one hand, looking out the window.

He was a math teacher, and when I was eleven, I decided to become a mathematician. I would be a citizen of the country of math, someone who covered chalkboards with dazzling numbers, elegant and intricate algebraic equations, lacy webs of thought spreading out and filling up all the available space. They would have to bring in more chalkboards on wheels, whole rows of chalkboards, to accommodate my brilliance.

– You can barely add, said Denis.

This was not quite true. But not quite untrue, either. All those sparkling numbers often tried to trick me in incomprehensible ways. Instead of performing on cue and then sitting obediently in their appointed spots, they would disappear and reappear, they would slide around secretively, they would become mean-spirited practical jokes. They made me so frustrated that I wanted to strangle them, to throw them against the wall until the right answers popped out.

– Relax, said my mother. You're trying too hard, Nicole. Just relax a little more, and it will come to you.

Of course, this was impossible. This was inconceivable. I was born with an errant gene that made me wildly, intensely engaged with everything. Relax? Not likely. Perspective? I didn't have it.

My mother did not normally offer advice, possibly because she felt she was not normal. She was failing wifehood, a large F on her transcript, and she was acutely aware that her credibility was low. We were embarrassed for her, and we tried to keep her deficiencies a secret, as if she had a drinking problem.

The deficiencies?

Her interest in housework was sporadic. Sometimes she would roam our house, a small brick bungalow in Rexdale, with a pail full of cleaning equipment, sponges and dusting cloths and furniture wax, a bottle of spray cleaner in her hand. Every surface in the house would be damp to the touch, and smell like lemon or bleach or baking soda. A few days later, she would announce that she had retired from housework.

– My June Cleaver days are over. That woman must be an idiot. Her and Betty Crocker. And Mr Clean. I bet they're all in it together.

My father would wince, and start straightening up the living room.

Her approach to cooking was also erratic. She found it extraordinarily boring, so she would make colour-themed meals to keep herself interested. One evening, all the food at dinner would be red – spaghetti, beets, tomato juice, canned cherries for dessert. Another evening, the theme would be white – cauliflower, mashed potatoes, fish, milk, vanilla pudding.

After school, she would drive us on an endless round of errands in an old yellow Mazda. This meant that she became very focused on parking spots, engaged in a constant battle to outwit the parking fates. Circling the block, she would mutter *merde, merde,* until she found a spot, and then she would give a whoop of triumph, and bang on the steering wheel with her hand.

– Look at that, will you look at that? This is the best spot I've ever had on this street.

Can you imagine these two people getting married?

– It wasn't as if she didn't have a husband already, I said to Denis, after one of the all-red meals. She wasn't desperate. And he could have found someone who was at least tidier.

Denis had a simpler explanation.

– They're both mental, he said.

She gave us French names, and then stopped at that point, as if this had discharged any obligation towards her origins. We certainly didn't speak French, other than the little that we learned at school, although we went through a period of think-ing that it was hilarious to use made up or misplaced French words. *Où est la poutine mal?* Denis would say. *Regardez la gros cochon*, I would reply, and then we would roll around in stitches at our own wit.

Perhaps we deserved our parents.

One minute, they said, my father was putting salt on a piece of potato, and a few minutes later, he was dead.

Really dead.

No paramedics, no heroic fellow diner clutching him around the abdomen, no near death experience, no doctors giving orders 'stat' or doing CPR or triumphantly finding a pulse. This was not a television show, where the people who died were either the villains, or people who were at least disposable in terms of the plot.

A lunatic event, corkscrewing off the page of the script.

One minute this. One minute that. Alive, dead. Alive, dead.

I thought:

I should have felt more grief-stricken.

I thought:

I should have been seized with a crystalline sadness, some-thing vaguely purifying. Instead, my body was crawling with a gritty mess of misery and longing and guilt. I thought he had died because of me.

Ridiculous? Of course.

You think a thirteen-year-old should have known better?
You're right.

In my dream, I wake up in the cottony darkness of my room.
The door is open, and light is coming in from the hall.

Someone is in the room, sitting on the edge of my bed. He
turns his head, and I see that it is my father. I see that he has a
small bulge in his throat, as if his Adam's apple is swollen, but
only slightly.

– You're not dead? I say, confused.

One minute this. One minute that.

– No, he says. Not at all, he says. No, it was all a misunder-
standing. I'm fine. Just fine. Good as new.

He pats one of my ankles through the blankets.

Good as new. Perhaps better than new. He is a more reliable,
kinder, more dignified version of a father. I can see with the certainty of nightdreams that he is the father I knew I had somewhere, the father I knew would show up sooner or later, the
father who would cradle me, and feed me small pieces of
cheese, and stroke my hair, and whisper to me, who would listen to me gravely, and cut my fingernails, and tell me how
much he missed me. He is here, this father. Now I am safe, with
this father. He is finally here. He is here at last. A little flap of
gladness starts to unfurl painfully inside me. That television!
What a kidder! Finally, the right plot.

And then he is gone.

Of course, the ambulance did reach my father eventually. You
must have been wondering about that.

It had been in an accident with a taxi along the way, with a
taxi driver who had turned up the radio in his empty cab so
that he could sing along with Aerosmith at the top of his lungs.
It was dark and raining a little by then, and he didn't hear the
siren until it was too late, until he hit the right side of the
ambulance as it went barrelling through an intersection on a

red light. He wasn't going very fast, and it only took a few minutes for the paramedics to make sure that he was uninjured, and to exchange insurance information in the rain.

Did they know that they were trying to reach a choking person?

Did they know that he was seconds from death?

Did they know it was a piece of potato?

What *did* they know?

Whatever they knew, they still had to pry the crumpled bumper of the ambulance away from the right tire before they could drive on. While they were searching for something in the back to use as a lever, my father was continuing to asphyxiate, the potato wedged into his windpipe, the other customers watching in horror, garlic bread forgotten in their hands.

– A doctor, we need a doctor, my mother screamed at them from the tile floor, where she was trying to get past his flailing arms and legs to bang on his back.

They eyed each other accusingly, suddenly aware of their own inadequacy. What? You're not a doctor? An electronics salesman? An office manager? How can you be an office manager at a time like this?

Windpipe. Wind. Pipe. A pipe for wind, a moist tube sucking air in and out of the body. Cold air, stale air, humid air, cigarette smoke, the tomato-coloured air of an Italian restaurant.

In and out.

Inhale and exhale.

Intake and exhaust.

The most intimate of orifices, leading deep, deep inside the body, bypassing the heart.

– By the time the ambulance got there, Stephen said to us, he was dead as a doornail.

– For God's sake, Stephen, said Alison.

They had come over to tell us, after my father had been

pronounced dead at the hospital, while my shell-shocked mother was still filling out forms. Denis and I were watching reruns in the basement and drinking pop in a temporary, television-induced truce. They had gently rousted us out and assembled us on the living room sofa. *We have bad news.*

– No point in sugar-coating it, said Stephen, defensively.

– He didn't really suffer. Not really. It was so fast, said Alison in a shaky voice.

An ant was crawling up the wall behind one of the end table lamps. It crawled in a zigzag way until it reached the ceiling, and then turned around and started crawling back down. Rain was splattering on the windows, and the backs of my legs were sticking to the leatherette sofa, even though I was cold. The air smelled sharp, a smell like wet electrical fuses.

– He's *dead?* My brother's voice squeaked up on the word *dead.*

– Right, said Stephen, although he passed his hand over his forehead and his hair, as if he wasn't quite sure himself.

– I could use a drink, he said, getting up and going over to the sideboard where my parents kept the liquor.

– Don't worry, we're here for you, I swear, you can count on us, said Alison.

Her face looked disorganized, and she was stroking my arm, over and over.

A little white explosion had gone off in my brain, leaving it empty. There was only one clumsy, naked thought lying around in the wreckage.

Would this make any difference?

Of course, it made *some* difference. This is only common sense. The question is: What? What was the difference? Was it possible to measure this in the absence of a control group? Should there be a way of evaluating the impact of fateful events? How do we know whether to sink into peevish victimhood, so poorly treated by life, or to thank our lucky stars? Compare and contrast two versions: life with a father, and life without one.

There are two sides to every story.

Or perhaps it's better not to know.

We are sitting around the dining room table on my mother's birthday, waiting for her to blow out the candles. My father has put canned icing on a supermarket cake, and in my eight-year-old enthusiasm, I have sprinkled red crystal sugar on it, then green, then coloured shot, and then tiny silver balls.

– You have to think of a wish, says Denis.

– I'm thinking, says my mother.

The candles are melting as my mother thinks, apparently considering and discarding a number of possibilities.

– Wish for a bigger television, says Denis.

– Wish for a swimming pool, I say.

My mother is still thinking.

– Wish for a faster car, says Denis.

– Wish for more cake, I say.

– Wish for anything, says my father. The damn candles are almost out.

My mother sighs, a long explosive sigh, and then leans forward and blows.

– You got it, you got it, I scream.

– Who knows? says my mother.

I picture her wish spiralling crazily up from the cake into the ceiling, through the ceiling and the upper floors of the house, bursting out of the roof where it zooms into the stratosphere, until it is just a tiny dot.

– What was the wish? I say.

– It's a secret. If you tell, it won't come true, says Denis.

– What was the wish? I say again to my mother later, when no one else is around. I am worried about this wish, this wish that took so long to make.

My mother beckons to me, and then leans down and whispers in my ear:

– It was nothing.

– Nothing? A nothing wish?

– Shhh, says my mother.

This is the second part of the story.

A stable, calm home is recommended for raising children (*Modern Homemaking with Helena Barker*).

My mother became more orderly, more like my father after he died, something that surprised her almost as much as it surprised us. Perhaps his death had seemed like a form of punishment for her, and she was eager to show that she had learned her lesson, and that no further tragedies were required to bring her into line.

So we became stable and calm at home, as recommended.

Except for me, that is. I had such a twitchy and melodramatic interior life that it was all I could do not to race around the house, banging my head against the grey-blue walls. Any increase in calm and stability seemed to have a perverse effect on me, elevating an already significant degree of internal chaos. In fact, at the precise point where my mother could be considered to have ceased flunking motherhood, I started flunking childhood. By the time I was sixteen, I felt as if were in a soft, colourless jail, and I married Joe a year later, just to get out on parole.

This is how I knew he was the right person.

A train terminal sat in a large tract of land between our house and the waterfront like a digitized octopus. Tracks spread out from the terminal, and six or seven sets crossed a road nearby, laid out next to each other. Driving over the tracks was a bone-rattling experience, because the rails weren't buried deeply enough in the asphalt. Most drivers slowed down to a crawl, and even drivers of music-thumping Camaros were instantly transformed by a kind of prim caution.

I spent a great deal of time in cars with friends because I was willing to go anywhere with anyone, as long as it involved getting out of the house. On this particular hot day, the city air was rough with hydrocarbons, and Joe was driving. When he saw the tracks, he speeded up.

– You have to hit them fast, he said. It's the only way to do it, he said. Hit them fast, and then you go sailing over them.

So I married him. Who wouldn't?

He was wrong, of course.

– Do you like children? I say to Joe.

We are sitting at the kitchen table in our flat behind a store, drinking orange juice without the pulp. The kitchen floor is uneven, and some of the tiles are coming up. The walls are painted yellow, and there is a row of scraggly plants on the window sill, a weedy ivy, a tired begonia, an anonymous plant which has lost most of its leaves, and an amaryllis which is an eye-rasping red. I am pretending to nurse these plants tenderly, but I am really waiting for them to die, especially the amaryllis, which gives me a headache.

Joe is reading the sports scores in the newspaper, and I am folding sticky roach traps, following the instructions, and trying to work up my nerve. *Ever thought about a family? How do you feel about kids? Aren't babies sweet? Do you like children?*

– I don't know, he says, still reading the paper.

– Maybe you should think about it some more.

He looks up from the baseball scores.

– You've got about five months, I say.

Pregnancy. Please take a number and we will be with you shortly.

– Is this going to hurt? I say to the doctor who is listening to my swollen stomach with a stethoscope.

– Having the baby? Probably, he says.

Tactlessness is an ideal quality in a doctor. A doctor should be someone who will tell all the truth, all the time.

– How much will it hurt?

– Do you get bad period cramps? he says.

– Very bad.

– Then it will probably be very bad.

Curses.

(Was it *mauvais*? says Denis, after it is all over. Very, very *mauvais*, I say. Death to childbirth instructors.)

Joe and I are both startled to find that I have expelled a live being from my body, even though we have read up on this at considerable length in advance. But what kind of being is she? She seems like a dear pet, or perhaps a spectacularly realistic and interactive doll. She has a long head with spidery veins, and a crumpled, soft body that is still unfolding.

– We love you, I say to her vaguely.

– We love you, says Joe uncertainly.

We look at her as if she will explain to us what this means, describe in more concrete detail the contours and features of what we should be feeling. She looks back gravely but uncommunicatively.

– What about Gwyneth? says Joe. All the names he suggests for her are the names of celebrities.

I stall, searching her navy blue eyes every day for clues for the right name.

– Believe me, says my mother. This isn't the hard part.

It seems presumptuous, though. She is still a stranger, we have only just met, and I am not even entirely convinced she is the same species.

– What about Brittany? says Joe.

Then I am swamped with primitive hormonal feelings so strong that I am afraid I might start washing her with my tongue.

Then I am blindsided by an achy, high-wire joy.

Should I have known about this? Was someone supposed to tell me, and simply forgot?

– What about Cameron? says Joe.

– What about Sienna? I say. This is a colour in a set of oil pastels I had when I was younger.

– Close enough, says Joe.

– Note that this is not a French name, I say to my mother. She looks at me as if I'm demented.

I throw myself into looking after the baby with the same reckless disregard for details that has worked so badly for me up until then. I descend into a voluptuous haze of infant skin and infant breath and milk-stained laundry. The days and nights roll around loosely, as if someone has dropped a handful of them on the floor, and they are caroming off in all directions.

I am hoping that if I fling myself at motherhood with my eyes closed, it will stick to me. But I feel as if I am trying on a costume that is slipping around my neck, or bunching up at the waist. I am worried that I have inherited bad motherhood genes. (Let me know if I start making dinners that are all the same colour, I say to Joe. Sure, he says, puzzled.)

I study my parenting books, all of which seem to feature blond, patient people who make their own baby food, and have babies with hair who like to play with rattles. My baby is bald and is only interested in dangerous objects. I read passages from the books to her, hoping this will help her to see the error of her ways, but she is unconvinced. Eventually, I throw out the books. As far as I can tell, Dr Spock and a punk performance artist have been wrestling for control of my neural net, and Dr. Spock has finally gone down for the count.

In my dream, I speak French, and my hands make small, silvery gestures. I speak a swan-neck French, a liquid French, and my hands float in front of me.

Stop, I say, holding my hands up gently.

Come, I say, beckoning tenderly.

What can I do? I say, with a sweet shrug, holding my hands apart, the fingers together, tracing a small arc of futility.

Who knows? I say, my hands waving intelligently.

Where am I? I say, my hands lost for a second.
Except that I say this all in French.

Time evaporates rather than passes, because I am doing the
same things over and over, and I am not sleeping. The baby is
nocturnal, a small night animal, and I spend my nights rocking
her, and watching the density and distribution of molecules of
darkness. Sometimes I put her in her car seat, and we drive
around the dark streets, the street lights creating a shadow and
light show for her in the car. After lengthy study, I determine that
darkness is not an absence of light, but a substance itself, something thick and soft that collects quietly at the end of the day. I
consider sending this discovery into a scientific journal, and
then I forget. During the day, I sweep the kitchen floor often.

At four, Sienna looks like this: she has fine, straight, black hair,
oyster-coloured skin, round eyes, long black eyelashes and
glasses. The glasses give her an unfocused look. Her head is
large and she often needs to rest it. She does this by sidling up
to me, turning my hand palm up, like a table, and then putting
her head down on it. It is heavy, and it makes me exhausted just
to think about her thin little neck, and her heavy head.

She is the kind of child who should have been born with
pointed ears.

– The rings of Saturn are *so* hot this time of year, she says to
me one day, like a rich socialite complaining about how boring
the Riviera has become.

For a second, this actually frightens me, because she is just
strange enough. It turns out that she has been learning about
planets in nursery school.

She doesn't like her name.

– I want my name to be Tiffany, she says to me.

I say: Oh?

It could have been worse, I want to say. You could have been
Raw Umber.

* * *

Joe is a good husband, except for the husband part.

He has his own business doing house inspections for prospective buyers. He checks for leaky basements, or old wiring or carpenter ants. He talks about houses with affection, as if each house were a tiny continent with its own internal geography (rooms), its own weather (drafts and forced air heating), a river system (water pipes), and its own geology (rippled basement floors). He writes this up in official-looking reports, with spiral binding and coloured tabs.

All his mould-detecting and mortar-scraping and wood-knocking coalesce around his other inspections, which usually involve the women who are selling their houses.

Why are they interested in him?

Of course, there is the way he looks: olive skin with rings around his eyes, black curly hair. Or the way he sounds: a dark hoarse voice, like coffee.

Or perhaps there is something erotic about his gentle, thorough explorations of their house foundations. Perhaps once he has run his hands over their cracked windowsills, opened their musty closet doors, poked around in their old wiring, it seems natural for him to go on to their own soft structures, to probe and evaluate them as well.

He falls lightly in love with them, but only for a week or a few days. I can see it coming over him, taking him in a queasy grip, and then releasing him just as suddenly. These are events that are devoid of moral content or harmful intention on his part. They simply occur, as natural and inevitable as the flu. For him, this is not a question of fidelity, but a matter of contagion.

Not all the women feel the same way, or are content to float into and then out of his radius. Sometimes they object to his here-today-gone-tomorrow approach, and become overwrought, calling him on his cell phone as he goes house to house.

Sometimes Joe forgets to turn his phone off at night.

The first time:

I pick up the ringing cell phone and before I have a chance to speak, a woman says:

Hi, baby.

I feel frozen.

This. Is. Such. A. Cliché. Each word is a small cube of ice that someone has carelessly dropped into my head.

Then I become instantly accustomed to it. I adjust to it. Everything is fine. I am fine. I am fine with the fact that he is only about one-third there, the other two-thirds of him channelled into a daytime soap opera with the customer de jour. I am fine with the fact that he is a full service kind of house inspector.

What else am I going to do? I say, with a small Gallic shrug. At least this way there is a real, live father around.

Does it bother me? *Mais oui*, I say. *Naturellement*, I say.

But let's face it: I don't have very high expectations.

– Here, says my mother to Sienna, passing her a book.

They are French fairytales, although they are written in English. Recently, my mother has become more absent-minded and more French at the same time, as if she put down her Englishness for a moment and couldn't find it again. *It was just here a minute ago.*

The fairytales are brutal old stories, in which people have names like Ti-Jean, and heads are severed from bodies and sometimes replaced, or golden apples stick to people's hands. The story Sienna makes me read over and over is called Clever Yvette. This is a short version:

Clever Yvette was a peasant girl who was known far and wide for her cleverness, and so Ti-Jean (of course), who lived in the next village, decided that he wanted to marry her. He went to visit her family to ask for her hand in marriage. While he was eating dinner with them, Clever Yvette went down to the cellar to draw some wine for him. As she was waiting for the wine, she noticed there was an axe stuck in the ceiling of the cellar. What if I get married, she thought, and we have a child, and he comes down to the cellar and the axe falls on him and kills him? She started to weep at the thought and forgot all about the wine. When Ti-Jean found her a few minutes later, he was so impressed with her foresight and cleverness that he proposed to her on the spot.

They lived together happily for several years, but soon Ti-Jean tired of her cleverness. One day, he told her to go to the fields and cut some wheat to be ground into flour and made into bread. She cut a lot of wheat, but the sun was hot, so she grew tired and fell asleep. While she was asleep, Ti-Jean came and threw a net of little bells over her, and then left. When she awoke, the bells jingled every time she moved, and confused her. Why am I jingling, she thought? Perhaps I am no longer Clever Yvette. Perhaps a witch has changed me into someone else.

She went to their house, and called out to Ti-Jean: Is Clever Yvette inside? He replied: Yes, she is right here by the fire, spinning flax.

Then, indeed, I must be someone else, she thought, and she set off down the road and was never seen again.

In other words, Clever Yvette was not very clever.

What does it mean to have your life changed by a piece of potato?

Does it mean that things seem more fragile?

Does it mean that things *are* more fragile? A trick of physics, perhaps, for the potato-traumatized person?

This feeling doesn't go away, of course. It simply gets buried in layers of subsequent experiences, so that underneath all the glossy, adult emotions, there is still a little piece of root vegetable stuck at the bottom, a little pivot on which everything else is balanced.

Good things can happen, even brightly coloured, sparkling things can happen, but the person with the potato is always listening for the first crack in the ice, or watching for some telltale sign of slackness in the guy rope holding up the tent. Any catastrophes that come along are instantly old acquaintances, almost a relief. Finally. I knew it. I knew it all along.

March, a month of cold mud and crocuses.

Sienna eats an almond and turns white, her eyes rolling back in her head. Then she faints. At the hospital, they revive her (stat!) and diagnose a nut allergy.

– But she eats peanut butter all the time, I say.

– Peanuts aren't really a true nut, says the doctor, an earnest resident with stylish narrow glasses. Peanuts are legumes. You'll have to keep her away from real nuts, almonds, hazelnuts, walnuts, brazil nuts, pecans, all of them, and when I say away, I mean *away*. Next time, she could die.

– Just like that? I say, stunned.

– Just like that.

Hazelnuts, walnuts, brazil nuts, pecans.

*Hazel*nuts, *wal*nuts, bra*zil* nuts, pe*cans*.

It sounds like a skipping rope song.

Sienna has inherited the family predisposition to death by food. The dyslexic version of nutrition – food as a serial killer.

– I can't believe it. Can you believe it? What are the odds? says Joe, rubbing his arms as if he is cold.

The doctor hands us over to a nurse, who shows us how to use an emergency injection pen, and gives us some pamphlets on taking precautions, and creating a nut-free house. (Does that include the parents? says Joe.) But how can we keep her safe when she goes to kindergarten every day, over to friends' houses, on class trips, off to birthday parties? Is there a god of child safety? Perhaps it would be more practical to start sacrificing goats on a daily basis.

– Now, is that all clear? Do you have any questions? says the nurse cheerfully.

– Yes, I say.

How do you tell a four-year-old that if she eats a nut, she'll die?

A brilliant, windy day, a few weeks after the trip to the hospital, still cold, but the mud is warming up and starting to smell alive. I drop Sienna off at my mother's house while I go to the grocery store and the hardware store and the cleaners and the library. When I get back, my mother meets me at the car.

– She won't come out of the bathroom, she says.

– What? Is she sick? Is there something wrong?

– No, says my mother. She's just been in there for an hour. I called Joe's cell phone, but he isn't answering.

– I'm in a hurry, I say. I'm busy, I say. This is not a convenient time for something strange and troubling to happen, I think.

– Well, you try. Maybe she'll come out for you, says my mother. She is shivering in the wind in her shirt-sleeved dress.

We go into the house, which is still blue-grey. As I walk through the door, I feel the usual second of panic that I am walking into a blue-grey maze in which I will be forced to sit still for long periods of time and eat monochrome meals. The bathroom door is closed, and I rattle the handle. The door is locked.

– Honey, we're in a hurry. Can you come out right now? I say.

The bathroom says nothing.

– What's the matter?

The bathroom is mute.

– I'm not going to say this again, I say. Come out of there this minute.

I can hear her rustling a little, a soft rustle like the shush of cloth against cloth, but she doesn't say anything. And she doesn't come out.

– Isn't there a key or something? I say to my mother unreasonably. I know this is not a door with a key. I know every cracked tile, every paint drip on the window glass, every water

stain on the ceiling of this bathroom, and I know there is a half
moon knob that turns one way to lock, and the other way to
unlock, all from the inside. I know this, but I want a key to
materialize in front of me, even a blue-grey key.

– What happened? I say to my mother, in the spirit of calm
investigation. What did you do to my daughter? I think.

– Don't take that tone with me, young lady, says my mother,
who can detect a subtext at twenty yards with her eyes closed.

– If you wanted to know what happened, we had lunch, vegetable soup and tuna sandwiches with pickles and potato chips,
we played Parcheesi and then she made a collage from pictures
she cut out of magazines and pasted together, and then we
played Snakes and Ladders, and then she went into the bathroom and wouldn't come out. That's what happened.

– Was she upset about anything? I say.

– How should I know?

I go back to my conversation with the bathroom door.

– It's Wednesday, I say casually. – You know what happens
on Wednesday?

The door stolidly refuses to reply.

– Pizza night! I say brightly.

Of course, Sienna does not really eat pizza in the usual
sense; instead, she scrapes off the top and eats pizza-flavoured
crust, but this is something she looks forward to all week. However, the door is still silent.

– And I was thinking of picking up some chocolate marsh-
mallow cookies, I say, bringing out the heavy artillery.

No reply. I hear water running in the sink, and then it stops.

This spate of bribery has exhausted my parenting strategies.

– Does the window open? I say to my mother.

– The sash was painted shut a few years ago, and there's one
of those wedge locks between the upper and lower frames.

I call the fire department on the theory that if they rescue
cats from trees, they can extract a little girl from a bathroom
with fish wallpaper.

– She'll get hungry sooner or later, the dispatch clerk says confidently. – The safest thing is just to wait her out. If you try to force the door or break the window, she might get hit with broken glass or a piece of wood. Just be patient.

The clerk sounds so authoritative that I wonder if people call in frequently with this problem. Either that, or they give the same advice for cats.

I call a locksmith.

– No problem, lady, I can be there in an hour, cost you about one hundred and twenty bucks, depending on the lock.

– Maybe later, I say.

I tell my mother that I am staying over, and we have a quiet, strangely normal evening, aside from the fact that Sienna is locked in the bathroom. Joe comes by at six, and has dinner with us. I make spaghetti in the hope that the smell will lure her out, but it doesn't. I make Joe go and talk to the bathroom door for a while in the hope that this will lure her out, but it doesn't.

– I've got some houses tonight, says Joe, fingering his phone.

– Sure, I say. There is always the possibility that he is telling the truth.

I read a copy of *Chatelaine* that is lying around, and then I read a furniture catalogue, and then I read the army jokes section of an old *Reader's Digest*, and then I read the television guide, and then I watch a game show with my mother, and then I study the new colour of the living room walls and decide that I will never paint anything this colour (Georgia peach, says my mother, but it looks like the orange skin colour on a diagram of the musculoskeletal structure in a doctor's office), and then I pace around the house until my mother yells at me.

Then I go to bed in my brother's old room, because I am afraid that if I sleep in my old bed, I will vanish down a time tunnel into a jittery, powerless adolescence. I lie in his bed with a soft, starchy taste in my mouth from the spaghetti and doze off for a few hours, a threadbare sleep just under the surface of consciousness. At 5:00 a.m. I call the children's hospital.

– How long can a child go without food? I ask.

– It depends, says the information nurse warily. – Why don't we start with your name and address?

I explain that I am not trying to starve a child to death. She asks me how much Sienna weighs, how old she is, and whether the water is working in the bathroom.

– Have you tried incentives?

By this time, I have promised her a movie with popcorn and ginger ale, a trip to the zoo to see the llamas, and a pet rabbit (How about a pet llama? says Joe). I have also tried delicate inquiries, trying to skilfully draw her out, telling her jokes, playing imaginary card games, speaking to her gently but firmly, speaking to her sternly and seriously, reading to her from *Reader's Digest*, and losing my temper.

– She should be all right for at least forty-eight hours at her weight, as long as she's drinking. It's preferable for her to come out on her own, so try waiting a little longer.

The day acquires a baffling elasticity, stretching and looping around the laws of physics. By the time evening arrives like a purple bruise in the sky, I am in a panic.

– Maybe we should get a child psychologist to come in and talk to her, I say to Joe.

– How about a hostage negotiator? he says.

– How about that locksmith? says my mother.

I try one last time. I lie down beside the bathroom door and put my face to the crack, the rough carpet against my cheek.

– Sweetie, I say, is there anyone else you want to talk to? I say. I say this in the most coaxing, persuasive voice I can muster, in a voice that I hope will curl into her head and warm up any little frozen parts of her brain, or relax any twisted little cardiac muscles.

There is a long silence. I wait. A piece of old tape is stuck to the carpet at eye level, and the carpet itself smells like dusty plastic.

Then I hear a rustle and the scrape of the shower curtain being pulled aside.

Another rustle.

I wait some more.

Then I hear a click.

I wait some more.

Then I stand up carefully and try the door handle, very slowly and quietly. It turns all the way, and I push the door open.

She has the toilet seat down, and she is sitting on top of it with her knees pulled up to her chin, her arms wrapped around her thin knees, and a bedraggled looking towel around her shoulders.

– Clever Yvette, she says.

– What? I say.

– I want to talk to Clever Yvette, she says.

My father has brought home a small cardboard box with a picture of a snow-covered mountain, and trees with cherry blossoms in front of it.

– This is for you, he says to Denis and me. For us? We look at each other, startled by this odd event. It is a week before his death, although none of us know this.

– *Très bizarre*, says Denis, under his breath.

Inside the box, there are small cardboard trees, a cardboard mountain, and a plastic tray. My father reads us the directions, which involve standing the cardboard cutouts in the tray, and pouring in a liquid from a plastic envelope that comes with it.

– Now, we have to wait. It takes a while, so go and do something else for a couple of hours, he says.

By late afternoon, the cardboard trees have soaked up the liquid and are sprouting tiny pink flowers, and the mountain top has grown a snowy crust. Even my mother is impressed.

– How does it work? I ask my father.

– I'm not sure. Something in the liquid, I guess.

I inspect the empty plastic envelope. All it says is Do Not Ingest and Made in Japan.

After dinner, I examine it again. The trees are in full bloom now, and there are small yellow flowers around their trunks. This small tableau is strangely compelling. The cherry blossoms seem to be swaying in the warm spring air, and the snow on the mountain looks cold and wet.

What is it made out of? Chemical crystals? Tissue paper?

I touch one side of the top of a tree, very lightly, but not lightly enough. Some flowers fall off in a clump onto the side of the tray.

– I'm telling, says Denis.

But I'm telling now. I'm telling this story, and one of the questions I have is about Clever Yvette. What was she thinking about when she woke up from her sleep with a bundle of wheat in her hand?

Was she thinking about baking round, floury loaves with cross-hatching on their top crusts?

Was she thinking about pressing wine grapes so ripe that juice was leaking out of splits in their skins?

Was she thinking about making blue flax plants into yards of smooth cloth?

Perhaps she was still not entirely awake, and all of these thoughts were mingled together in her mind, becoming more and more blended until they turned into something else, something she was desperately tired of watching for.

Something she was desperately tired of waiting for.

Like a sharp metal axe head stuck in the ceiling.

I think she had a moment of cold clarity then, a moment when everything went out of focus and then came into focus again, looking brighter and dirtier and different.

I think she decided she wasn't waiting any more.

Acknowledgements

I have been daydreaming about writing acknowledgments since I started writing this book. Of course, this was largely to avoid doing any work on the book itself. And in fact, these daydreams didn't produce any actual acknowledgments, possibly because when my mind started to wander from the book, the next step was to lie down on the floor with my eyes closed, hoping fervently for a bolt of creative energy to strike.

Fortunately, The Porcupine's Quill sends their authors a couple of pages of advice from author Ray Robertson, which includes a few words about acknowledgments. His advice on this subject is to keep it short, and avoid statements thanking all the wonderful people out there – you know who you are! – who have made my life so wonderful in so many wonderful ways! I shuddered dutifully when I read this, and resolved that my lists would be short, and that nothing as awful as this sentence would ever come from my computer.

However, such excellent advice doesn't really address the dilemma of authors who have a large number of people to whom they are justifiably grateful. There are the patient family members, in this case, my partner Peter Dorfman, the most intelligent, witty and supportive person I know, who never once laughed at the idea that I might be a writer, even when it seemed laughable; our children, Julia Dorfman and Daniel McCormack, whom I am shamelessly wiggling in here simply for being their fascinating and remarkable selves; my twin sister, Naomi McCormack, an award-winning filmmaker, a trapeze artist, and a capoeira practitioner, who has been a role model of artistic talent and integrity, as well as a very kind, helpful and fun-to-be-with sister; and my parents, Thelma McCormack and the late Robert McCormack, thoughtful and generous people who raised me in a house where every surface in every room was covered with books.

Then there are the authors and other literary people. They

include the late Timothy Findley (and the unlate Bill White-head), both exceptionally unstinting in their nicotine-flavoured encouragement and assistance; Nino Ricci, not only highly encouraging but willing to roll up his sleeves and provide gentle but crucial advice on an earlier draft of 'Ipso Facto'; John Metcalf, the editor of all editors, a word junkie who sent me elegantly hand-written letters full of deeply sustaining and stimulating wisdom on all things writerly, and who exercised a refined and subtle editorial eye; Tim and Elke Inkster and intern Amanda Jernigan at The Porcupine's Quill who provided their enthusiasm, guidance, and talent in designing and publishing matters, and who are (happily for their authors) demented about their books; The Fiddlehead (and especially Sabine Campbell, another warm person who aids and abets neophyte writers), for printing both my first short story and an earlier version of 'Plural'; *Descant*, which printed an earlier version of 'Hardiness Zones'; the 2000 *Journey Prize Anthology* jury; Maggie Helwig and Oberon Press who included earlier versions of 'Plural', 'Hardiness Zones' and 'Ipso Facto' in *Coming Attractions*; and all the other workshop leaders who said skillful and insightful things, including Susan Musgrave, Michael Helm, Elizabeth Harvor, M.T. Kelly, Anne Montagnes, and George Fetherling.

But this long list doesn't even include the many friends to whom I am wildly grateful as well: the friends who hid their surprise at the lunatic idea of being a writer as well as a lawyer; the friends who read early drafts without holding their noses; the friends who inquired about and listened tolerantly to the travails of writing; the friends who good-humouredly voted on various titles or launch locations; and the friends who generally cheered me on in many ways. You are all truly remarkable, and you certainly deserve to be listed here, but I think I have already pushed the limits of these acknowledgments as far as I can.

And well, you know who you are.

Judith McCormack was born outside Chicago, and grew up in Toronto, with brief stops in Montreal and Vancouver. Her first short story was nominated for the 2000 Journey Prize. Her second won an honourable mention in *The Fiddlehead's* Fiction Contest, and has now been optioned for film. Her third story was published in *Descant,* and in 2001 she was one of three authors featured in the *Coming Attractions Anthology.* As well as being an author, she is a lawyer, a twin and an insomniac. She lives in Toronto with her partner, Peter Dorfman, and their two children.